"Can a single organism subsist for half a billion years?" Brigid asked

The round man shrugged. "Some creatures appear to continue living and growing until something kills them. Many dinosaur species are believed to have been that way. So are some modern carp. The point is that not everything dies of old age."

Wu held the skull up to examine it in the morning light dribbling in through water-stained windows. "Or maybe our Leviathan was an extraordinary individual, a freak—a mutant. Although I personally favor the hypothesis that he survived all these millennia on the basis of unbendable willpower alone."

"So he just kept eating," Kane said, "and getting bigger. And meaner. And smarter."

Wu nodded. "Precisely."

"What does he eat?" Kane asked. "Seems pretty damn desolate down there, except for the black smoker farms."

"Forgive me, Doctor," said Brigid, perching on her stool as if she were too worked up to commit to just sitting on it, "but your biography seems to leave a very great deal unaccounted for."

"Very perceptive, Ms. Baptiste."

Other titles in this series:

James Axler
Outlanders®

LORDS OF THE DEEP

A GOLD EAGLE BOOK FROM
WORLDWIDE®

TORONTO • NEW YORK • LONDON
AMSTERDAM • PARIS • SYDNEY • HAMBURG
STOCKHOLM • ATHENS • TOKYO • MILAN
MADRID • WARSAW • BUDAPEST • AUCKLAND

*For Randy "Skids" Clark,
artist extraordinaire, Big Daddy Goth*

First edition August 2006

ISBN-13: 978-0-373-63851-2
ISBN-10:   0-373-63851-5

LORDS OF THE DEEP

Copyright © 2006 by Worldwide Library.

Special thanks to Victor Milán for his contribution to
this work.

"There's a divinity that shapes our ends…"
—William Shakespeare, *Hamlet*

"There is, one knows not what sweet mystery about the sea, whose gently awful stirrings seem to speak of some hidden soul beneath…"
—Herman Melville, *Moby-Dick*

The Road to Outlands—
From Secret Government Files to the Future

Almost two hundred years after the global holocaust, Kane, a former Magistrate of Cobaltville, often thought the world had been lucky to survive at all after a nuclear device detonated in the Russian embassy in Washington, D.C. The aftermath— forever known as skydark—reshaped continents and turned civilization into ashes.

Nearly depopulated, America became the Deathlands— poisoned by radiation, home to chaos and mutated life forms. Feudal rule reappeared in the form of baronies, while remote outposts clung to a brutish existence.

What eventually helped shape this wasteland were the redoubts, the secret preholocaust military installations with stores of weapons, and the home of gateways, the locational matter-transfer facilities. Some of the redoubts hid clues that had once fed wild theories of government cover-ups and alien visitations.

Rearmed from redoubt stockpiles, the barons consolidated their power and reclaimed technology for the villes. Their power, supported by some invisible authority, extended beyond their fortified walls to what was now called the Outlands. It was here that the rootstock of humanity survived, living with hellzones and chemical storms, hounded by Magistrates.

In the villes, rigid laws were enforced—to atone for the sins of the past and prepare the way for a better future. That was the barons' public credo and their right-to-rule.

Kane, along with friend and fellow Magistrate Grant, had upheld that claim until a fateful Outlands expedition. A displaced piece of technology…a question to a keeper of the archives…a vague clue about alien masters—and their world shifted radically. Suddenly, Brigid Baptiste, the archivist, faced summary execution, and Grant a quick termination. For

Kane there was forgiveness if he pledged his unquestioning allegiance to Baron Cobalt and his unknown masters and abandoned his friends.

But that allegiance would make him support a mysterious and alien power and deny loyalty and friends. Then what else was there?

Kane had been brought up solely to serve the ville. Brigid's only link with her family was her mother's red-gold hair, green eyes and supple form. Grant's clues to his lineage were his ebony skin and powerful physique. But Domi, she of the white hair, was an Outlander pressed into sexual servitude in Cobaltville. She at least knew her roots and was a reminder to the exiles that the outcasts belonged in the human family.

Parents, friends, community—the very rootedness of humanity was denied. With no continuity, there was no forward momentum to the future. And that was the crux— when Kane began to wonder if there *was* a future.

For Kane, it wouldn't do. So the only way was out— way, way out.

After their escape, they found shelter at the forgotten Cerberus redoubt headed by Lakesh, a scientist, Cobaltville's head archivist, and secret opponent of the barons.

With their past turned into a lie, their future threatened, only one thing was left to give meaning to the outcasts. The hunger for freedom, the will to resist the hostile influences. And perhaps, by opposing, end them.

Prologue

"Deep Probe 23 approaching the target," Warden Lang reported. Ostensibly he was addressing the submersible's right-seater and commander, Senior Technician Zoster, but really he was speaking for the benefit of the ultra-low-frequency broadcast by which every detail of their mission was being tracked in the great submerged dome of Lemuriaville.

"Idiot," Zoster snarled from beside him. "I can see that as plainly as you can."

He gestured irritably with a moon-pale hand at the armaglass front viewscreen. Below and ahead of the descending craft the deep Pacific floor scrolled slowly beneath them in the light of twin spotlights. A mile or so ahead lay a black line like a knife cut across the sinuous ridges and silt-filled valleys.

The image was not altogether real; down here, four miles beneath the surface, no light penetrated. Even the hundred-million-candlepower fusion-driven beams could do little to pierce the eternal gloom. They were assisted by a variety of forward-looking sensors ranging from sonar to millimeter-wave radar to gravitic anomaly detection, which was computer-translated into visual representation and painted on the viewscreen by micro-lasers mounted in the console.

Lang jerked a thumb toward the thin microphone curving from his headset in front of his mouth. "For base," he mouthed. Zoster was nominally his superior on this mission—and certainly Baron Lemuria would enforce the chain of authority with the same imaginative zeal he enforced all his laws, not to mention passing whims—but one of Lemuriaville's elite Wardens of the Deep could only put up with so much from a mere civilian.

Zoster only glared. The prick. He had black hair like sparse steel wool receding from a bulging forehead that glowed faintly blue in the lights of the panel. His eyes, a blue somewhat less faint, stood out from his head. His beard had twin stripes of gray down the sides; Lang would bet he wore it to conceal a weak chin. His breath stank like a long-uncleaned pisser.

That was the sort of thing you became acquainted with on a long voyage in a cramped deep-sea vessel. Intimately acquainted.

"Deep Probe 23, do you see anything yet?" came the voice of the controller sitting back in Central Control in Lemuriaville.

"Prime Base," Technician Zoster said importantly, "we have sighted the undersea canyon."

"Proceed as planned."

"Affirmative," Lang said. He resisted an urge to flick a glance at the technician beside him.

In fact, he felt anything but affirmative.

The seabed below was devoid of apparent life, as it generally was at this depth. Yet *something* supposedly lived down here. Farther down, in fact, deep within the canyon ahead.

So patrol reports claimed. Remote sensors periodically showed what appeared to be enormous, unexplained masses moving about this region.

Such reports weren't what were making Warden Lang's palms moist and his mouth dry. They were all bullshit and anomalies. Nothing really lived way down here, except the strange sulfur based life-forms clustered around deep-sea vents. And they were nothing but tubeworms and bacteria and a few mutant crustaceans that fed upon them.

What Lang feared was crush depth.

The submersible was enormously strong, a titanium shell sandwiched in polymerized ceramic wrapped around a collapsed-crystal lattice framework. Submerged, the craft was driven by jets of water sucked into ducts, ionized and then accelerated by fluctuating magnetic fields, with no moving mechanism whatever. It was designed to resist not only the unimaginable pressures of the deep ocean, but also the stresses and projectile impacts of high-speed surface combat.

Nor was Lang a stranger to the concept of being at a depth at which he would be instantly crushed if for any reason the circumambient pressure ceased being resisted for even a microsecond. He had been born and raised in Lemuriaville, sealed within in its great dome three hundred fathoms below the Pacific's seldom peaceful surface.

But this was an extreme depth indeed. The Lemuriaville whitecoats assured him the craft was good to at least three thousand fathoms, but how would they know? There was never a call to send a craft this deep.

And besides, Zoster was a Lemurian tech, too. And just look at him.

Though he could never admit it, for fear of being yanked from warden duty and dropped into the Bilge— or just being recycled—Lang had a fear of being crushed by the awful weight of water at depth that bordered on the phobic. Though nobody he'd ever met had been fused-out to say so out loud, he reckoned he was far from the only one.

Maybe everybody in the dome had it. To judge by all the times he'd been wakened by someone screaming in their sleep in the dorms, until he reached pilot status and rated his own tiny closet of a compartment. To judge by the strange, strained silences in the mess and wardroom, the haunted glances people cast overhead and toward bulkheads when they thought no one was looking at them. Though it was said that the dome had been built centuries before, before the nukecaust even, and thus had survived the awful shocks sent crashing through the Pacific seabed by the Soviet earthshaker nukes that sank America's West Coast and lit off Ring of Fire volcanoes like so many firecrackers, Lang wasn't reassured.

The sea had its way. He'd been on enough patrols to know that. He'd known enough men who never came back from patrol, known of enough seafloor mining and aquaculture accidents. Even away down deep in Lemuriaville, where even the most violent surface storms were as remote as if you were off perched on the Moon's pimply ass, the brutal Cific would always find a way to reassert its terrible might.

So he reckoned it was just a matter of time before the dome cracked. Hell, it wasn't as if surviving the nuke-caust was such a good thing. What if the shocks had caused some tiny imperfection, a crack in the foundation, a flaw in the armaglass bubble of the dome itself, and it was even now building, slowly and inexorably, toward failure?

Being out in a pod, as the Deep Wardens called their dual-purpose submersible craft, was worse, of course. Barring accident or enemy action, they didn't fail often.

Often.

Lang shook his head, blew air silently out bearded lips. And we're going deeper still….

The pseudopicture painted on the inside of the front viewport was deceptive. What at first glimpse appeared to be a cut in a flat floor was in fact edged with what would, on the surface, have been a range of young mountains, and jagged as a moray's lower jaw. He could feel Zoster tightening up beside him in instinctive dread as they skimmed the fang peaks, and the abyss dropped away before them, black, right down to the heart of the world.

Chickenshit civilian, he thought. He acts so high and mighty, but once the pressure gauges start to get near redline, his shit turns to water.

"Entering canyon now," he reported. He thought it was chickenshit that he had to report everything verbally, too. It wasn't as if Lemuriaville wasn't monitoring everything within the pod and everything its sensors detected through telemetry. But that was procedure, and as a warden, it was in his job description to come down hard on anybody who thought to break or even bend the rules, including his fellow wardens. Independent thinking was not considered a virtue in Lemuriaville. It was the kind of thing that caused unrestrained humanity to blow up the world, he'd always been taught.

"Pilot," Zoster commanded, eager to impress himself on the action again, "start your descent."

Descend on my chubby, Lang stopped himself from snarling. "Aye, aye, sir," he said, as he worked the controls to use jets and gyros to direct the submersible's nose fifteen degrees downward.

In tomb stillness the craft dived toward the blackness. The chasm was swallowing their floodlights like a blue whale imbibing plankton, and for some reason the sensor suite wasn't sucking in enough information to image whatever was down there. Lang had a flash fantasy that there *wasn't* anything down there, that they had come into a rift not just in the seabed but in the fabric of reality itself, so that he and Zoster stared down into the naked void.

"Curious," Zoster murmured, a trickle of sweat down

his bluish balding forehead giving the lie to the studied detachment of his tone. "Shouldn't we be, well…seeing something?"

"Don't mean nothing," Lang said. "Software just takes its time updating the display sometimes…sir."

"Ah. Of course."

Then he scowled. "What's that?" he asked.

Lang glared at him. "What's what?"

The senior technician pointed ahead. Lang's gaze followed his finger.

Down in the black blackness, blackness stirred.

"Deep Probe 23." The voice from the speakers was harsh and peremptory. "Deep Probe 23, what is happening?"

Turbulence began to rock the deep sea vehicle. Zoster was babbling questions. His nervous spittle pattered against the side of Lang's face.

Lang didn't hear him. He was fighting to hold the craft steady against the buffeting of some kind of mysterious current.

The blackness below reached for them.

It reached with waving sinuosities. "Tentacles?" Lang said, more disbelieving than frightened.

Like ink diffusing through water, the tentacles flowed out to surround them. Lang furiously worked the controls, but it was already too late to escape.

Zoster emitted a strangled sound. A black bulk of unimaginable size heaved itself up from the darkness of the abyss. Lang had a sense it was vaguely triangular.

A giant eye, luminous and red, startlingly human, opened in the center of the black triangle like a hatchway into Hell.

The tentacles closed in. The submersible jerked as they seized it and wrenched.

Lang just had time for one scream of searing agony as the piston effect of water blasting at unimaginable pressures through half a dozen hull breaches simultaneously sent the temperature of the air within the submersible soaring to crematory temperatures in a fractional second, igniting his hair and skin. He had a brief glimpse through his own private Hell of Zoster burning yellow like a wax figure.

Then a fresh hypersonic leak cut through his head like a diamond saw and put an end to pain.

Chapter 1

Brigid Baptiste was sitting bolt upright with her H&K clutched white-knuckled in both hands before she realized the 9 mm handgun would do no good against the terrors that had wakened her.

The black, she thought, shivering as if in the throes of fever. The cold. The crushing…

Voices drew her attention, and the flicker of pale light. A campfire burned on the beach. The others sat clustered about it.

She put the handblaster away and stood up. Her legs shook slightly beneath her. She frowned, inhaled deeply. Get control of yourself.

She raised her head and smoothed back her hair. Then she made herself walk steadily toward the leaping orange-and-yellow light.

Kane sat directly across the fire from her. At her approach, although she knew she moved very quietly indeed, he raised his dark shaggy head to gaze directly at her. Yellow flames danced in his wolf-gray eyes.

"Dreams again, huh, Baptiste," he said. His voice was a baritone, rich but roughened by hard use.

He hadn't asked a question. She answered anyway. "Yes," she said, nodding and smoothing back her hair again. Her hair was much the color of the flames, as her eyes were green like the sea beyond in sunlight. The leaping campfire brought the true colors of both to rich light where it struck them. She sat down, careful to arrange the tails of the man's tan shirt she wore between her bare legs for modesty's sake, although she wore underpants.

To her left, Kane's right, knelt Grant. His big, slightly grizzled head was sunk to his muscular bare chest in a meditative pose. He looked like an idol carved of mahogany. A god of strength, hidden wisdom—and anger, which smoldered sometimes deep, sometimes near the surface.

"We all had them," Grant said. His voice rumbled like a boulder rolling down a rocky chute. His own amber eyes were turned down so that Brigid could read no reflection in them. He wore loose camou trousers; his feet were bare. Though shirtless, he wore his Sin Eater in its power holster on his right forearm. Kane wore his, too, visible below the short sleeves of his khaki T-shirt.

The Sin Eaters were the badges of the Magistrates, once the terrors and tyrants of the nine villes of North America. Since the barons had apotheosized into living gods—the original Annunaki reborn—the villes had slid into decline. Some persisted as power centers; others had fallen to internal strife. Some Magistrates hung on in the remaining occupied villes to enforce the will of whichever power figure claimed their allegiance.

Others roamed the countryside like the masterless samurai or *ronin* of Japan, especially in the days following the overthrow of the shogunate by the Meiji Restoration in the latter half of the nineteenth century. Like the *ronin* of old, some had become mere laborers or even mendicants, some mercenaries hiring their blasters to whoever was willing to offer pay or loot, and some outright bandits. They had become one more of the pervasive evils the growing complement of Cerberus redoubt fought against.

Kane and Grant were different. They had become renegades through their own choice, rebels against the tyranny of the barons and the vast secret conspiracy they once served. Although as in the case of Brigid herself, an erstwhile archivist who had fallen from grace and escaped Cobaltville with the pair, how big a role free will or choice had actually played in their exile was subject to debate. All had on one level or another been manipulated by Dr. Mohandas Lakesh Singh, the scientist who had been one of the architects of the program of Unification and the baronial system, and who subsequently had betrayed both—ostensibly in the interests of humanity. He was now director of Cerberus, and de facto commander of the resistance based there.

Kane and Grant, sometimes even Brigid herself, had repeatedly rebelled against Lakesh's arrogance and manipulation and assumption of command. Yet somehow he remained in charge. Perhaps, in the end, Brigid reflected, because no one else actually wanted his job.

"Same as last night," Grant said. "Same as every night, lately."

"What?" a female voice asked. Domi appeared like a photonegative shadow out of the darkness. She wore a brief red top and loose khaki shorts against the warmth of the Snail Cove night.

Domi was a small woman. She was an albino, her skin the white of milk or sun-bleached bone, as was her hair, which she wore trimmed to a silvery plush. Ruby highlights glinted in her eyes in the firelight. Though she was slimly built, her breasts and hips and buttocks were full, and her legs long for her inconsiderable height. With her pert, gamine features and a web belt cinched about her narrow waist to hold a holster for her Detonics Combat Master .45 counterbalanced by a sheath for her pet knife with the nine-inch saw-backed blade, she looked like a naughty elf.

The elfin resemblance didn't carry too well—unless, as Brigid knew, one looked back at the old myths to learn what the elves were *really* like. Although physically the least imposing of the four fugitives who had fled Cobaltville together to wind up in Cerberus, Domi was as casually deadly as a krait.

Domi plopped down on the sand across from Grant and sat with the soles of her feet together and her legs carelessly splayed. "What every night?" she asked. "Did you start getting some, Grant? Shizuka-*san*'ll be pissed."

Grant's dark cheeks actually flushed—he was comparatively light-skinned for a black man. He lowered his head and his heavy brow furrowed further.

"The nightmares," Kane said. "Same ones we've been having for weeks." He looked up at Brigid. "Seem to be getting stronger."

"What nightmares?" Domi asked brightly. "I didn't have any nightmares."

"You really don't have the dreams, Domi?" Grant asked. Only occasionally did Domi's needling get under his skin; he was, as he said, used to her bullshit.

She shook her head, her ruby eyes wide. "No. I really don't."

Watching her narrowly, Brigid could see no signs she lied. It meant little, Brigid was painfully aware. Having grown up in the desperate Outlands, a forager, scammer and survivor, Domi was a skilled dissembler, while Brigid was only slowly and painfully building the most basic skills of reading and understanding other people, which formed no part of her training and practice as an archivist. Indeed, interaction among people on any but a duty basis had been kept to a rigorous minimum throughout the Cobaltville Enclaves, and particularly in her Historical Division.

Around them the night lived with the rustling of the palms and the inland vegetation, the twittering of night birds and the variegated insect noises. The sea was relatively calm, the surf a soft susurration. The air was warm and soft. The waning moon had fallen away behind the island hours before. The stars' reflections floated and played in the gentle waves out beyond the shore, like schools of phosphorescent fish. Just another night in Paradise—except for the dreams.

"What was your dream, Baptiste?" Kane asked. Challenge rang in his words, though they were softly voiced.

She flushed and made herself meet his gaze. Their fates, their very souls, were linked—throughout time and space, if the jump dreams were to be credited. Yet they also seemed fated, at least in this incarnation, always to rub each other the wrong way.

Nor, Brigid knew, was Kane always at fault.

"You know I'm uncomfortable talking about such matters at the best of times, Kane," she said.

"I'm not asking out of idle curiosity."

She felt her cheeks tighten, drawing her mouth out into what some—Historical Division archivists, perhaps—might mistake for a smile. She lowered her face.

"Of course. There was the blackness. The sense of crushing pressure. The menace, terrible and terrifying as anything I've known. And…the eye."

"The eye in the pyramid," Grant said. His voice seemed to emerge from him without motion of the lips, as if an idol spoke in fact.

"A big red eye in a black triangle, anyway," Kane said.

"Why would we all be dreaming about an ancient symbol of the so-called Illuminati?" Brigid said.

Kane shrugged and scratched meaningless ephemeral patterns in the white sand before his feet with a stick.

"Mebbe because we all used to work for the bunch that was really behind all the tales about the Illuminati?"

"But why do you all keep dreaming the same thing?" Domi asked. "Lakesh, too."

The other three looked at her intently. Grant even raised his head. "What's this about Lakesh?" he asked.

She shrugged. "Something he let slip. He's been having bad dreams, too. He was cagey about the details, like he's always cagey about everything. But I think he sees the eye in the black pyramid, too."

Kane grunted. At one point Lakesh had been rejuvenated through the actions of Sam the Imperator; it had proved a temporary effect. When it was in effect, he and Domi had become lovers.

Although middle age had reclaimed Lakesh, the affair seemed ongoing. Despite that fact, she got as exasperated with Lakesh as any of them, at least as often. It tended to express itself, as Domi's emotions did, in periodic outbursts of pyrotechnics. Still, they seemed to share a definite affinity, the ancient whitecoat and the white-haired wild child.

"Naturally he didn't say anything about it to the rest of us," Grant said.

"It is a fairly private matter," Brigid said. Her three companions glared at her. Why do I feel the need to defend him? she asked herself. He had been her mentor in Cobaltville—and had set up her like an ancient glass bottle a coldheart put on an Outlands fencepost for target practice. She remembered shivering naked in the tiny cell, awaiting execution of her own personal termination warrant—Lakesh's doing. As, allegedly, had been her eleventh-hour rescue by Kane.

"It's a potentially important data point," Kane said. "I'm not usually the sort to get too worked up over dreams. But something is going on when we all keep having the same ones."

He glanced at the albino girl. "Most of us, anyway."

A rustle of brush, a thudding of footsteps in the night. Brigid jumped up and spun, heart in her throat. A shadowy humanoid figure resolved out of the dark, shambling toward them.

At the very edge of the illumination cast by the driftwood fire it stopped short. It held up two hands. Yellow-pink palms became visible.

"Sorry," a British-accented voice said. It was young, male and hesitant. "Sorry. I keep forgetting."

"It'll kill you someday, kid," Grant said. His big black Sin Eater snapped back into its holster. A heartbeat later Kane's handblaster whirred back to its customary resting place and Brigid lowered her handblaster.

The rest of the figure emerged into light from shadow: a gangly young man with dark sheepdog hair framing a long face, dark eyes, nondescript nose and a generous mouth. He was dressed in a light-colored shirt with long sleeves rolled down against the bugs, which seemed to single him out for abuse, and the shirttails hung over the khaki cargo shorts most of the research personnel wore.

He had a floppy-puppy manner about him that was disarming even to the likes of Kane and Grant.

Which was unusual: Simon Jenkins was among the youngest of the refugees from the Manitius Moon Base, and usually that bunch didn't get along any too well with the senior Cerberus operatives. He wasn't as young as he looked, which was about fourteen; in fact he was a trained marine biologist who had been involved in looking after the various aquatic forms cultivated in the lunar base. He had always harbored a passionate interest in ocean life-forms. When offered a chance to join the contingent from Cerberus he had jumped at the opportunity.

"I certainly hope not," he said. "Might I join you?"

"Looks like you already did," Kane said.

He plopped down on the sand between Domi and Brigid. He was particularly partial to Domi, although from time to time in the days since the four had arrived on this Pacific island outpost he had made it clear the sight of Brigid didn't pain his eyes, either. Brigid was mildly exasperated by the attention; Domi tended to encourage it.

"You people do seem set rather on a hair trigger," he said, nodding at Brigid's USP, which she still held. She hurriedly holstered the blaster and sat back down.

"Snail Cove isn't exactly a green zone, kid," Kane said, "if there even is any such thing on this tortured mudball. There're critters out in the bush on these islands that'd be more than happy to eat your head."

"Not to mention the raids," Grant added. It was why they had been dispatched to the island in the first place.

"Or the snails," Domi offered.

Of the four only Brigid seemed to know or care exactly what Lakesh had in mind with the remote research facility he had established, with personnel from Cerberus, recent recruits from the Outlands and a labor force hired from the largely Polynesian-descended population of the eastern Pacific islands, most of which had appeared during and after the upheavals of the nukecaust, two centuries before. The others knew they were cultivating creatures known as cone snails in shallow wooden pens in the surf near shore.

The cone snails were fascinating creatures, even to Brigid, who was not keen on living things or the smelly, gritty world outside the cool, reasoned calm of the records room. They were tiny, the largest only about fifty millimeters in length, with colorful, intricately patterned shells. They customarily buried themselves in the sand, pushing up trunklike snouts when disturbances in the water indicated the proximity of fish—or incautious humans. They would then whip out astonishing organic harpoons to sting their prey with lethal cocktails of assorted neurotoxins.

Somehow Lakesh had learned about a particular species of cone snail that lived in the shallows of this particular volcanic pimple on the Pacific's immense face, southeast of the Hawaiian chain. He had dispatched a team to begin collecting the creatures, breeding them, observing them and milking them of their venom. From a bit of research before coming out here Brigid knew the various component toxins of assorted cone snail species had once been studied for possible use as nerve blockers and treatments for Alzheimer's and epilepsy.

What got Lakesh so excited about these particularly lovely if nasty organisms he had not shared with his four main operatives, even Brigid. She had not failed to realize that, although the literature didn't say as much, the snail venom—which usually worked by inducing quick paralysis of the respiratory system—might prove useful for assassinations and such.

"But we've not seen hair nor scale of the raiders since you got here," Simon said, smiling loosely and moistly at Brigid. "Not to mention the fact that with all the razor-tape tangles and sensors and whizbangs surrounding us here, neither tattooed cultists nor fish men are at all likely to fall on us unawares, are they?"

Someone had taken an interest in the proceedings on Snail Cove. While Kane and Grant discounted reports of nocturnal sightings of strange outsize figures resembling hybrids of men and fish, there was no question that a bizarrely tattooed tribe or cult had been raiding the facility sporadically. They had left behind corpses to prove it. The night before the four were sent out, a Moon base refugee scientist named Cannondale had been snatched and three local laborers killed.

Grant fixed the youthful whitecoat with an eye. "If you only had a clue how many men have got chilled because they relied on passive defenses like fences and sensors to keep us out," he said.

"If only he had a clue," Kane said.

The kid's cheeks turned bright pink. "I suppose I forgot about all that," he said. "Sorry. I admit I am rather new to this rough-and-tumble stuff."

"It's all right, Simon," Domi said, stroking his arm as if he were a favored pet. "You're a scientist. You're not supposed to know all this snoop-and-poop stuff."

He nodded to her half-absently and turned back to gaze at Brigid. Adoringly.

Brigid felt both irritation and something akin to sympathy for the boy. Admit it—you find the attention flattering.

Domi formed her right hand into a Phoenix-eye fist, first knuckle protruding, and jabbed the young scientist briskly in the biceps with it. "Hey, at least look at me when you talk to me!"

"Ow!" He jumped, turned, rubbing his injured arm. "That hurt!"

"Supposed to," Domi said dangerously low.

Simon had learned what it meant when Domi started losing parts of speech. "I'm sorry, Domi," he said. "It's only that I'm distracted by—"

"I *know* what you distracted by!" She punched him again. "If you can't tear eyes from her big boobs—"

They were interrupted by one of the Cerberus techs. "We just received word from Lakesh," he said, not sure whom to address.

"What does he want this time?" Grant demanded, not even bothering to look at the tech.

"Something about having just received a most re-markable communication," the tech answered.

"From where? Outer space?" Kane said.

"Not Sindri again." Grant said.

"No," the tech said hesitantly. "Lakesh said it appears to originate on the seabed eight hundred miles from where we are now!"

THE SLEEP OF A BARON was not like the sleep of apekin. Even that of a baron who wasn't a true baron, but rather a sort of penultimate draft, genetically speaking. Although Baron Lemuria didn't encourage talk on the subject, even sympathetically couched.

Nonetheless, sleep Baron Lemuria did. And he dreamed.

He saw again in his sleeping mind's eye the final images relayed from the doomed submersible: a roiling blackness in the abyss and then the opening of a fearful glowing eye.

But the eye was staring at *him* now, at Baron Lemuria. It knew him; its awful intention had sought him out here in his inner sanctum in his subterranean fortress.

It found me.

He rolled and cried out in his bed, unaware he did so. He was aware of struggling to awaken. Awaken before the terrible black tentacles closed around him…

"Wake if you will," a voice said. "It won't stop you from knowing my thoughts."

"What are you?" the baron cried. He didn't know

whether he shouted the words with his mouth or in his mind alone. Either way they were a desperate ragged scream.

"I am Leviathan," the voice said. "This day you beheld me. Know that you have experienced only the minutest fraction of my might.

"I am Lord of the Deep, who dwelt in undersea canyons before the Annunaki evolved from swamp geckos, much less arrived upon this Earth. I am older than humankind itself, older than the dinosaurs. This world is mine."

The words were terrible—blasphemous, to one such as the baron. "What do you want of me?"

"Your kindred and rivals, the barons of North America, have transformed into what they laughably imagine to be gods, and become possessed of the souls of the ancient Annunaki. They seek to rule Earth. The time has come for me to confront them and reassert my dominion over all this globe, not just that majority which lies covered by water. My will be done.

"And you are going to help me."

Chapter 2

"We're being attacked!"

The words rang like steel clashing on steel. Popping gunfire punctuated them. A thrill of fear ran through the chest of Kiri, fleet mistress of the Shark People tribe of the Children of the Great Wave, as she stood on the deck of her trimaran *Great Sky Reef*.

My son! she thought. Reva!

Today they harvested kelp several hours' sail from their current harbor on Camel Island. Her son rode in an outrigger several hundred yards away. A dozen or so vessels of various sizes were spread about the water around Kiri's ship.

The day had been calm. Sunlight danced on the waves. White clouds rolled and piled up along the western horizon. They receded slowly from the fleet, posing only a small threat of a storm. Like all island people, Kiri knew too well how quickly the Pacific mood could turn ugly.

But no one anticipated *this* kind of ugliness.

Like the sound of evil insects the whine of engines cut across the morning's peaceful rhythms: of wind in rigging and sea slapping multiple narrow hulls. Clapping a hand to her dagger's man-bone hilt, Kiri looked wildly around. One-man skimmers forked by men in indigo wet suits and formfitting dark-visored helmets popped out of the sea like blue-and-green bubbles from a submarine gas release all around. Apparently weighted, once emerged they rolled quickly upright and began to scoot across the waves. She could only guess they were being released from some submerged vessel.

The skimmers fired forward-fixed machine guns. The fleet mistress watched in horror as one raked a thirty-foot outrigger canoe from prow to stern. At least half a dozen bare-chested men and women, caught in the act of hauling aboard whalebone racks overgrown with lank purple-green kelp tangles, swayed as bullets punched through their bodies, throwing out sprays of fine red mist that quickly puffed away on the freshening breeze. Some slumped in place, their lifeblood leaking into the bottom of the boat. Others slumped across the low gunwales or pitched into the sea.

None had anything resembling the ghost of a chance.

She snapped her head in the other direction, heavy purple-black locks whipping her cheeks. Her son, Reva, a clever, mischievous boy of 110 moon cycles, rode an outrigger five hundred yards in that direction. Ironically its duty was to keep watch.

But there was no watch-keeping against attack from underneath.

Her eyes, palm shielded from the sun, sharpened by

many watches by day and dark night, quickly picked out his craft. What she saw made her knees weak. The boat rolled empty on the slow swells.

Across the water came the buzzing blare of a conch shell blown by lusty lungs. Three long notes repeated over and over: the signal for the fleet to return to base.

"No!" she cried. "Tupolu, you coward!" We mustn't abandon my son! she thought wildly. She ran back a few paces to where Big Tony, her own conch man, stood gaping from the doorway to the main cabin, with his big belly hanging over his loincloth and his conch-shell trumpet hanging from a shark-leather strap on his shoulder.

Punching him on the arm to gain his attention, she shouted, "Countermand the war leader's order! We must fight."

Big Tony turned to her. His big fleshy face was slack and gray at the shock of the attack.

"We have no chance to outrun them," she insisted. "We have no choice but to fight."

Some vessels like the *Great Sky Reef* possessed engines, which burned alcohol fermented from coconuts and other plant matter, including the seaweed they harvested today. But the engines weren't powerful, the Shark People craft not built for speed. And the wind still blew offshore—as if with the fairest of winds they could hope to outsail these raiders on their gleaming blue-and-green skimmers.

At least a dozen of the fleet one-man craft had popped from the sea. They buzzed around and through the harvest fleet, firing at random. As Big Tony raised the conch and blew the falling-rising-falling fanfare that was her own personal signal of command, Kiri realized that the only thing saving her people was that the marauders could only aim but poorly from their fast-moving craft.

Big Tony blew the notes conveying fleet mistress's commands, which superseded all other orders. The Shark People were warriors, men and women alike, although when possible men bore the brunt of war, ranging afield to intercept foes while the women stayed back to defend their homes and children. Gunshots banged from the score of craft of varying sizes, single shots only. The Shark People commonly carried only a few bolt-action rifles and somewhat more muzzle-loading black-powder rifles, to conserve their stocks of precious ammunition. Arrows arced ineffectually from rolling canoes. Kiri pumped her fist and cheered aloud when she saw a thrown fish spear impale one of the synthetic-clad riders, causing him to tumble like a flung rag doll, limbs sprawling, off his speeding platform. He vanished from sight beneath the water. The skimmer itself proceeded straight ahead for another twenty yards or so, then slowed and began to wallow broadside to the seas.

"Kiri, look!" a crew woman shouted from the far side of the trimaran's main hull. Kiri ran that way to see a bizarre sight.

A craft like some kind of smooth seed pod or a sea-bird's egg appeared on the surface two hundred yards off their starboard beam in a froth of green foam. Noiselessly, so far as she could hear, it began advancing with remarkable speed.

A blue-green beam stabbed from it. It didn't seem bright in the intense sunlight, yet it dazzled Kiri's eyes and left a pulsing magenta afterimage that persisted when she shut them. The main cabin of a larger twin-hulled vessel exploded in flames.

Big Tony stood beside her, conch shell hanging loose as his jaw. "Deviltry!" he blubbered.

Kiri had experienced too much to doubt the existence of the spirit realm. But she was well educated, even—perhaps particularly—by the standards of the wretched landlubbers. The Wave Children were more than they seemed to the outside eye.

"Lasers!" she snapped back. But her heart sank within her to a stomach gone cold and curdled. *How can we fight such weapons?*

Thought of her son snapped her back to intense focus. She ran into the cabin, snatched up a rare treasure from brackets on the wooden wall: an ancient Springfield Armory M1A rifle. Seizing a web vest with spare 20-round magazines of .308 cartridges, she ran out again into the sunlight.

Her craft had begun to gather together so that they could more effectively support one another with their pitifully limited firepower. Clumping also made it harder for the far swifter enemy vessels to dart among the canoes and catamarans like barracuda through a school of pilchards. Unfortunately, it also made the harvest fleet a more concentrated target.

The fight was not entirely one-sided. More than one hundred of the tribe crewed the flotilla, most with access to some sort of projectile weapons, if only spears and bows. The skimmer riders were armored only by their speed. Great as that advantage was, their number had already been reduced by a third.

But the pod craft seemed impervious to anything they had. Kiri wound the sling around her left forearm, snugged the butt of the longblaster to her shoulder and drew a bead on the nearest enemy through the peep sight. The enemy craft moved at right angles to her. She led it slightly, squeezed off a round.

The rifle kicked her shoulder. She was no large woman, rather small by her people's standards in fact, no more than five foot eight. But she had wiry strength. And she knew how to shoot: she rode the recoil, allowing the barrel to rise inevitably but slightly, never losing the weld of cheek to stock.

She was fairly sure she had struck her target, fast though it was. It showed no effect. Increasing her lead slightly, she fired twice more.

Nothing.

Despairing, she lowered her rifle. One of her vessels—the *Squirrelfish,* she thought—blazed end to end. As she watched, what she hoped was the last of its crew dived overboard to flee the flames.

Around them, tall dorsal fins began to knife the water. Sharks! Kiri thought. A thrill ran through her.

A skimmer cut near her vessel. As it did, a mako shark performed one of that breed's trademark flying leaps from the water. Its jag-toothed gape struck the rider at the shoulder. He shrieked horribly as it bore him off his craft and into the sea with a mountainous splash.

A wine-dark stain seeped to the surface as the waves closed over him, rapidly turning pink as it diffused.

With their allies joining the battle Kiri's people seemed to have the skimmers more or less in hand. But nothing they could do seemed to faze the pod craft. As the thought flashed through her mind, there came a smell of ozone, a dazzling flash, a crack like thunder. The whole upper half of Big Tony's bulky body vanished in an eruption of pink-tinged steam and black squirts as the powerful cyan laser flash-boiled the water in his tissues. Stern and seasoned warrior though she was, Kiri winced as bits of hot tissue splattered her face and clung, stinging like hot tallow.

Wails rose from the ship. From her own deck. The hand-shaped planks of hulls and cabin seemed to groan in sympathy.

Furiously she spun to the crew, staring horrified at Tony's flopping legs and hips.

"It's war!" she cried. "People die in war. But we make them pay!"

"But the egg ships," someone said. "We cannot touch them."

She threw her rifle to her shoulder and fired at another of the closed craft. "Then we die like warriors!" she shouted as her ears still rang from the head-splitting report.

Her second in command, Timu, seized her arm, pointing off to the north. A skimmer whose rider had been shot out of the saddle suddenly righted itself. A female figure straddled it, brown skinned, slim, like Kiri herself naked but for a loin strap, with a great cloud of dark dreadlocks hanging to bare shoulders.

"That's Tessa," said Margene, Kiri's sailing mistress, who had the sharpest eyes. Kiri, whose eyes were also keen, quickly recognized the rider, as well.

The one-person craft surged into purposeful motion. The Shark People made sparing use of technology advanced beyond the bare Paleolithic level of stone, wood, bone, shark tooth and shell. But that owed to the steep resource costs of obtaining or maintaining higher tech. They were neither superstitious nor ignorant, as were some peoples they came in contact with on their ocean rangings. Indeed they possessed certain items of a sophistication that would take the breath of any mainlander unfamiliar with their history—as most lubbers were.

Tessa had received sound training from her tribe and spent a wander-year on the mainland as an adolescent, as Kiri had herself. She knew machines. And like most of their folk, she was resourceful and bold to an extreme.

If they weren't, their ancestors never would have survived being swept out to sea during the great deluge two hundred wheel-turnings before.

A pod craft moved with menacing purpose toward the clustering fleet from Tessa's left. Kiri felt the sense its occupants were toying with the Shark People. Her lithe body filled with rage and frustration.

The white-foam V of Tessa's wake curved as she turned her skimmer toward the pod craft. The skimmer accelerated.

"Tessa, *no!*" Margene exclaimed from Kiri's elbow.

Skipping across the water like a flung stone, the skimmer rammed the shiny egg-shaped craft amidships. The impact flung Tessa cartwheeling across the surface for fifty yards before sinking, broken, out of sight.

No explosion followed. The eggshell visibly cracked where the skimmer struck. Parts of it and the smaller craft flew out to drop into the sea in white splashes. The pod rolled toward the side on which it had been struck as water rushed in, then sank from sight almost before the slamming, rending sound of the collision reached Kiri's ears.

She hoisted the M1A's not-inconsiderable weight over her head and led her crew in a booming cheer.

"The wave skimmers flee!" shouted a crewman from a nearby craft. Looking around, Kiri quickly saw a good reason, as a great white shark surged half out of the water to seize a rider's leg and pull him screaming down below the waves.

The *Great Sky Reef*'s mainmast parted with a crack. Her mainsail whoomped into flames as the sundered mast brought it crashing down on the afterdeck. A laser blast from another egg craft had struck it. Kiri's ears and nostrils filled with the seafarer's greatest dreads, the crackle and boom and acrid smell of a ship burning.

She snapped orders to her crew to fight the blaze. Her voice rang with command, as she knew how to make it do, despite the tears of rage and frustration rolling down her brown cheeks. She longed to rend and tear the evil crew inside those glittering seamless craft as the sharks were tearing their comrades from the skimmers. Running back to supervise the firefighting, she saw one of the hateful ovoids through eye-stinging smoke, scarcely a hundred yards off the starboard quarter and closing for the kill.

Water began to roil about it as if coming to a boil. The submersible wallowed. It had a clear viewscreen for the top of its rounded prow. Kiri fancied she could see two faces inside, dark bearded ovals pale with lack of exposure to sun—and sudden fear.

A shape exploded from the water. Not a shark this time, but another sea predator scarcely less fearful to the lesser fishes, if not—usually—so menacing to man: a great bluefin tuna, a full fifteen feet long. It landed smack atop the egg craft with a resounding crack that caused it to wallow momentarily deep in the water.

Flopping feebly, its back undoubtedly broken, the great fish slid off into the sea. Instantly two more exploded from the sea in geysers that glittered in brief rainbow clouds, to likewise strike the enemy vessel like living artillery shells. Other big blue-backed shapes were leaping on all sides of the embattled craft, not playfully, but in evident panic.

And Kiri understood: they were being driven. Stampeded by a shoal of hunters far more terrible than themselves. Stampeded with purpose.

Deadly purpose.

"Reva," she breathed. Then she shouted, "Reva! My son! He leads our brothers and sisters against the foe!"

Dark heads were already bobbing in the waves as people who had abandoned their own stricken or strafed craft for the sheltering embrace of the sea swam strongly toward the enemy ovoid, now under a constant battering by great shapes massing half a ton or more, leaping into it in self-sacrifice born of the sea thing's greatest dread. The swimmer showed no fear of the pointed dorsal fins that poked from the water on all sides of the terrified tuna school like an animated picket fence.

It was perfectly natural for siblings not to fear each other, after all.

Part of the egg craft's upper surface opened as a curved hatch. A bearded head poked out, the cord of a headset dangling visibly by a shoulder clad in cloth only the brilliance of the noontime sun showed to be deep midnight blue rather than black. Perhaps not seeing the sharks circling at some distance, or prepared to risk them rather than drowning trapped in the egg, a crewman was attempting to bail out.

Not all of the nearby Shark People had dived off their own craft, or perhaps some had reboarded when the enemy crew found better things to do than hunt them. Kiri lifted her rifle to her shoulder—and saw a puff of dirty bluish-white smoke from an outrigger forty yards on the far side of the egg craft. The head, dark-haired or hooded—impossible to tell which, given the distance and sun glare off the water—snapped sideways as a maroon cloud gusted away from it. The crewman flopped down half in his craft, half out.

At once he began to retract into the vessel. His companion or companions now tried desperately to haul him back, failing to do the coldly rational thing and jettison him before slamming shut the hatch.

Three swimmers clambered up onto the craft's sleek back. The rest turned back to swim lustily for the nearest boats of their own side. Most folk of Kiri's fleet possessed the gift of empathy with their finned and gill-slitted brethren, if few to such a degree as Reva, tender as his own years were. That rapport told them what they, like any of the Shark People who survived from earliest babyhood, already knew well from observation and experience: the sharks, these mostly a mix of makos and tigers, tasted blood spilled in the sea. That began shifting their keen but limited minds into a state memorialized long before skydark as a feeding frenzy. They now could barely restrain themselves from tearing at anything that came within reach of their terrible jaws, even one another. Soon they would no longer be capable of even trying to refrain.

The three tribesfolk swarmed toward the hatch. A

flash lit the inside of the open hatch for an eye blink, and another cloud of dark red spray appeared behind one man's bare tanned back. He fell into the water. The crack of a handblaster shot came to Kiri as the surviving man and woman dived into the hatch with steel knives glittering like white flames in their hands.

From port and starboard of *Great Sky Reef* two egg craft moved to the aid of their stricken fellow, converging at about forty degrees. The sharks herding the tuna school had been released to feed. The bluefins were if anything more utterly panicked than before as the sharks ripped through them like animated chain saws, tearing away whole fins or ham-sized chunks of flesh at a pass. The tuna leaped into the merciless blue Cific sky, but no longer were their frenzied jumps focused on the first egg craft.

A bluefin sounded in a fifteen-foot leap. The whole last third of body and forked tail vanished in a sudden scarlet-shot cloud of milky steam. Realizing the ovoid had been commandeered by their previously helpless enemies, the egg craft coming in from Kiri's right had opened fire on it. Almost at once more bluefins began jumping from the water between the two similar craft.

"Truly, your son's skill is great," Timu murmured in unfeigned admiration.

Kiri nodded, heart swelling with pride. Yet she still knew fear: the ovoid obviously intended to get near enough to put a certain kill shot in the hijacked vessel. As low as both rode the sluggish waves, it was likely no easy shot even with advanced electrooptics and computerized targeting systems, such as Kiri took for granted the enemy seamen possessed.

She raised her rifle and methodically cracked out the shots remaining in her 20-round box magazine, though the sustained firing jackhammered her shoulder brutally in spite of her snug marksman's hold on the semiauto longblaster.

The bullets produced the results her mind expected and her heart feared: nothing.

A cloud of spray erupted from the slow moss-green back of a swell. A truly colossal figure rose in the sky like a big-bellied cloud, its back gray, its swollen-seeming belly white. It was a great white that really honored its name, at least thirty feet from pointed snout to the tip of its upper tail fin.

"Old Grandfather!" Kiri's crew sang out in awed unison. And there was more: a dark figure, ridiculously tiny against the monster's awful gleaming bulk, straddled its back, legs almost at full split, small, wiry arms clinging to a dorsal fin taller than the tallest Samoan.

"Reva!" Kiri shouted, waving her rifle over her head.

The great shark came down right on the back of the egg craft attacking its fellow. Tons of mass drove the craft downward from view in a cataclysm of prismatic spray. The sea closed over where both had been an eye blink before, slow-rolling mounds laced with white froth.

Kiri's triumphant cry died in her throat. Then the sky filled with water yet again as Old Grandfather

leaped forth, flashing its own scythe tail as if in triumph, with Reva clinging to its back with one arm as
the other waved insouciantly.

A moment later cyan light stabbed from the craft the
Shark People had entered. Its ovoid shape, again intact,
showed they had closed the hatch after them. The remaining egg craft, its crew now distracted by the buffeting of bluefin bodies flying all around them, exploded
with a white flash, foundered and sank in seconds.

If any skimmer jockeys survived they had long since
fled, no doubt far more fearful of being eaten alive in a
frenzied airless thrashing below the surface than the few
projectile weapons of their intended victims. At least two
of the egg vessels remained in view. But not for long: they
dived from sight as Kiri's osprey gaze flicked across them.

The egg craft Old Grandfather had struck never re-
surfaced. Whether it was sunk or merely chose to flee,
the tribespeople would never know.

"REVA! MY SON, today you have shown yourself a man!"
Kiri caught up the dripping slight form that had clambered over the gunwales and squashed him fiercely
against her bare breasts. A great fat torpedo of white appeared three yards from the big trimaran as Old Grandfather flashed its belly in a victory roll. The mighty
shark was immensely old, wise and frighteningly intelligent, although of course its thoughts were not those of
any human. Kiri could feel them now, like the kiss of a
feather on the surface of her mind.

For just a moment, she tasted blood, salt as sea water, iron as nails.

Kiri's crew cheered the great beast. It rolled onto its belly, its immense isosceles dorsal fin jutting high in the air. Then it disappeared with a surge of its tail that sent a wave of water sloshing across the deck and the laughing, shouting crew as the shark patriarch swam away for a well-deserved gorging on the flesh of tuna—and men.

As its kindred did already, Old Grandfather would feed as eagerly upon the flesh of dead Shark People. This, too, was part of the ancient compact between shark and human that had helped the Shark People to survive so long in a pitiless world. Some day Kiri herself would go to be food for the shark brothers and sisters—if she were lucky, Old Grandfather itself. And if the fact failed to fill her with the sense of religious purpose as it did some of her more susceptible tribespeople, neither did she feel any apprehension. It was the natural way of things.

She set her son down to allow him to be enfolded by the arms of her jubilant crew. A call took her to the deck toward the stern.

An ovoid rolled just a few yards from the trimaran's starboard outer hull. Its hatch stood open once more. Standing half out of it was none other than Tupolu, his hair hanging almost dry in purple-black waves to his broad brown shoulders.

"Well done, War Leader," Kiri said, though her frown belied her words. "You show courage after all, it seems."

Tupolu's handsome face clouded like a sudden squall line on the horizon. "And I gave the fleet mistress cause to doubt my bravery?" he said.

"Was not your first instinct to turn tail and flee?" she said with a sudden bitterness that surprised even her.

An arm around her should made her jump. It was Timu, her second, his old sun-seamed face tight with concern.

"Come, let our hearts harbor no discord," he said. "Surely there is glory and joy in this victory enough for all our people to share."

She glared at him a moment, her brown eyes deadly as a shark's steel-gray ones. Then the hardness passed and tension flowed from her shoulders. She nodded.

"You have right," she said. She turned to face her crew, and the crews of the other flotilla craft, all now crewed once more.

"Hail to the people! Hail to the sharks, our brothers and sisters! Hail to my son, Reva, and Old Grandfather whom he rode to victory! Hail to Tupolu, who seized the enemy ship!"

She sang out the last lustily as the paean to her own son's heroism. The look that passed between her and the strapping war leader, as her calls were taken up and repeated again and again by the flotilla, said that neither was fooled.

And that, unlike the battle with the strange submarine marauders, this matter was far from finished.

Chapter 3

Kane came instantly awake with his Sin Eater in hand. Its holster lay in white sand beside the depression his body had made. It was too risky to sleep with the power holster strapped to his forearm, where forming a half fist in the grip of a dream could bring the blaster slamming into action, its guardless trigger setting it instantly to spitting noise and copper-jacketed 9 mm death.

Especially the dreams he'd been having the past few weeks.

Grant stood on the other side of him from the blaster as Kane sat up. His long, strong face was impassive. For all Snail Cove's paradisiacal aspects, they were there on business—and as everywhere else on Earth, any and all business on the island could turn deadly without warning.

But after all, for them, that was business as usual.

"You got the call, too," Grant said, low.

"Got the same damn voices in my head you do," Kane moaned, rubbing the back of his skull with the Sin Eater's butt. In this case Domi's voice, via their implanted tactical transceivers.

He stood. "Trouble?"

"Always got trouble."

"Granted. Which particular trouble?"

Grant grinned through his gunslinger's mustache. "Kind we came for."

"Lucky us."

The crackling of distant gunfire rippled beneath the belly of the night.

A scream pealed through both their heads.

THE CAR-4 SCREAMED as Domi ripped out a burst. Blue-and-yellow pulses from the flash suppressor blanked out most of her night vision. But she still saw the hunched, shambling shape fall to the sand not ten yards from where she crouched behind an overturned boat.

Then, groaning, the misshapen shadow rose and resumed its seemingly inexorable advance from the sea. Right toward her.

"Fuck all mouse guns, anyway," she said aloud. Rising, she braced herself with the extended butt snugged into the pocket of her shoulder, took aim in the green-white light of the moon at the humped mass that had to be the head and squeezed off a single round. The carbine made its terrific crack and slapped her face with muzzle-blast. The recoil was negligible and made the muzzle rise only slightly. Not enough to prevent her seeing the shadow figure drop with the rag-doll finality that indicated instant death from a brain shot.

Something whispered through the peripheral vision to her left. A scream came from behind a dormant alcohol-fueled generator. The figure of a Cerberus tech reared up from hiding, clutching at a barbed spear through its throat.

More of the larger-than-human shapes lumbered past to Domi's left and right. "This is pretty fucked up," she said. "Kane? Grant? Where the hell are you? I'm getting surrounded here."

Ripping a burst from the hip, she turned and ran for the shadows of the underbrush upslope from the beach.

IN HER PREVIOUSLY DREAMLESS sleep Brigid suddenly dreamed a clammy, fish-reeking cloth had covered her mouth and nose, rendering it impossible to breathe.

Then her eyes snapped open and she looked into a pair of bulging baseball eyes that glowed with their own green witch light. The creature's hand was wet and scaly and chill on her face.

She screamed into its palm. The reek of fish almost overwhelmed her. The hand muffled the sound.

The thing hunched over her was a mass of blackness blocking the stars in the clear sky overhead. Its silhouette was manlike but seemed in no way human. She caught the impression the creature was bigger than a man, but enough presence of mind had returned to her that she realized that might be an artifact of surprise, the darkness and panic, as adrenaline filled her veins with its crackling song and distorted all her perceptions.

But then, maybe it wasn't.

With a grunt of minor effort and accompanying exhalation of breath that stank so intently of rotting fish that it filled her eyes with tears and made her gag, the monster stooped lower and slid a hand beneath Brigid's back.

He's trying to pick me up! she realized.

She caught a mental flash of the reproduced images she had seen of early- and middle-twentieth century pulp science-fantasy magazines, showing beautiful women—clad even more scantily than she was now, in her T-shirt and underwear—being carried off by monstrous green aliens. For what purpose she had never been able to fathom, since the pink-skinned human females should by rights be as repulsive to their goggling eyes as they were to human ones.

Now she seemed on the verge of suffering that same fate.

It was too ludicrous to be borne.

Even as the creature clasped her to a strangely sharp-keeled chest and began to lift her, she slid a hand beneath the towel roll she had used for a pillow. As it straightened to a hunched stance, she pressed the muzzle of her USP against the cold scaled skin and began triggering off rounds.

Strobing yellow-orange flashes lit a face with a sharp protruding jaw filled with jagged teeth. The face seemed to consist of two bony planes that came together in the middle. Double nostrils trailed from the apex above the mouth. The two huge oval eyes were set above, giving it a sort of binocular vision with more peripheral coverage than a human. Brigid took the impression of ragged excrescences set low and back on the glistening skull, couldn't tell if they were external ears or just fins. Blood splashed her hand and soaked the front of her T-shirt, surprisingly hot.

The being grunted and dropped her. In her occasional moments of awkward vanity she feared she was big and ungainly, especially by contrast to the lithe Domi or Shizuka. Now she was glad for what she considered the extra padding of her rump. She landed hard.

Even by starlight she could see blood twining down the looming horror's right leg in black streams. It stood steady for a moment, showing no sign it was even aware of being shot, although clearly it was or it wouldn't have dropped her. Then it bent forward, reaching with webbed claws that each looked large enough to enfold her whole head.

She shoved the handgun up before her with both hands and blasted off the rest of the magazine as fast as the slide would cycle.

The creature came on. It seized her shoulders as she pumped her finger spasmodically on the now inert trigger, even as her brain registered her slide was locked back. She screamed in frustrated fury.

The monstrous head exploded.

She was aware of shattering noise from her left as the contents of the misshapen skull streamed away like fleeting storm-wrack against the stars to her right. The great green lamps of eyes stared unblinking down at her.

The glow dimmed, flickered once, went out. The towering mass toppled. Right toward her.

For all her vaunted mental discipline she barely remembered to roll to the side and out of harm's way at the last second. The fish thing slammed down on the blood-soaked mass of what had been her bedroll with a thud that actually lifted her off the ground.

She jumped up. A strong arm went around her shoulders. She sensed without knowing how the presence of Kane.

"I'm fine," she said, nodding convulsively.

"Good. Then reload. An empty mag'll just get you chilled double-quick."

"Just a fount of comfort, aren't you, Kane?" She stooped to grab a fresh magazine from the harness next to the bloody morass that was her roll, eject the empty box and slam home the new one. She stuffed the USP in its holster. Then she stood to buckle the belt around her slim waist.

"You look like you took a shower in fish-guy blood," Domi said, slipping out of the night with a carbine in her hands. "Hard-core!"

"Plenty of time for warm fuzzies later," Kane said. "Right now we got a fight to win."

"Where's Grant?" Brigid asked.

"Pulling sec. We need to get a feel for the tactical situation triple-fast and then counterattack."

"What *are* these things?" Brigid asked, gesturing a little too abruptly at the great mass that lay huddled and shapeless on its side on what had been her bed.

"That one's dead. Right now all we need to track is how to make all the others get that way fast."

"That won't be easy," Brigid said.

"Tell me about it," Kane said.

From nearby a Sin Eater erupted on full-auto.

"They're moving on us," Grant called.

"Time for us to move on them," Kane said. "We need some heavier blasters. And we need some data. Let's fall back to base camp and arm up—"

"Kane," Brigid said.

He was already turning away, already swinging into action. Prolonged reflection was not for him.

"Make it snappy, Baptiste."

Her cheeks burned. "That thing—" she gestured toward the dead creature on her bedroll "—it tried to pick me up."

"So it's got good taste for a walking fish. So?"

"It didn't try to kill me, Kane, it tried to capture me."

"Things were chilling everybody they got close to that I saw," Domi said. "Some of 'em throw some nasty spears. Be on watch for those."

"What if it's us they're after?" Brigid asked, eyes wide.

Kane shrugged. "Then we make sure they don't get what they came for. Enough jaw aerobics, people. Time to move."

"I'M OVERLOOKING THE BEACH, Kane," Grant's voice whispered into the Commtact, the implanted communications device. "Don't see any boats but ours."

"Roger that," Kane replied via his own Commtact. "These ugly bastards look like they can swim. Submerged, too." He nudged a scaly corpse sprawled across a bush with his boot. "Got gills and everything. All right. They came out of the sea. Let's roll 'em up."

He glanced at Brigid, who stood by with a black-and-chrome-finish marine-model Mossberg 20-gauge shotgun in her hands, looking pale but determined. A single slug through the keelbone of the chest had brought down the nine-foot-tall monster who had suddenly roared out of the brush at them as they approached a lava trail that formed a ridge overlooking the eponymous sheltered cove on the eastern coast of the island, where their boats were moored.

They stood at the top of the ridge, which was the highest point on this side of the island. Sweeping the harbor area with his 8x21 microbinocs, he could see at least half a dozen dark shapes shambling around, some clutching short spears, apparently in search of humans to destroy. The things hardly showed as greenish glimmers on infrared, as he ascertained when he swept the area with a separate IR scope. They were hot-blooded, as Brigid had testified after being drenched with the stuff. Evidently their thick, scaly hides or perhaps a layer of subcutaneous fat that they didn't much show insulated them well against the chill of the water.

As Kane watched through the microbinocs a webbed claw darted with surprising speed to knock over an inverted dugout canoe used by one of their islander allies and laborers and the families they had brought with them. A small girl, no more than ten, cowered beneath.

She raised her hands above her shaggy mop of dark hair and opened her small mouth in a scream.

The monster looming above her raised its scaled arm for a kill stroke.

"Damn," Kane said. Stuffing the binoculars in a pocket of his tan cargo pants, he unslung the heavy rifle from his shoulder, took a turn of the shooting sling around his left forearm and threw the longblaster to his shoulder.

It had a standard 3x9 telescopic sight, no night-vision capability. He had to rely on his sense of where the target was to acquire it in the dark glass. He hunted briefly, muttering another curse.

And there it was. A blur of motion as the raised arm swung down to smash the child. Kane dropped the crosshairs on the head sunk low between the shoulders without apparent intervention of a neck, and pulled the trigger as the peal of the little girl's scream rang thinly in his ears.

He pulled way too fast. The heavy Browning A-Bolt roared and kicked his shoulder. The massive .338 Lapua bullet smashed through both wings of the monster's pelvis, jellying a few loops of gut on the way.

Kane knew what he'd done before the crosshairs settled back onto the target two hundred meters below him on the beach. The creature had dropped to its knees. One hand was down to support it on the sand. The other was extended to paw at its intended victim, who shrank back but did not run. Obviously the beast had terrified all strength from her bare pipe-stem legs.

But its terrible injury had slowed it. Kane had sufficient if not ample time to line up the shot he wanted and pull off a proper trigger squeeze. The gun roared and kicked itself off-line again. Kane opened the off eye he had squeezed shut in violation of usual marksmanship practice to preserve its night vision against the bright muzzle-flash. Even as his left hand drew the rifle back down into line while the right worked the bolt to send a smoking-hot empty spinning into the weeds and crank a fresh round into the chamber, he saw a black fan flicker out from the far side of the monstrous head.

The fish man fell straight over to his right with the no-volition finality of a good head-shot kill.

"Finally," he grunted. "I pulled that first shot off like an Archives Division amateur. Forgive that, Baptiste."

"Don't trouble yourself," she said, crouched beside him in the sand. "When I was an archivist I would have sprained my shoulder and dropped that thing if I tried to shoot it. But you need to worry about something else getting to you right now, Kane. Those things saw the muzzle-flashes. They're headed this way."

Kane raised his head from the glass, where he'd been confirming that the fish thing was a chill and the child, aside from being scared into seven kinds of hysteria, seemed all right. He saw black shapes converging toward them from the beach.

"Ace," he said. "Make my shots a lot easier in this crap light if they come to me. If any of their pals try to jump us from the sides or rear, you spank 'em for me, Baptiste."

LIKE A WHITE SHADOW flitting between trees, Domi fled lumbering monsters three times her size. Except white shadows didn't emit shrill screams of terror, customarily.

The fish things converged from several directions. In her flight the albino girl occasionally swung back to fire single shots, blastingly loud, from her stubby black carbine.

They had no effect on the forms that pursued.

She vaulted a log, fallen and liana twined. With a cry she fell, clutching her ankle with her free hand. She got up barely in advance of a humming swipe of a fin-gar-landed arm, hobbled forward sobbing in desperation.

There were a dozen pursuers now, grotesque mutated shadows in the moonlight. Though they uttered no sounds other than gurgling breaths they seemed to quicken their pace somewhat, as if sensing the climax of the hunt.

Domi limped through a bush gray in the starlight to find herself hard against a lava cliff. Its face was pocked with innumerable honeycomb holes, offering plentiful handholds. It was an illusion: the razor rims of the ancient stone bubbles would shred her hands, her shoes, her milk-pale feet. A better avenue was the creepers that veined its face like green lace—had she not injured her ankle.

She turned. Boulders thrust from the molten-stone flow had channeled the fish men into a knot behind her. Swaying side by side, waving their long arms before them, they came, hunched and eager.

Suddenly she stood upright and faced them. She no

longer favored her left ankle. "Oh my," she sang out in a theatrical voice, "I'm trapped! Whatever shall I do?"

She dug into a pocket of the bulky vest she had thrown on over her tube top. "Mebbe *this?*"

She flung her hand forward. Nine little spheres the size of boulder marbles flew from her palm. They bounced across the overgrown black soil and rocks toward her pursuers. They didn't react.

The girl did a sort of scissors-vault backward over a hump of lava rock about a yard high and a bit over twice that long. It was very fortuitously placed.

Or would have been had Domi, wild waif of the Outlands wastes that she was, and with no scientific expertise to distract her, not spend the past week on the island roaming every one of its rugged hectares and learning its features by heart.

The microgrens started cracking off. Domi had wondered if the fish things could scream. They could and did, strange shrill whistling, piping cries that sounded more mechanical than organic, as fragmentation grenades shredded their legs and bellies and cracked their bones, tore legs whole from two unlucky enough to be standing astride the death balls when they went off.

Then they began an ungainly dervish dance, as the white phosphorus pellets the incens had dusted them with began to eat into their bodies like incandescent insects. White tendrils of smoke wreathed them as they writhed.

From above came a booming like the thunder of a

nearby lightning strike, but repeated over and over. A great black form seemingly not much smaller than the fish things, silhouetted against the stars at the top of the twenty-foot cliff, had risen up and was slamming shots into the hissing, squealing fish men. Grant had appropriated a Franchi SPAS combat shotgun from the stores at the permanent camp near the island's center, where he and his comrades had herded such survivors of the Cerberus techs and island laborers as they could together to fort up in the wooden buildings and stand the creatures off with blasters while they mopped up. The shotgun flamed like dragon's breath.

Domi rose from behind her boulder refuge and, screaming wild raptor triumph, joined in spraying the fish things with needles of death from her CAR-4.

Chapter 4

"We must seek help," the proud young woman said to the council assembled in the long house by the orange smoky light of a hundred torches. Had the palm fronds of the roof not been fresh and green and moreover just wet by a brief passing squall they might have been in danger of taking flame. Outside night insects called to the darkness. "It gives me no pleasure to say so, but we cannot face both the undersea raiders and the cannibals alone."

"At what price, child?" The voice of Ramapua, first speaker in council, quavered with age. As did his thin limbs and stooped frame, although when he went about he customarily had two strong young maidens to support him.

Kiri felt a thrill of annoyance. She suppressed it at once. Although she was the youngest fleet mistress in many cycles, and renowned among not just the Shark Tribe but all the Children of the Great Wave for her derring-do and skill, the people had high regard for age. And Ramapua, weak though his body had grown with the passing of many cycles, had been a mighty speaker to sharks and warrior in his day.

"What do you mean, Elder?" she asked, forcing her words into shapes of respect.

"In this world all things have their price," the oldster said. "What you would ask of others is that they put their treasured goods, their boats and nets and weapons, at risk along with their very bodies, to aid us."

"More than their bodies," another elder muttered. A murmur of agreement ran around the council chamber like a fugitive rat.

"For such risk, they will demand a price of us," Ramapua said. He now held himself erect with two canes made from the shinbones of enemies he had slain in battle; a necklace of shells around his neck, light as a bird in fact, seemed to bow him forward with its weight. His maidens, garlanded in flowers, dressed only in grass skirts, knelt at his side, eyeing him attentively lest he falter. "I don't think they will settle for pretty conch or cowry shells."

"We have rifles to sell," said a younger woman from farther back in the dark.

"I fear a deeper price," the old man said. "Our independence. Our life free as the ocean waves that brought our people here many cycles ago."

"You summon strange sharks from the deep where no fins are seen above the water, Elder," Kiri said, keeping her tone level with effort. "We can negotiate price."

"We must be sure the terms are explicit and well understood before any bargain is struck," Ramapua said. "Alliances are like nets—it is easy to become entangled in them and drown."

"What else are we to do?" she demanded. The old man bobbed his head of taut gray curls. She realized he had trapped her in glib nets of his own. Inwardly she cursed his liver.

"Precisely the question we should be asking," he murmured through his beard. Despite the fact he spoke as if musing to himself the words rang clearly from the rafters.

"We have allies among the other wave children."

Kiri scowled openly now. The speaker was Tupolu, hereditary war leader as she was fleet mistress. Her rival. "I take it you urge us to seek allies beyond their fire circles. What means have the other ocean tribes which we have not? What advanced or heavy weaponry do they possess? Their numbers might aid us against the man's-blood cultists and the sea devils. But what of the men from below the sea?

"It was by foolish luck and sheer courage that we defeated their last attack upon our fleet. Yes, your courage prominently, Tupolu, as well as the resourcefulness and skill at shark speech of my own son." She smiled quickly down at Reva, who sat in the front row facing her with his arms around his knees. He smiled back, and a rush of love suffused her cheeks, swelling down throughout her body.

"Yet how long do you think sheer courage will avail us?" she asked. "Against armor that turns the bullets even of our heavy mainland rifles? Against their efficient motors and light weapons? Had those raiders not chosen to toy with us instead of finish us right away, our whole flotilla would now be smoking husks, and we floating food for crabs and our shark siblings. Or perhaps slaves with heads bowed and hands bound behind our backs, to labor for others in the false sunlight of a crystal dome on the ocean floor."

"The Mother Ocean is broad. Her breadth has saved her people many times before," Tupolu argued.

"But these enemies may pursue faster than we can flee."

Tupolu pulled his head up and back, and made a brief noise in his throat. Kiri knew her harpoon had struck home.

"What price will the mainlanders exact for helping us?" the war leader asked.

"I don't know," Kiri said. "Nor do you."

She shook back her ringlet mane. Her high forehead and cheeks gleamed golden in the torchlight. "But I for one am not afraid to find out!" Despite the deadening effects of the palm-frond ceiling and many bodies, she made the great house ring with her challenge.

She stood there with arms crossed while the members of the Shark Tribe muttered among themselves. The sound washed over her like surf. She was hot; she glowed in exultation.

The people would seek consensus, and then she would be directed to act upon that consensus. Such was their way. But she was confident what that consensus would be.

She understood what her handsome male rival did not: because consensus was based upon hurting the fewest possible feelings, it tended to accommodate the emphatic. While mainland academics among whom she had studied as a girl thought of the system as a perfect collective, she knew from experience that in practice the community would seek to appease the most vociferous will.

In other words, the perfect commune was decisively swayed by the most vigorous display of sheer individualism. Of will. And will, she thought with blazing contempt, was the war leader's weak point, for all his mere physical courage.

She felt a warmth against her leg. She looked down into her son's smiling upturned face. He had moved to sit beside her. Filled with maternal pride now, as well as lioness's pride, she tangled loving fingers in his hair and stood to await her triumph.

Blue-white glare, diamond and electric as a rogue star, filled the long house from its doorway at the far end which gave out upon the harbor. Choking out a curse, Kiri threw up a hand to protect her eyes.

ASSEMBLED ON THE BLACK SAND between their beached lesser craft, the people of the Shark Tribe stood squinting into the blaze of light from half a mile offshore. Usually they chattered like the bright birds that made the days colorful among the inland forests. Even in council, the most serious of social events, they never ceased

whispering and murmuring, gossip mostly, unless someone most compelling were speaking.

Now they were silent as so many idols.

A bubbling in the water offshore. Like an ideal inva-
sion beach, Mako Harbor had been formed by armlike
lava extrusions when the island had thrust itself in fire
and fume above the waves in the days following the
nukecaust. It was ten fathoms deep in the middle, shelv-
ing steeply up to the land. That allowed the dugout canoes and lighter outriggers to be brought close inshore
and dragged up onto the land, and piers to be built out
to allow bigger vessels, even deep-draft mainlander
freighters, to offload directly onto shore.

Now, scarcely ten yards from where black sand was
swallowed by the restless sea, the water began to foam.
Light blazed up from beneath, staining the turbulence
bubbles like blue ink.

Slowly a shape bulked up through the roiling water.
A dome, shedding water like the back of a sounding
whale, of crystal. A gasp rippled through the crowd as
they glimpsed human forms within.

The dome came out into air with the water streaming down its globe sides like the tears of the families of
the drowned. Kiri could see the dome rested upon a
slightly wider circular platform. Presumably it housed
the mechanisms that drove the curious craft through the
water, as well as provided life support for the two visible occupants.

That craft is not built for speed, nor yet for long

travel, she thought, her mind spinning quickly but under full control of the indomitable will that had made her a captain and allowed her accede to fleet mistress before her years. It's a landing craft, come from that submersible offshore. Or another that lies beneath the water, out of sight.

She thought of sending her mind casting out, for the sharks that always circled just outside the harbor to look and see. Or quietly asking her son to. He was a far greater speaker to sharks even at his tender age than his mother ever would be; she had always been deficient in matters of empathy. But there was no point, after all. Given the weapons the high-tech undersea marauders had demonstrated in past depredations the larger vessel had to carry enough firepower to scour the beach of life, if not the entire island. They didn't need a second craft.

With a hiss of equalizing pressure the seal popped. The bubble opened, lifting up and back like a lid opening. The two occupants stood, one man tall and slim with broad shoulders, the other shorter and squatter. Both wore formfitting uniforms of what looked like black but Kiri knew to be the deepest indigo. Each one's head was bulked out by a helmet that came to a point on top, like a short, fat bullet. The tall man's visor was raised to reveal a pale, dark-bearded face. The face of his companion, hunched over an obvious control pedestal, was obscured by his dark faceplate.

"People of the Shark, I salute you." The voice

boomed out from hidden speakers. "I am Commander Zeno of the Barony of Lemuria."

He waited. Eyes turned toward old Ramapua, who looked more stooped than usual despite his canes and the aid of his bare-breasted maidens, as if the sight of enemies in his people's safe harbor was an unbearable weight piled upon his old shoulders. He looked to Kiri. They all did.

She said nothing.

"You have fought us well, despite your limited means. Yet the time has come for an end of games. A time has come for change, across the whole Pacific. Great storm clouds pile on the horizon. They threaten the whole world. We can no longer afford to use your folk for live-fire training exercises. You can no longer afford to resist us."

Kiri made a brave show of sweeping the dark horizon with her eyes, moving her head from left to right. "I see no clouds gathering. I see threat from below the waves, not above."

The man laughed with full lips. "Well said. To whom have I the honor of speaking?"

"I am Kiri Far-Seer, fleet mistress of the Shark People." It should be Tupolu who takes the lead, she thought. How fortunate for us all that he has no stomach for that. He would surely surrender to what he imagined to be the inevitable.

"Well, Fleet Mistress Kiri. The threat is real. Both threats, if you will. For now you must take our word.

When you have joined us, we can give you a more complete picture."

She threw her hair back in a defiant toss. "You cut our nets. You burn our boats. You murder our people. Now you want us to join you? As slaves, no doubt!"

The people raised a great shout of defiance at that, shaking fists at the intruders. Kiri's heart swelled with pride at their spirit.

The strange man in the strange craft seemed unfazed. "We could compel your obedience. Our patience is not unlimited."

"For no reason you have been attacking us sporadically for tens of moons. It seems to me that you have tried to conquer us. And failed."

"It has not been so imperative before that all Pacific peoples cooperate before. Your refusal would be selfish. It would threaten your survival, and more. Are you so self-centered, then?"

"Your words are water," she said. "They sink into sand."

"Think about what I say," Zeno said. "Make the proper choice, the wise choice. It may be that you benefit. And certainly acquiescence will be more to your benefit than defiance. I go, but I shall return. And when I return you shall submit. One way or another."

Reva darted forward, a coconut in his hand. He ran splashing into the phosphorescent lace fringe where the surf was retreating back into the harbor and hurled the coconut with all his might at the helmeted head.

The clear dome had already begun to close. The coconut, well thrown, bounced off it. The shorter man inside flinched. Zeno did not.

The dome sealed. The bubble craft vanished, the only sound a murmuring of waters closing where it had been. A moment later the blue floodlights blasting the beach from the sea switched off.

Blinking, Kiri saw a long low black whale-shape likewise slide beneath the waves. She could make out no details.

For a moment all was still but for the rhythmic slog of the surf and the whispering of the wind. A night bird cried somewhere high overhead.

"The fools," Kiri said, pitching her voice to carry to the crowd. "If they had only known, they could have come close to wiping us out here and now, with their mighty weapons."

"Perhaps," Ramapua said, his voice quavering, "this Commander Zeno understood that, and is confident in their ability to wipe us out whenever they so choose."

Kiri scowled but she forcibly swallowed her anger. "You may be right. We should disperse to other islands before they come back with their heat beams and their rockets."

"But if we do not concentrate our strength, how can we stand against them?" Ramapua asked.

"We cannot stand against such weapons as they possess. If we clump up, they'll slaughter us, the way shark herd a school of mackerel together so they can feed more efficiently."

The old man gasped. "But you yourself threw defiance in their faces! You all but spit on them!"

"We cannot stand against them. Not alone. But there are others who can."

She sensed Tupolu's heat nearby. She turned to him with her arms crossed beneath her proud bare breasts. "What say you now, War Leader?"

The man glared at her for a moment. He stood a head taller than her, yet didn't seem to overmatch her.

"You have right," he said slowly. "We must try to enlist the mainlanders' aid."

"And what of the price they might ask?" Ramapua asked. From his uncertain tone of voice, he wasn't trying to pile on the war leader for his capitulation, but was genuinely astonished.

"Better to be in the mainlanders' debt," the strapping young man said, "than caught in the nets of the men from beneath the sea."

Chapter 5

"'Help me, Obi-Wan Kenobi,'" Domi stage-whispered as the hologram flickered in the darkened room. "'You're my only hope.'"

"Hush," Brigid hissed, cheekbones practically glowing pink in gloom enforced by heavy Army blankets hung over the window to block the strident oceanic sunlight.

"If you've quite finished your puerile displays of impatience," the image said with sibilant asperity, "perhaps we can engage in meaningful activity."

"I thought you called us here to talk at us, Lakesh," said Grant, sprawled in his own wood-and-canvas folding chair with his arms crossed like buttressing hardwood logs across his mighty chest. "When do we get down to the 'activity' part?"

"Very clever, friend Grant. Those who dismiss you as a mere blunt instrument do you small justice, as I am once again reminded."

"I'd think he was making that up to yank your strings," Kane said, "if not for the existence of Philboyd." The physicist, one of the Manitius fugitives and perennially self-promoting candidate for command of

Cerberus—not to mention ever-hopeful candidate for Brigid's lover—was a bitter and persistent rival to the pair of operators.

"Will you all please pipe down and listen to what he has to say?" Brigid said, exasperated.

"Excellent," the simulacrum of Lakesh said. He smiled beatifically. "Now that we have the levity out of the way, perhaps we can get down to business.

"Brigid dear, I must commend you on your excellent job performing preliminary examinations of the bodies of the fish creatures. We have begun dissecting the specimens you returned by interphaser to Cerberus. Really fascinating adaptations. For example, they are apparently fully amphibious. They possess both lungs and fully functional gills. That means they can survive indefinitely both on the surface and beneath the water."

"Adaptation?" Kane asked. "You mean they're naturally evolved?"

The nebulous head shook. "By no means, friend Kane. Among other things, sequencing reveals that their DNA is almost identical to human. They are the products of genetic engineering."

"Pantropic science?" Grant asked.

"Precisely."

Rummaging in a cargo compartment of her voluminous shorts, Domi came up with a bag of sun-dried fruits for which the personnel of the island frequently traded with the surrounding tribes. She began to eat.

"So they combine the worst features of men and… fish?" Domi asked. "What's up with that, anyway?"

"I was unaware the Archon Directorate had any interest in aquatic adaptations," Brigid said.

"To the best of my knowledge and belief," Lakesh said, "they did not."

The four Cerberus operatives looked at one another. They sat in the room of one of the cluster of prefab buildings brought by ship from the stores of Redoubt Yankee on Thunder Isle and assembled by laborers hired from among the populations of the widely scattered eastern Pacific islands. It rested on Snail Cove's blunt summit, which, like many of the extensive chain stretching south and west from Hawaii, was in fact the very tip of a seamount, thrust upward from the seafloor during the eruptions that followed the nukecaust. The volcano was dormant, although Kane was uneasily aware that meant the same thing as "could blow at any minute." It did comfort him some that volcanoes usually gave some warning before acting up.

Usually.

Around the bases of the walls, fragments of glass caught the light from the hologram and cast it back like polychrome animal eyes. The cleanup from the battle several days before had missed them. The fish creatures had smashed in windows in their attempts to get at the technicians and laborers forted up inside. A slight but unmistakable—and nauseating—stench of blood and fish permeated the darkened room, despite several applications of cleaning solution. The personnel of the island were well-armed. Although they had fought inexpertly, they had plied their shotguns, handblasters, axes, shovels and clubs with such vigor that they had suffered no more than a few light wounds by the time the four Cerberus operatives had finished rolling up the aquatic invaders from behind.

Those who had been caught outside and unawares by the fish men had not been so lucky. Seven had been killed, three technicians and four islanders. Ten more had been injured, three badly enough to require evacuation to Cerberus.

"You mean to tell us," Grant said deliberately, "that somebody else is making monsters?"

"It would certainly appear so," the ghostly apparition of Lakesh said.

"Could the overlords have gone into the business of making sea monsters?" Kane asked.

"That seems improbable, Kane," Brigid said. "If these beings are truly of predominantly human genotype, it seems extremely likely that their growth cycle takes as long as it does for normal humans. If not considerably longer, given their immense size." The largest chill measured almost ten feet tall and close to 450 pounds.

"Mebbe not, Baptiste," Kane said. "Don't forget about forced growing in vats."

"I don't know about that," Grant said. "It looked like some of them had led a pretty hard life. Even before they ran into us."

Lakesh nodded again. "Our examination of the bodies revealed numerous instances of long-healed injury. Nor did their tissues reveal any trace evidence of the sort of hormones usually used to accelerate growth. Our best surmise is that they matured naturally. Whatever that may entail, of course—the excellent Brigid is correct that the most likely hypothesis is that it takes them a comparable period to us to achieve their full growth. Therefore, the overlords, recently emerged as they are, could not have created them."

"So someone else *has* gone into the monster-making business," Kane said. He turned to his partner. "I'm really liking this. How about you?"

"Too much," Grant said, employing the island slang they'd all begun to pick up.

"But who could be making them?" Brigid asked.

"Ah, but that's the mystery. However, an explanation might soon be forthcoming."

"Those mystery broadcasts of yours?" Kane said.

"Indeed. We continue to receive them. They are as yet…scrambled. They unmistakably address themselves to myself and Cerberus. But the contents are often unintelligible. Apparent nonsense."

"Have you instituted two-way communications?" Brigid asked.

"We have made attempts in that direction. Our success remains uncertain."

Kane turned back to Grant. "How can you not know if you've communicated or not?" he mouthed silently. His partner shrugged mountainously.

"Something I don't get," Grant said. "We've been out here ten days pulling sec because our people reported frequent attacks from some kind of blood cultists. Humans, more or less. Nobody's said jack about these fish guys."

"Maybe they're new players," Kane said.

"Ah, perhaps not." Brigid had her head down. Her cheeks flushed pink. "As you know, Lakesh, I've been interviewing our native contacts to derive as much information about possible threats as I could. The most consistent stories concern groups of what our personnel term cultists, perhaps a tribe or large extended family, whom the islanders regard with loathing and trepidation. Their behavior exhibits extreme violence— they apparently make a regular practice of human sacrifice, if not cannibalism."

"That's what we're looking for," Domi agreed. "Only they haven't put in an appearance yet."

Brigid nodded. "However, I have heard certain other reports. These have concerned strange devillike creatures emerging from the sea."

"You don't mean to tell us that you sloughed those off as mere native superstition, Baptiste?" Kane said. "That would be insensitive."

Grant guffawed.

Brigid blushed again. "No. I did think the name was metaphorical, based on the attackers' behavior and appearance—whether contorted expressions, or some kind of facial decorations such as paint. Or even tattoos or ritual scarification. It never occurred to me they might be describing nonhumans."

"You should back off her, Kane," Grant said. "It's a pretty long stretch to believe in fish devils. Just like the stories we've heard once or twice about Jet Ski-riding rangers from the depths attacking the fishing fleets."

"What's that?" Lakesh asked sharply.

"Nothing," Kane said. "Just sea stories."

Domi snickered. "You mean like sea monsters?"

"Perhaps it would be of benefit to you to take any and all potential intelligence under investigation, rather than deciding a priori that it is worthless," Lakesh said. "It should be obvious even to the untrained mind that there are phenomena in play here about which we know little to nothing."

"Tell us something new," Kane said, slumping in his chair with an arm over the back.

Lakesh opened his mouth to say more.

Somebody pounded hard on the door to outside. "Kane! Grant!" one of the techs called. "Are you in there?"

"Don't knock the door down," Grant said. "What do you want?"

"We've a native war fleet standing right offshore," came through the door. "They demand to talk to whoever is in charge. Right effing now!"

THE WOMAN ON THE BEACH was tall, half an inch shy of Brigid's height. Her skin was medium brown, her hair a tumble of black curls with purple highlights. Her face was broad with high cheekbones. Beneath fierce unplucked black eyebrows her eyes, almond shaped and subtly tilted, were pale amber with gold-and-topaz highlights. She wore a sort of lightweight shift or smock of some light white fabric that looked to Kane's sartorially inexpert eye like cotton or linen. It came down to the tops of smooth-muscled brown thighs.

The way her nipples made dark peaks plainly visible within the fabric suggested she was indifferent to nudity and had only clothed herself to this extent out of respect for mainlander modesty. Handsome bronzed bodies along the rail of the vessel that floated a hundred yards out on the slow green slog of the sea, male and female alike bare from railing upward, bore out his surmise.

Terns with gray-blue backs and wing tips wheeled and screeched, their thready cries riding the sea breeze. "You are the leader?" the woman challenged in good if exotically flavored English. It was no surprise to Kane; English was the trade language of most of the widely scattered Pacific-island peoples, and while some affiliations used Anglo-derived pidgin as their native tongue, few resorted to it in dealing with outsiders.

Kane looked left and right. Brigid stood stiffly on the one hand, Grant on the other, Domi slightly apart on the big black man's right, wearing her scarlet tube top, baggy cargo shorts and a slight smile.

"You know me, Kane," Grant said sideways.

"Don't want any part of running anything. I'm just looking to put in my twenty and retire." Domi laughed silently.

"That's me," Kane said, stepping forward.

"I am Kiri Far-Seer, fleet mistress of the Shark People."

"I'm Kane Who Leaps Before He Looks, of Redoubt Bravo. These here are Brigid Baptiste, our chief scholar, Grant the Sierra Hotel pilot, and Domi the huntress."

She laughed. "You don't have to patronize me, Kane-Who Names Himself Truly. Still, I think you choose well with the appellations you give your folk."

She turned to indicate the outrigger canoe, formed of a big hollowed log and tapered at both ends, which waited on the beach behind her among the Cerberus contingent's grounded light craft. Standing by it were the crew who had rowed her inshore: six strapping dark men, each taller than Grant and with tree-trunk arms crossed over chests even more impressive than his. Lot of Samoan blood in this bunch, Kane thought. He guessed they had been selected to impress the outlanders.

Which worked. Anybody who looked as if he could pick up Grant and toss him commanded Kane's respect from a purely physical point of view. Of course, lifting weights, even mighty heavy ones, was one thing, and real fighting another. Judging by the occasionally mashed nose and sundry nicks and scars, somewhat paler against tanned purplish-dark skin, Kane guessed this particular crew weren't exactly strangers to combat, either.

"Why not come discuss the matter upon my vessel, the *Great Sky Reef?*" she asked.

Kane didn't look around to consult his comrades. "Why not?" he replied.

Chapter 6

The screaming girl in the pool was young, scarcely eighteen surface years. She was light skinned for one of the island savages, and her hair showed pale streaks against her seal-brown shoulders and back. With her hands tied behind her back by polymer restraints, she had to kick constantly with her long, slender legs or drown in the shallow water, there beneath the baron's spired palace in its domed city beneath the great ocean.

That gave free scope for Mi!k-Mi!k, a young dolphin, to thrust his long yellow-pink penis freely and furiously into her vagina despite her best efforts to fend him off.

Overlooking the tank, Baron Lemuria sat on a throne of white marble veined with sea-green on a low dais. He wore a sort of white chiton trimmed in gold. He had his bare, lean-muscled legs crossed, elbow on knee, pointed chin in palm. Though his long aquamarine eyes watched the dolphin rape the captive with apparently fixed interest, he was bored almost subsentient.

He lacked a sexual impulse. He had never known whether his finished kindred possessed one or not; it was his impression that it had been deliberately engineered out of the strain that had become, first his kind, then the true barons, to differentiate them from the ape-kin with their untamable drives.

Nor was he sadistic. He took no pleasure in cruelty; lacking compassion, he could feel neither sympathy nor its reverse. He was, so he characterized himself, supremely objective and supremely rational.

His ape underlings were distinctly otherwise. It reassured him very little to have that displayed quite so graphically.

The bulk of his Trust, half a dozen elderly human males in long robes, stood by watching with boiled onion eyes, occasionally moistening thin bloodless lips. Though they would never admit the supreme sexual degradation of a physically attractive female of their species excited them beyond what their years were accustomed to, the thin nostrils inset in the baron's fine but tiny nose could smell the hormone-dump of their lust.

Somewhat aside stood the youngest and newest—and, whether he knew it or not, highly provisional—member of the Lemuriaville Trust. It was Commander Zeno, tall and lean in blue-green tunic and trousers with dark silver stripes. Empty holsters gaped on his belt where baronial guards had relieved him of maser side arm and shark knife. Just as the open bearing of weapons was a badge that set him unmistakably apart from the common run of Lemurians, so their absence emphasized the gap in status between him and his master.

Zeno alone showed no interest, much less stimulation. Although neither his face nor his posture, nor even his respiration and skin tone, betrayed any sign, he was distinctly uncomfortable. The baron could smell that, too. Over the years, he had learned to discriminate among a wide range of apekin smells.

He'd spent more than enough time in proximity to them.

The girl's head broke surface again. Her scream pealed in the tiled chamber. It began as a gag and ended as a gurgle as the impassioned dolphin rolled her over again and pumped her energetically.

"Your pardon, Excellency." Zeno's voice crisp as a whip crack. "With all deference, may your servant inquire as to the purpose of this demonstration?"

The other Trust members uttered a collective gasp of astonishment at such impudence. They were all gray men. Gray, of course, in that almost everybody in Lemuriaville was gray, from lack of exposure to sunlight and ultraviolet radiation, except the baron himself and his designer-gene guards, who had skins of alabaster. But gray in a far more fundamental sense, at once numinous and substantial.

Perhaps that is the true purpose of this distasteful exercise, reflected the baron. To remind me that I myself have need of change, and not just the necessity of accommodating my new…partner.

His new ally, the dream invader, who had suggested

this means to begin creating the moral environment needed for conquest.

"F-forgive us, Excellency," Tolwyn almost blubbered. He was the tallest of the Trust, the youngest, the fattest, his own pate bald as the dolphin's glabrous hide and scarcely drier for sweating in this humid pressurized-saturated chamber in which no water would evaporate. He had charge of life support within the Lemuriaville dome, including provision of fresh water, as well as food, grown internally or harvested from the ocean. "This man obviously has no idea of the gravity—"

"The honor—" said Bennett.

"The great benefits—" said Malatan, the chief scientist and technologist.

Baron Lemuria held up a long, white, fine-boned hand. "Enough," he said in a voice like honey. "Perhaps the purpose, Commander, is to ascertain whether I have subordinates with wit to think for themselves, and courage to speak for themselves."

Certainly Baron Lemuria didn't encourage independence of thought, at least among the lesser orders. As one of those charged to actively discourage such independence, Zeno knew that far too well. Strong man though he was, Zeno couldn't help going slightly pale behind his own tan which, though certainly light by surface standards, rendered him as conspicuous in the ville as his midnight-blue uniform and his side arm. But neither his eyes nor his expression flickered.

With a splash and a scream the girl rolled to the surface again. Mi!k-Mi!k obviously did not intend his partner to drown. At least too soon. Instead he stayed on his back, thrusting rhythmically with all the force of his powerful flippers.

The six senior men of the Trust shook visibly now, in transports that were neither pure fear nor lust but a dynamic flux of both. "We must make an example," the baron said, pitching his beautiful tenor voice so high and carrying it was almost contralto. "We must teach the surface people to submit, must teach the price of disobedience."

"For years it has been your policy to tend to our gardens here on the bottom of the sea, my lords," Zeno said, pitching his own deep voice to carry over the cries and splashing and the triumphal bugling and tweeting of the sea beast. "Is it wise to try to extend our sway above the waves, especially now?"

The baron's sculpted brows knit in a slight frown. Really, the man does go too far, he thought. Perhaps his own appointment with our delphine friend? The Lemurians made great use of dolphins; the baron understood well that Mi!k-Mi!k was unlikely to care overmuch which gender of apekin he violated.

No, the baron decided. I don't want to risk breaking his spirit, much less killing him. He had quite enough gray apes in his service already. He could always destroy Zeno if the commander became too troublesome.

"The situation in the surface world is highly problematical," the baron said. "You have been privileged to review such data as we possess. Much of the data. But there are things you do not know, cannot know, Commander. The time has come for decisive action. Decisive."

The officer kept his face turned toward his leader. His eyes did not flick aside as the captive's screams turned to sobbing gasps.

"Very well, Excellency. As you know, I have many duties in order to prepare to take such action. I humbly request that I be released to pursue them."

One of the Trust elders emitted a low whimper, quickly stifled. The baron nodded precisely. "Your zeal does you credit, Commander. It pleases me to grant your request. Dismissed."

Zeno clicked the heels of the shiny black boots together, pivoted as if one of those heels were bolted to the floor and marched from the chamber.

"Your Excellency!" Bennett's voice quavered. He was marshal of the sea wardens, meaning Lemuriaville's sec boss. "My profoundest apologies, Excellency. I had no idea the man possessed the capacity for such rank insubordination. I will have him severely punished. An injection of nerve fire should do it. Or perhaps an accident—"

Baron Lemuria raised two fingers from the arm of his throne. The security chief instantly shut his mouth.

"No such thing, Marshal," the baron said. "I find his vigor altogether commendable. Now, I have provided entertainment for the benefit of my loyal servants. You should relax and enjoy it." He gestured magnanimously toward the pool.

The young dolphin male's motions had become more frantic as his excitement grew. The woman's sobbing turned to staccato moans as her upper body was whipped from side to side. The right side of her head cracked against the rim of the pool with a sound like pistol shot. It made the men of the Trust jump. The noise echoed between the walls of the tiled chamber for what seemed an impossibly long time.

The breathless cries ceased. So did the woman's struggles. A pink tinge began to seep away from her head as the dolphin pinned her body against the pool's side and spent himself in a final frenzy of furious energy.

The baron's mouth puckered in disappointment and irritation. Is it possible, he thought peevishly, that the woman is dead? He could scarcely credit it. The apekins' skulls were so thick—their heads contained so little.

He had intended to return the bitch to her people more or less intact, so that she might enlighten her fellow beasts as to the consequences of defying their natural masters. It would be most vexatious were she dead. Perhaps she is only stunned.

He heard a soft moan. He leaned forward intently, perceiving at first it came from the captive. Then he realized it had escaped the lips of one of his Trust members.

He turned to them with a blank smile and nodded in what he hoped was a benevolent manner.

So Leviathan was right in what he told me. What the

monster had told him via mind link was true after all: that it understood the minds of mere humans better than he did. He had to admit the apekin remained a mystery to him, the supposedly more elevated specimens of his Trust scarcely less than the most wretched laborers.

But after all, Leviathan claimed to been observing them rather longer than he had.

Unbidden to his mind sprang images: the last seconds of the video broadcast from the lost deep sea vehicle. Alone in his chambers, the baron had reviewed them again and again. There could be no possible question. In the deep ocean chasm before it, a gigantic black creature had stirred. And it had opened a titanic glowing red eye.

An eye that the baron could see now. Peering deep into his own soul.

He became aware of pain and stabbing of his wrists and forearms. He came back to himself, and realized that he was gripping the arms of his throne so tightly the muscles and cramped. Then he realized his Trust was staring at him with eyes bulging in frank terror.

He smiled in a way meant to be reassuring and nodded. "Very well, gentlemen. You know your duties. Get to them now."

He glanced at the pool, and his fine upper lip curled back from his perfect teeth. "And send some workers to drain and clean the pool at once."

Chapter 7

"We need your help," the woman said.

Kane leaned on the rail. The morning sunlight seemed to skitter across the surface of the water between ship and shore, or slide and float like a film of levitating mercury. Seabirds skimmed just above it, sometimes flying straight through the tops of waves.

"With what?"

"We are being destroyed," she said.

He turned to look at her. It wasn't an unpleasant task, he thought, as he leaned back with an elbow on the rail. She had skinned off her smock unselfconsciously as she came aboard her vessel from the outrigger canoe that had brought her and the four Cerberus exiles and tossed it aside with a toss of her huge mane of hair as if ritually shedding the land.

"By what?" he asked.

She shrugged. "Many things," she said. "The sea has always been our friend, our mother. Our home and the source of our livelihood. And yet now it almost seems to have turned against us. It is not enough, the blood cultists who have preyed for years upon our ships and settlements. Nor the fish devils. Now we are attacked by submarines and high-speed surface craft. With machine guns and even great lasers."

It occurred to Kane to wonder how she knew about things like machine guns. Or lasers, anyway. He decided not to ask.

Mebbe I'm learning tact, he thought.

Grant stepped forward. "Wait a minute here. Did you say something about fish devils?"

"Yes," Kiri said.

"Could you describe them, please?" Brigid's previous stiffness was replaced by forward-leaning intensity.

"They are fish who walk like men. Although we have speculated that they are men who have been somehow melded with fish."

"Pretty good call," Grant murmured.

"Our people on the island here have been having trouble with low-tech attackers," Kane said. "It's what we're doing here. Our local contacts say they're blood cultists."

"So they are. They sacrifice humans to their gods. No one knows who those gods may be. Captured cultists only giggle madly when questioned, even under torture— they appear to be insane. Nor have we or any of the other nations we know of been able to infiltrate them. But we have successfully spied upon their rituals. What our spies report is truly horrifying."

Kane wasn't cherry enough to have been appalled by the woman's casual reference to using torture. He was surprised, mildly, by her use of a term like "infiltrate."

"That squares with what little we've been able to find out," he said.

"Who are they?" Brigid asked. "Where do they come from?"

"Everybody," Kiri said. "Everywhere. Our people have long whispered rumors of degenerate sea nations, different than pirates and far worse, who prey on other humans like shark among fish. That may be so. Certainly many of the cultists we have killed or caught have been people of the ocean. But many are not. There are Asians, and mainlanders, and Chinese pirates from the east among them."

"Wei Qiang's bunch," Grant said.

"Yes. There have even been those of our people who have joined them, I am ashamed to say. But we have never taken any of them alive. Perhaps we haven't tried sufficiently hard. We have no idea how they came to join the cult, whether they were approached, or perhaps whether they somehow learned about the cult and sought it out through such means as we cannot guess."

"Have you thought about dreams?" Domi asked.

Kiri looked at her sharply. She wasn't the only one.

"We are people who put a certain stock in dreams," Kiri said deliberately. "I didn't know you mainlanders did."

"Some of us have been having the same dreams, over and over, since we got out here," the albino girl said. "I haven't, but others have."

Kiri looked narrowly at her four guests. Her people, gathered at polite distance on the deck and atop the cabin, began to mutter suspiciously and cast dark looks in their direction.

"Way to go, Domi," Grant said under his breath. "We have to swim for it, I'm chucking you in first to give them something to keep busy with." He nodded toward the triangular fins cutting the water to seaward. At the moment at least seven were visible.

"I'd be just a mouthful," she said with a wicked grin. "Just an appetizer before they started chewing on your big butt."

"Put a lid on it," Kane said. "Nobody's swimming anywhere."

"My butt isn't that big," Grant muttered.

"No one here will harm you," Kiri said, raising her voice and sweeping her crew with a fierce gaze. "You are my guests, aboard under my protection. But these dreams intrigue me. Do they tempt you? Make offers?"

"Yes," Brigid said. Her voice was muted, hard to hear above the boom of the wind and the creak of the rigging and the moaning of the anchored vessel as it rode up and down on the waves. "You could say they make offers. Horrifying ones."

"Hard to see how anybody might be tempted by them," Kane said. "Unless from fear."

"Or to be done with the damn dreams," Grant said.

"What you say may be true. You will forgive me if I wonder why whoever—or whatever—the source of the dreams may be should have picked you out for temptation."

We've been around, Kane thought. Made some noise, made a name for ourselves. After a quick consultation of the expressions of his three companions he chose to answer with a shrug of his own. "Good question. I'd like to know the answer myself. Could be important."

"What about these new marauders?" Brigid asked. She was clearly not unhappy for an excuse to change the subject. "The ones with the submarines and skimmers. What can you tell us about them?"

Concisely Kiri recounted the attack on her kelp-harvesting expedition and subsequent ultimatum. "We have had sporadic dealings with the undersea folk for years," she said matter-of-factly. "My grandmother told stories of them. They call themselves Lemurians, and their place of habitation Lemuriaville."

The mainlander quartet exchanged a look.

"Sometimes they have traded with us. Occasionally they have raided us. But now they have declared war upon us."

"You've dealt with these people?" Kane asked, surprised.

"Not in person. But our people have, as well as others of the ocean folk."

A cry from the sentry high up in the rigging. "Fleet Mistress! Your son—"

Kane looked out to sea. An outrigger canoe approached, propelled by several rowers. It was already within fifty yards. Apparently the lookout had recognized the new arrival, and only thought it worth mentioning when she recognized the boy.

Brigid cried out in alarm. A small, brown boy had stood up in the outrigger—deftly, so as not to upset it, although its outboard float provided extra lateral stability—and waved. Then he dived overboard.

Into the midst of the circling pack of sharks.

Kane and Grant ran to the far rail. Their Sin Eaters were in their hands. Kane wasn't sure what good the handblasters would do against sharks, but slapping the weapon into its hand from the power holster strapped to his bare forearm had long been his default response to crisis situations.

Grant waved his gun arm. "Get out of there!" he shouted. "Go back!"

But the boy swam forward in a good, clean crawl, moving like a racer. The fins jutted from the water to all sides of him now, ten, maybe twelve.

"Somebody help him!" Brigid cried.

Yet the sharks did no more than circle. With surprising speed and deft strokes the boy swam up toward the port outer hull of Kiri's flagship.

And then, when he was within a literal yard of safety, beneath him appeared a gray shadow, a finned-torpedo shape the size of a cigarette boat....

COMMANDER ZENO STALKED echoing corridors of vanadium steel. Technicians in the color-coded jumpsuits of various divisions dodged quickly to get out of his way.

His skull within its blunt-spired helmet was crowded with thoughts.

My duty, he thought over and over. Reminding himself that it was up to him to keep down the chaos, to restrain human nature: weak, selfish, passionate, ultimately destructive. The oath and burden of a Deep Warden.

The question, though unasked, was unavoidable: how was what I just witnessed not chaos?

He came to a door that opened to a scan of coded patches incorporated into his uniform as he faced it. He turned aside from the main corridor of D Section, down to which he had ridden in a secret elevator from the baron's apartments at the pinnacle of the submarine city, almost touching the vast armaglass bubble of the dome itself. As he stepped through into a narrower, less garishly lit passageway, the door whispered shut behind him.

As he walked down the maintenance gangway, which smelled faintly of cleaning solvents, he breathed deeply from the pit of his belly in self-mastery exercises he had been taught as a solemn child, years before in the lyceum. What is happening? he asked himself. The bizarre and obscene exhibition to which his baron had subjected him was totally out of phase with the whole of his prior existence. And the way the Trust—his superiors, the very men who bore the greatest burden of holding back the oceanic disorder that sought to drown them all—had reacted....

He came to a set of elevator doors. The nearest opened to his approach. He stepped inside. As that door closed, he ignored the buttons, opening a panel beside the door and typing in a sequence on a keypad instead. With a smooth hiss of a perfectly functioning mechanism, the elevator began to descend.

He had learned so long ago to suppress his personal inclinations and desires in service of baron and ville that he could scarcely remember a time when he'd had them. Yet he had also been trained to serve Lemuriaville's interests to the best of his ability. He had done many things in its service that, had he been a different man in a different job, even within Lemuriaville itself, he would never have done.

Individualism was not encouraged in the ville. Yet as he rose through the ranks of the elite wardens who kept order within and without the crystal dome, he was called upon to display ever more initiative. Accordingly he had developed it. If that accorded strangely with what had been engrained in him from infancy, he chose not to dwell upon it. And besides, he could always tell himself that as he served and learned he was ever more able to conform his thoughts and will to those of Baron Lemuria.

The door opened. He went down another passageway, this one murkier, with some illumination panels dark. It decidedly did not smell as if disinfectant had ever existed inside it. The walls were splashed with dried encrustations, and the flexible nonskid padding underfoot was spongy from accretions of various organics.

The odd light panel wasn't the only thing that didn't function in this noisome hallway. Neither did the surveillance cams. Every inch of the domed city was supposed to be under constant surveillance. Professionally, Zeno knew all too well that that was a sheer impossibility.

Unless some untoward incident drew attention to the fact, it was vanishingly unlikely anyone would even notice the gaps in surveillance here.

There were other entrances into the underworld. They were more pleasant, cleaner, more secure than this reeking utility access. Also better watched.

Even a man like Commander Zeno sometimes had reason to move beyond the scope of the security that he himself was tasked with maintaining.

He opened another door by presenting his identification panel to a sensor. A brawl of noise and stink and swirling activity struck him in the face as he stepped forth into the Bilge.

It was not dark so much as sporadically lit by eye-searing lights. Huge pumps throbbed, drawing waste and seepage through torso-thick conduits. Among the great hunched machines a society of outcasts lived and excreted and fought and fornicated and died.

A hag with seaweed hair and a mildewed, faded orange scrap of cloth tied at a bias around her waist, to maintain, perhaps, the illusive hint of possibility that what lay beneath was more appealing than the pale, gray, big-pored skin and shrunken dugs otherwise exposed, gyrated to tinny electronic music from a CD player. She laughed, her mouth a toothless gape, as she deftly evaded a clumsy grab from a potato-white man who slouched around her.

She uttered a raucous cry of recognition and waved at Zeno. He knew her as Cross-Eyed Mary. She was less than thirty.

Life was hard and miserable in the Bilge. Yet its denizens clung to it as tenaciously as multicolored algae on the bulkhead walls. So tenaciously that, a generation before Zeno's own birth, the baron had directed the Deep Wardens to give over sporadic efforts to eradicate the Bilge scum. Had he simply given in to the urgings of certain past marshals and flooded the bottom levels to insure the problem went away, it would have compromised the machinery that kept the delicate and intricate systems of the city alive, possibly fatally. And as it happened the Bilge denizens proved to have their uses, especially for scutwork that even the lowest-level technicians balked at doing.

It also proved useful as a means of social control. While the bureaucrats who administered in the baron's name were no more inhibited about signing termination warrants than the wardens were in executing them, a standing threat of internal exile was, for some citizens, a threat more horrifying than death. Or even banishment to the terrifying untamed surface world.

Zeno made his way among hulking machines and the people who squatted among them, noisily bargaining, drinking swill, gambling, laughing. He passed a knot of men kicking and beating another man—past death, if the limp way he flopped and limbs flailed in response to the blows was any indication. Although Zeno wore the uniform, and hence was in his own persona the official hard arm of the might and right of Lemuriaville, he paid no heed. It was no crime to kill Bilge scum, even for each other. The only law imposed from above was that the only capital crime was to inconvenience the great city above.

He passed through an open hatchway into a storage area. Ramparts of metal containers rose toward a distant ceiling. Between them scraps of trash and detritus had been knocked together into dwellings and kiosks. In a cleared space in the middle a thieves' market was held, with the pallid darkness-crawlers selling each other booty for which Zeno could imagine no use.

A few scabrous leper-pale whores called raucous solicitation from in front of a container made into a makeshift tavern and gaudy. Synthetic Moroccan-roll skirled out the open door, drowning out the clamor within. He ignored them as he ignored the inch of what appeared to be plain sewage sloshing beneath his waterproof boots. There were other services than Bilge-mucking that the scum were sometimes called upon to perform for those above....

He walked with the iron authority of a living statue. But his eyes were never still: because the prevailing state of life in the Bilge was total hopelessness, you could never be sure one of the scum wouldn't make a play at a warden. The fact that the response to assault by a lone fuse-job would likely be a spray of submachine fire or maser beams that would kill or cook half a dozen uninvolved bystanders would not inhibit them. Compassion was as unknown down here as hygiene.

He entered an alley between stacks of containers. Turned and turned again, as the gloom thickened until it rivaled the stench.

He came to a door of mottled and warped synthetic that had been rudely fastened across a low doorway laser-cut at some point into an empty container. A muffled call from within.

"It's me," he called softly, trusting his voice to serve as identifier. Without waiting for response he pushed inside.

Candles of wax rendered from the fat of human corpses sent yellow glows dancing over bits of cloth hung on the walls to soften the echo-chamber effect of metal walls, and for a kind of decoration. Smoldering incense added another layer to the stria of stink that hung in the air from the foul flooring all the way up to the metal rafters of the storage hold outside.

A slender youth rose from a pallet covered with stained silks. He glided forward, arms spreading wide. He had elfin features and huge green eyes.

Zeno accepted the embrace, enfolded the slight form in his own arms, tousled amber hair. "Robert," he said.

For the moment, one rare moment, he felt peace. Although to be here would be disgrace and death, were his presence to become known.

Chapter 8

"We can't save the world," Domi said. She bit the head off a pilchard, freshly caught and newly dead, given to her by Kiri's crew.

"But that would seem to be the description of the job we've all taken on willy-nilly," Brigid said.

She tried not to wince. But her stomach did a slow roll inside her. She had eaten distasteful things before in order to survive; doubtless she would do so again, provided she did survive. Anyway, Brigid was pretty sure Domi did things like this in part to gross her out.

The four stood on a high point overlooking Snail Cove, where soil had collected over the years. Lush green grass had sprouted from it, cushioning the harsh and jagged lava extrusion beneath. On the black sand of the beach itself, laborers and technicians were at work cleaning up the aftermath of the fish-man attack. On a similar grassed knob fifty yards to her right, Brigid could see a crew of burly brown islanders scraping a pit, with sandbags piled ready nearby. They were doing what Kane had ruefully probably admitted they should've done at the outset: emplacing a .308-caliber

M-240 machine gun to cover the beach. A second heavy
blaster from the Cerberus arsenal waited in its crate just
inland from where the four stood, with empty jute bags
lying atop it, waiting to be filled with black sand.

"Yeah," Domi said, munching contentedly. "That's
why we need to be choosy about which parts of it we
try to save."

"But doesn't your feminine heart just bleed for the
plight of that cute little kid of Kiri's?" Grant asked dryly.

Domi just laughed at him. While the others knew her
to be subject to occasional jags of sentimentality, in
general she was about as soft and sympathetic as a plate
of Sandcat armor.

"Yeah, I'm just overcome with worry for a kid who's
got a thirty-foot shark for a playmate," Kane said.
"Mebbe we should be protected from him."

Young Reva had made quite the impression. The colossal shark rising beneath him had breached, flying
out of the water in an eruption of spray for half its pro-
digious length. It looked like a submarine sounding.

Its wedge snout had propelled the boy upward. He
had jumped forward off it, somersaulted to land on the
deck beside his mother. The shark slid back beneath the
water and vanished with a swirl of a tail fin longer than
Kane was tall. Leaving the Cerberus crew standing at
the rail brandishing their guns and feeling foolish.

"Nice kid, though," Grant said. "Uh, as kids go." He
seemed embarrassed by his own brush with sentimentality.

"If we're going to operate in this part of the ocean," Brigid said, "we could probably use all the goodwill of the inhabitants as we can get."

"But it's a big ocean," Kane reminded. "We can't go fighting everybody's fight for them."

"But isn't this our fight, too? They have the same problem with the human-sacrifice cult we came here to correct. It looks as if we're about to start having the same problems with fish men they have."

"We need to go looking to tangle with these undersea guys, though?" Grant asked.

"What's the matter?" Domi asked banteringly. "Afraid of a fight?"

"Always," Kane said. "He's right. In a world as full of trouble as this sorry-assed one is, we can't afford to go looking for it. More of it already finds us than we can ever hope to handle."

"I thought you were against us getting involved?" Grant asked the albino girl. She shrugged and grinned an infuriating Domi grin.

"Surprisingly," Brigid said, "you're right, Kane. And just exactly how long do you imagine it will be before these undersea raiders seek us out on their own? Especially after Kiri told us where they claimed to come from."

"Uh," Kane grunted. "She asked. Not just Lemuria, but Lemuriaville. Which implies pretty strongly there's a baron involved."

"Or, to be precise, one of the preliminary-draft baron types we've encountered before, who scattered around the world after losing a civil war with the true barons and their creators," Brigid said.

"Why would they look to start trouble with us?" Grant asked.

"Other than the problems we've caused their kind in the not so distant past?" Kane said. "We might as well ask why've they started leaning on the ocean tribes in a heavy way, after years of only sporadically brushing up against them?"

"Think there's a connection?" his partner asked.

"I don't say there's no such thing as coincidence," Kane said. "Except where we're concerned."

"What about those dreams you've been having?" Domi asked.

The others looked at her intently. "Why would you think there could be a connection?" Brigid asked.

"Kane just said there's no such thing as coincidence with us."

"That was just what you call a figure of speech," Kane said. "Don't go all literal-minded on us, like Baptiste."

"Domi," Brigid said, "you have an exasperating habit of being right sometimes when you're at your most flippant."

She turned to the males. "Don't you think this really would be stretching coincidence past its breaking point?"

"What could the connection be?" Grant asked.

"Connect the dots however you like," Kane said caustically. "What it means is that our asses are on the line—again."

"AND SO IT PROVED," Kiri said, standing in the bow, "that we had something to offer you in exchange for your protection after all, Mr. Kane."

He was a splendid-looking man, she thought. For a mainlander. Although he was pallid to her eye, almost unhealthily so, he had about him a splendid lethality, like a great lean shark, and his eyes were the gray of a great white's eyes.

"Who knew that you people would have a ship like this?" the man called Kane said, gesturing aft past the white-gleaming superstructure with its antenna array and rotating radar dish.

"We're not savages, Mr. Kane," she said. "We have many resources."

"Then why do you need our help fighting the undersea raiders?"

"As you're aware this is no ship of war," she said. "In fact the people who built it considered their mission one of peace. As for the Children of the Great Wave, we are not rich. We possess little manufacturing capability, at least where elaboration of metals is concerned. We have such few firearms as we've found useful to trade for. Actually, what limits their utility to us is the poor availability of fixed ammunition for magazine weapons. Other than that we are armed with bows, arrows and harpoons, mostly. And some black-powder guns, for which the ammunition is more easily made."

"But you're a warrior people."

"We can fight when we have to. Mostly against people much like ourselves—pirates, predatory clans. Against more powerful foes—well, as an associate of mine said recently, the ocean is broad."

"But you don't think you can escape the Lemurians?"

"No. For whatever reason, they seem determined to make us submit. I suspect they need bodies—or hands."

He raised an eyebrow and leaned on the rail. Beneath them their progress raised a mustache of white foam that streamed away like catfish feelers to either side of the exploration ship.

"What makes you say that?" he asked.

"They make no secret of the fact they live in a dome somewhere on the sea bottom," she said. "That imposes certain strict limits on their population, does it not?"

She laughed at him. "Why such surprise? Didn't you expect a half-naked island woman to know about things like population pressure?"

"I don't know if I'd exactly associate the two."

"We are a complicated people, Kane. Our ancestors were among the peace-loving types who built this ship—and her cargo."

"I thought it was built by some kind of oceanographic research institute on what used to be the Pacific Coast," Kane said.

Her grin was startling white in her dark face. "Those were some of our ancestors. Oceanographic researchers."

"I thought you were Polynesian," the mainlander said.

"We're that, too," she said. "What we really are is complicated."

The fluting wail of a blown conch shell floated back from the small flotilla of islander craft that surrounded the larger powered ship. Those that had engines of their own, alcohol fired or powered by sophisticated solar accumulators, towed those dependent upon sail and oar, although with the wind fair for their northwestward course, sails were set for what boost they gave.

The outlander fumbled in a buttoned breast pocket of the white muslin shirt he wore, brought out a cunning pair of miniature binoculars, which he brought to his eyes. A glimpse awakened desire for them in Kiri's heart; like most of her people she had a magpie fondness for small and readily portable items of high technology. Evidently we've a basis for continuing trade, she thought on the fly. I wonder what he'd take for them?

Shading her eyes from the glare of the early-afternoon sun with her hand, she'd already spotted what the advance lookouts were calling to the attention of the fleet. Sudden white blemishes appeared on the rolling swell. Slim silver shapes glinted in the sun before disappearing back into more patches of white.

"Dolphins," said the *Auguste Piccard*'s boatswain, a huge broad brown man with shags of graying black hair hanging like a fringe from a balding dome. His name was Bukowski; Kiri had seen how Kane's eyes widened at the name when they were introduced. He still doesn't understand us, she thought with amusement.

The big bosun spoke the word with evident distaste. He punctuated it by spitting over the railing.

Kane looked at him in surprise. "I thought everybody liked dolphins," he said. "They're friends of seafaring men and all that."

"Not hardly," the boatswain said in the voice that made Grant's sound like a tenor.

"Dolphins are enemies to sharks," Kiri said. "We are the Shark Tribe. Work it out."

Kane turned to the big shipman. He was clad only in a batik lava-lava with flowers printed on it, maroon on brown and beige beneath a great swag belly. "I thought you were with the, uh, Albatross People." Actually the name they appeared to use for themselves was Booby People. There were some things even Kane couldn't say with a straight face.

"Yeah," the boatswain said. "We ain't cozy with sharks like Kiri's mob." Belatedly, Kane realized he had a faint Australian accent. The man was so quiet they'd already spent a day and a night on ship together without discovering that. "But the Lemurians use 'em for spies."

"So everybody knows about these Lemurians but us," Kane said.

"Pretty much."

"They haven't exactly gone out of their way to make themselves popular with the Great Wave Children," Kiri said. "It's just that they haven't declared open war upon us until now."

Peering through his microbinoculars, Kane saw white smoke puff away from the lead ship, a fairly sizable catamaran with a butter-colored hull a lot like Kiri's own *Great Sky Reef*, which had been left behind with the bulk of the Shark People. The pair of leaping shapes vanished below the waves and didn't reappear.

A breath later the sound of a musket shot poked Kane in the eardrum.

"Does this mean they're about to attack?" he asked.

Kiri shrugged. "Probably not," she said. "Since they have submarines, they can attack without tipping their hands like that."

"They're watching us, though," the big Samoan-looking boatswain said. "Bad thing."

He spit over the rail again.

Chapter 9

The ship's Klaxon jolted Kane from uneasy sleep.

Before he was fully sentient he was on his bare feet, strapping a belt laden with magazine carriers around his waist. Grant thumped down to the deck on his own bare feet from the top bunk, flexing his knees slightly to ease his landing. His Sin Eater was out.

"I do not *believe* this shit," Grant said.

"Bring grens," Kane muttered. He was having trouble with the web gear's black synthetic fastener. "Many, many grens."

"Incens'll work great," Grant said, grabbing at a pack. "Everything on a boat burns."

"Isn't this thing a ship? And isn't it made out of steel? We're not still on Kiri's piece of handmade furniture."

"It floats. It's a fucking boat. The hull and the bulkheads are fucking steel. Covered in fucking paint. Paint burns. The furniture burns. The wood paneling burns. *We* burn—"

"I get the picture. Let's go. You go low and left."

"Roger that," Grant said. "You first, high right?"

"Always." Kane tipped a forefinger off his eyebrow.

It was a sign between them, meaning it was a classic one-percenter. Meaning the chance of survival on their usual mission. "I am the point man."

As Kane stepped into the passageway a body tumbled down the ladder from the main deck. It thrashed and mewled in mindless agony. The blood spurting from the spear thrust clear through the island man's belly so that its head stuck out just beneath the ribs, and next to his spine was almost black in the dim amber safety lights of the gangway.

"Shit!" Kane said. He raised his Sin Eater with both hands and triggered a blast up and out the open hatch. The noise bounced off the claustrophobically close bulkheads and threatened to implode his skull, to say nothing of his eardrums.

"Double shit," Grant called from behind him. "There goes our night vision *and* our hearing."

"Better that than have four hundred pounds of fish thing land on me when I swarm up the ladder," Kane said. "I want the fuckers standing back."

He thought of popping a microgren—not incendiary—out the hatch but decided instantly against it. There was no knowing if friends might be up on deck within the blast radius instead of foes. Normally Kane tended to do what seemed needful to survive the moment for himself and his comrades from Cerberus, and if friendly natives got caught in the overkill, oh, well.

But the poor bastard kicking and crying and shitting into the widening pool of his lifeblood on the nonskid deck runners was one of their limited contingent of Wave Children who knew how to maintain and operate *Piccard*'s vital cargo. Aside from the fact they were hung out here in the middle of the infinite damn Pacific and totally dependent upon the islanders' goodwill to keep from having to swim a few hundred miles to the nearest land, provided they could find it, they couldn't afford to chill any of their own specialists.

Kane didn't bother telling Grant to cover him as he went fast up the ladder; he took it for granted. He burst out into the thick humid tropical night air and rolled up to kneel in the shelter of a corner of the superstructure, covering aft with his blaster.

A figure approached. Tall, somewhat lanky and, despite the utter lack of detail, especially after Kane's eyes had been dazzled by his own muzzle-flare, unmistakably human, not fish man. He eased his forefinger off the Sin Eater's guardless trigger.

Approaching almost to the perforated muzzle, the figure suddenly swung up an arm. In the dull orange glow spilling from the open hatchway Kane saw features more bestial than human, distorted by far more than transforming rage.

And the gleam of rusty light upon the blade of a machete raised to split his skull.

Before Kane's lightning reflexes could react, the flame-edged black blade hissed down.

Light and noise exploded in Kane's skull.

By sudden strobing yellow-white radiance Kane saw

his attacker's face start to crumple in on itself to the hammering impacts from Grant's Sin Eater.

"It's not like you, falling asleep at the switch like that, Kane," Kane heard through the ringing in his ears.

"Damn," Kane said. "They've got humans with them."

"Must be the cultists we've been hearing so much about," Grant said.

A yellow glare off the starboard bow showed where a boat burned from stem to stern. Shouts, screams and the clash of arms drifted across the ocean. Somewhere off on the other side of *Piccard*'s superstructure, a musket banged.

The exploration ship itself was oddly quiet. Kane heard a soft scrape from above. He ducked, wheeled, bringing up his Sin Eater. A humanoid shadow blocked stars above Grant. The light of the burning boat glinted off the blade of the spear aimed at the back of the former Mag's neck.

Kane's forefinger had already taken up the trigger slack. A red dot appeared in the center of the shadow mass. Kane squeezed off a quick double tap.

Grant threw himself into a forward roll aft past Kane. At the same time the ship canted to starboard to the motion of a wave. The shadowy figure fell into the sea with a scream.

Kane lowered his arms. At once strong arms enfolded him like iron bands, pinning his two hands, holding his Sin Eater, against his sternum. A blast of hot breath hit him full in the face. His attacker had come at them from the direction of the bow. The man's breath—if he was a man—stank like an open grave.

Kane brought his knee up to slam between his attacker's braced legs. He felt his patella slam against the man's pelvis, felt the weight shift as the man's weight momentarily broke free from the deck.

The grip never slackened. Kane saw a mottled gleam in the light from the hatch as lips grinned around filed teeth.

Kane snapped his head forward, felt cartilage splash. A squeal vented from the man's open mouth. Cannibal bastard never had his nose broken, thought Kane. Way past due.

The barrel-band grip relaxed. Kane pulled his hands down and pressed his foe away. The perforated muzzle-shroud of his handblaster slid under the other man's chin.

Kane triggered a burst.

Flame from the muzzle played up the attacker's chin like a blowtorch. Kane caught a glimpse of a face distorted by rage, jagged tribal tattoos and scarification. Then teeth shattered in a welter of blood, and it was as if the man's face was torn away upward as by the claws of a giant beast.

The man fell away. Holding his handblaster again at the ready, Kane quickly wheeled, checking forward to the bow, then swept his gaze around toward the stern. Grant, crouched next to the superstructure, covered its upper levels with his weapon. Otherwise nothing moved.

Until reeking bodies swarmed over the gunwales and swamped the two men.

CLAWLIKE FINGERS gripped Brigid's arm. These caught her higher up, on the biceps. They were smaller than the hands of a demon lover whose finger impressions she could still feel in the warm and pliant flesh of her thighs.

Beneath her, she perceived a triangle of deeper darkness against the chasm's black. In the midst of it something opened. Red light streamed upward to strike her face with an almost physical force, like the opening of a furnace door.

But it was no furnace. It was an eye.

"Brigid!" a feminine voice shrilled. "Wake up! Now!"

The tentacles turned to dust before they touched her, to shadow, to nothing. Brigid's stomach seethed in confusion.

A voice spoke in her head: *One way or another I shall have you!*

From somewhere far off came a quick insistent rapping, like a woodpecker boring for a weevil in hardwood bark.

Or gunfire.

She snapped her eyes open. A white oval swam close before them, with two ovals like smears of fresh bright blood above a bloody gape. Her breath caught in her throat.

"Brigid," the open wound said urgently, "snap out of it!"

"Domi," she said dreamily, recognizing the albino

girl as her eyes finally won focus. "I was having a night-mare—"

"The nightmare is happening in the real world," Domi said. "We got trouble by the shitload."

"It was the dream," Brigid said vaguely. She still was not connecting very tightly to the here and now. "It was the dream again. Only—"

She heard a shout from hard nearby, muffled only by the bulkheads of what she belatedly remembered was her compartment on board *Piccard*. It was followed at once by the boom of an obvious shotgun blast, strangled cry, a thud of something soft and heavy. Indeterminate noises followed.

"Blast the bugger again," a male voice bellowed. "He's still living!" Another slam of noise told that his suggestion had been followed promptly.

"Get it together right now!" Domi commanded. "We've been boarded by a pack of tattooed fusies with filed teeth."

She dragged Brigid from the bed.

"And get some clothes on, quick." Brigid saw that Domi was dressed in khaki shorts and a man's blue shirt, untucked and unevenly buttoned. "You'll just distract the men if you run around bare assed like that."

Brigid caught the white blouse Domi tossed at her face and shrugged into it. Next the albino tossed her a pair of cargo shorts from where they lay neatly folded on the little dresser in her cabin. Bridget hesitated, then, hearing more distant blasts of full-autofire and screams, stepped into them and pulled them up without bothering with underwear.

Her Heckler & Koch lay in its holster on the bedside table. She picked it up, drew it, tossed the holster on the bed. Reflex ground into her by Grant and Kane caused her to wrap her hand over the top of the back of the slide, press forward with the hand that held the grip. A gleam of silver case inside—she had confirmed the blaster was loaded.

"Fill me in," she said.

"You've heard most of what I know," Domi said. "I think the boys are fighting them topside. Some of them have gotten in, like you just heard. The islander crew is pretty tough, but our techs are gonna get chopped to pieces."

"Then let's get them forted up down in the main bay," Brigid said.

PAIN STABBED through Kane's hand and down his forearm as his Sin Eater was wrenched away. I hope that wasn't my trigger finger breaking, he thought.

The reek of foul bodies and carrion breath clamped his lungs as fiercely as arms did his limbs and body. His stomach lurched. The weight of bodies pressed him down.

A knee slammed painfully on the deck as his leg buckled. The pain jolt called him to himself. One thing a Mag didn't do was go down easy.

He pushed hard with his left hand against a midsection like a slab of oak, then yanked it back, swiveling his hips counterclockwise as hard as he could. His left arm popped free momentarily.

It was enough. His hand snatched his Magistrate's combat knife from its sheath on his belt. Holding it tip down and blade forward, he lashed out across himself, then upward.

He felt resistance as skin parted to the keen blade. Hot fluids spattered his bare face and arms. The cannibals had been fighting in a deadly silence more unnerving than battle cries would have been. Now several voices screamed at once.

He slammed his head up and back. He heard the jarring impact and felt teeth shatter as his crown slammed into a tattooed face of a man on his back. Jagged stumps gouged his scalp through his hair.

He stood, the weight still on his back, and drove backward with his right elbow, felt ribs give. With a strangling yell the man fell off his back.

Holding his blade straight outward from the bottom of his fist, he punched forward and across himself. A fine spray of black jetted as the combat knife sliced through a cultist's Adam's apple, severing his carotid artery. The man staggered back, clutching futilely at his neck. He fell down. Kane found himself momentarily in the clear. In front of him, toward the stern of the converted freighter, a pile of bodies writhed like a snake-mating ball.

"Grant!" he shouted. A man lunged at him from his left, swinging a club in an overhand blow like an ax. He ducked, quarter turned away, then backed straight into the man's attack. The man's right arm came down hard across his left shoulder.

He grabbed the right wrist with his right hand. Straightening his knees, he stood forcefully and pulled down with his hand. His attacker's elbow broke.

With his other hand he stabbed backward. He felt the blade sink into flesh. His opponent gasped, dropped his club and flung himself backward with a bubbling shriek.

Painted and tattooed bodies erupted in front of Kane as if Hell had blown a gasket. From their midst Grant snapped upright, arms extended like spring-driven levers that had thrown his foes aside. One man landed on his back on the starboard rail. His spine snapped with a sound like a muffled gunshot. He screamed, teetered a moment, waving his arms; his legs hung limp. Then he slipped over to fall from view, into the waiting arms of the deep Pacific.

Grant still had his handblaster. He pointed it down and to his left, then triggered a long, jackhammering burst as he swept the weapon right across his body. Cultists howled as jacketed 9 mm slugs punched through the great muscles of their thighs, smashed their pelvises, pulped their bowels and splintered their lower vertebrae.

But Kane's own dancing partners weren't done with him yet. A man whose bobbing mass of dreadlocks contrasted with the shaved heads of most of his companions jumped onto the hold cover with a thump of splayed bare feet and ran at Kane with a short spear with a jagged head.

Kane took a step back as the madman lunged at him, but stepped in the middle of a warm, slimy pool of the spilled guts and body fluids of the man who'd jumped on his back.

Kane sprawled over backward with hot pale guts twining about his shins like the inky tentacles that haunted his dreams. The deck slammed his coccyx and sent lightning flashes of pure white agony jagging up his spine to explode in his brain.

He wasn't the only one having trouble with the blood-slick decks. The spear man had slipped a whole ten feet to slam into the railing with enough force to knock the breath out of him and bust a short rib or two. But he was high on adrenaline and fanaticism, if not some kind of psychotronic assistance. He deftly twirled the short spear in his hand and raised it above his head to throw it at Kane, who was still wallowing in the slippery, shit-stinking intestinal tangle.

A roar broke the night from somewhere behind Kane, so fierce and close that it drove his head forward and threatened to burst his eardrums. He smelled the hair on the back of his head crisp, felt a slap of moving air on his cheek as something rushed by.

The twisted grimace of hatred and triumphant fury on the tribal-tattooed visage collapsed at the point where the right cheekbone flanked the broad nose. The man's head snapped back. The spear dropped from his hand to thunk point first into the deck. He toppled over backward.

To reappear an eye blink later, limbs thrashing to either side of the maw of a leaping great white. A surge of foam slopped over the deck, glowing greenish white with either the light of the brilliant stars or tiny self-luminescent organisms.

His ears still ringing and reverberating to the blast of a shotgun from about a yard behind his head, Kane faintly heard shrill screams and an orgy of splashing from somewhere beyond and below the gunwales. It was drowned out by the thunder of a high-powered blaster on full-auto. Flashes as long as one of the *Piccard*'s lifeboats lit up the whole stern of the oceanographic vessel like a strobing spotlight from a point high up on the superstructure.

One of the cultists Grant had shot off himself had struggled to his feet. The front of him from belly downward was painted shiny dark with somebody's blood, his or one of his buddies'. He was clawed right off his feet by three crunching impacts of high-velocity bullets. The flickering garish illumination of the muzzle-flares showed other cultists racing toward the stern in fear as bullets thunked home or spanged off into howling ricochets all about them.

At least two threw themselves straight over the taffrail. Suddenly shrieks of intolerable agony showed what a mistake that was.

As three of their companions braked themselves like

characters from a comic twentieth-century cartoon vid, Kane wondered if the first pair had been sucked into the ship's propellers, which still turned and churned to keep the two-hundred-ton vessel under way. In the context of what had happened to the last poor bastard gone overboard, he doubted it.

The fleeing cultists still couldn't save themselves. Two more mind-shattering blasts knocked them straight over the railing to join their buddies, presumably as shark entrées.

"Looks like our islander friends have brought some of their little finny playmates to the party," Kane said, reaching up gratefully to accept the hand Brigid extended to help him off the befouled deck. Her right hand still held a Benelli shotgun pointed skyward with its butt resting on the swell of her hip.

He noted with approval that she didn't wince away from touching a hand dripping with blood and bellyooze and bits of tissue. Indeed she grasped it with surprising strength and half hauled him to his feet, then managed not to smirk at the way his bare feet slipped on the slick mess beneath.

"Thanks, Baptiste," he said. "You're turning out to be pretty hard-core."

At that she did wince. "I suppose you think that's a compliment, Kane."

With a hiss and a pop, a launched flare burst high over the scene. The blue-white artificial moon illuminated Grant, crouched with his handblaster at the ready, and a flotilla at least twice as large as it had been when the sun went down. The newcomers were mostly outrigger canoes. A lot of these bobbed empty, as did several of the islander craft escorting the *Piccard*.

Some of the interloping craft still had crews. Kane saw a dark finned-torpedo shape fly from the water, land midships of one of these with a splintering crash and a splash. Shrieking cultists tumbled into the water, which was churned to a boil about them by sharp dorsal fins.

The machine gun in the superstructure snarled again. A line of miniature water spouts appeared between two of the cultists' canoes. A second burst clawed across one, knocking two frantic paddlers into the drink.

Kane's hearing and general composure had recovered enough that he winced from the terrific racket the gun made.

"What the hell," he said, "is that?"

"A Browning Automatic Rifle," Brigid answered. "It was in the ship's stores, of all things." She shook her head. "I think Domi has a new favorite toy."

"Strike," Kane said. "We are never going to hear the end of this."

Chapter 10

"You were wondering how the cultists managed to catch up with us without motors in their craft," Kiri told Kane, standing beside him in the bow of *Piccard*. The sea stretched out apparently infinitely before them like an uneasy desert. A few albatrosses bobbed white on the water among the fleet of a dozen Wave Children vessels currently surrounding the ship. Others skimmed just above the waves

"Yeah," Kane said.

Peals of childish laughter rang out behind them. Kane glanced back. Though he knew the sounds portended no harm, he was not of a disposition to like or trust sudden loud noises.

Especially now.

Kiri's son, Reva, was racing forward along the starboard rail, with Domi darting in hot pursuit. Both were barefoot, and neither showed any sign of feeling a deck that had to be blistering hot in the intense sunlight. Both were laughing like crazy people.

The boy deftly avoided crewfolk, from both *Piccard* and Kiri's *Great Sky Reef*, weaving around them as they went about their business. Domi slipped between them fluidly. Grant, wearing camou trousers and an olive-drab shirt, stood talking with Ollie, Kiri's boatswain. Not unusually for the Wave Children, Ollie was even taller and broader than Grant himself, with leathery skin and gray-brushed steel-wool hair that hung like a kinky curtain around the rear fringe of his great dome skull. His capacious belly overhung a pair of shorts that looked like cutoff blue jeans, although untold years' exposure to the sun had faded them to a white almost as milky-pure as Domi's skin.

The boy ran right up to Grant and grasped him by his left leg. Without missing a beat in his conversation, the big mustachioed man hunkered down, picked up the boy and stood with him seated in the crook of a massive arm.

"That's quite the boy you got there," Kane said. "Grant doesn't even like kids."

Kiri looked back and her face lit with love. It made her even better to look at. "He is an unusual boy," she said. "I know every parent says that."

"Not every parent has a kid who swims with man-eating sharks."

She laughed easily. "You're right. I'm doubly lucky."

She crossed her arms beneath her breasts. They were covered today: she wore what looked suspiciously like a gray T-shirt hackled off at midriff length, although her lower garment was black and little more than a thong. Kane was just as glad she had put on a few more clothes. It wasn't as if he lacked the self-control to keep himself from being distracted; he just didn't need anything tugging at the edge of his attention, as it were. Besides, it put Baptiste's back up to be around a half-naked woman as damn handsome as Kiri, although currently the former archivist was belowdecks, poring over charts with members of *Piccard*'s crew.

The fleet mistress walked a few paces away. "But you were wondering how the evil ones caught us without mills. Easy—they sailed to a point athwart our course, which they expected us to reach well after sunset."

"Which means they know our course and speed."

She nodded grimly. "Which means we have a traitor in our midst. Or traitors."

"Mebbe," Kane said, "mebbe not. We don't know our Lemuriaville friends didn't scope us out and pass the info along to the cultists."

"Why do you say that?" she asked, looking at him with raised brow. "We've never seen any sign of cooperation between the undersea folk and the crazy ones in the past. Fact is, the Lemurians have indicated they've had their own problems with them during our—I won't say friendly—*neutral* dealings in the past."

Kane shrugged. "I don't know why I say that. Just call it a hunch. It does seem a little too coincidental to have both of them jumping our case like this."

"Perhaps. But we already know we have traitors. Or at least defectors."

Kane grimaced. Cannondale, one of the techs missing from the cone-snail farm had turned up.

It had been he whose elbow Kane had broken preparatory to gutting him like a fish the night before.

Despite the bright and stinging sunlight, Kane felt a chill wave pass through his body like a cloud before the sun. For the erstwhile Moon base scientist had babbled as he spiraled down toward death, Brigid reported. About the dreams.

His last words had been a scream: "The tentacles! The black—"

"Okay," Kane said to the fleet mistress, shrugging it off. "Point to you. But I don't see how that means it can't have been the Lemurians scoping us out."

She smiled sweetly. "Ever heard of Occam's razor, the principle of not multiplying explanations?"

"Yeah. Vaguely. Baptiste said something about it. Where'd you hear about it?"

"We're not just naked savages, Kane," Kiri said. "Even if we tend to spend a lot more time naked than you mainlanders are comfortable with."

"I'm belatedly beginning to figure that out," Kane said. "Uh, the bit about you not being just savages, that is."

"Not the naked part?"

"Give me a break here. I'm trying to keep this on a professional basis." Not, he thought, that that was particularly easy. Kiri was considerably more than just a good-looking woman, and her friendly yet challenging manner made her more intriguing than otherwise.

"Don't take this the wrong way, but you seem to live by a pretty…traditional style out here. That makes the occasional high-tech flash a bit disconcerting, okay?"

She nodded. He enjoyed watching her luxuriant long hair with its purple undertones bob about her broad shoulders. "Our story is maybe a bit more complex than you'd imagine. I'll tell it to you later, if you're interested, Mr. Kane."

"I am. And skip the 'mister,'" he said. "It makes me sound like somebody else." Somebody I don't even know, he thought—that honorific had never been used in the Cobaltville Enclaves.

"Fair enough. I'll look into our internal housekeeping. Meanwhile—" she turned and paced to the bow and pointed straight ahead "—at our current course and speed, we'll reach the latitude and longitude you've given us in a little over twenty hours."

Lakesh, as usual, was playing his cards close to his skinny chest. Evidently their mystery correspondents had been heard from again and had provided detailed instructions on how the Cerberus operatives were to proceed. For her part, Kiri—to the best of Kane's knowledge—hadn't so much as glanced at a map or chart to fix the location of the oceanographic vessel and attendant fleet since receiving the coordinates. She just simply seemed to know where, in that vast, featureless open water, they were and where they were going.

He suspected that was it, too, that she did just know. That she wasn't playing tricks on the mainlander and sneaking off for some quick calculations and consultations when he wasn't looking.

"Well," he said, "so far, so good."

A sound like an ax striking distant wood reached his ears. A moment later motion pulled his eyes to his right: a puff of smoke, tinted faintly green, rolled into the Pacific sky from a large outrigger canoe five hundred yards off their starboard bow.

"Damn," Kane said. "You'd think I'd know by now never to say shit like that."

"Danger signal," the fleet mistress said unnecessarily. "*Sunfisher* has seen something."

Right off *Piccard*'s port bow an egg-shaped object surged from the depths. It raised a glistening skin of foam-dappled seawater, which broke in a gush of spray to give birth to a sleek Jet Ski with a man in a blue-black wet suit riding it hell-for-leather across the waves.

Gunfire crackled from across the little fleet.

Chapter 11

"Hit it!" Kane yelled. "Battle stations, everybody!"

He immediately felt like a dick for saying it. His people knew the drill. And even if it had been his place to give orders to Kiri's motley crew, they'd already amply shown they knew what to do when attacked.

They were briskly doing it, too. Briskly and professionally. A young woman grabbed Reva from Grant and ran him belowdecks. Others emerged through hatches, carrying uncased weapons and heavy bags.

The sea boiled around *Piccard*, giving birth to the Jet Skis like so many wasps. Black-powder rifles banged. Kane saw an indigo-clad rider, struck by a lucky shot—not so lucky from his viewpoint—sprawl sideways out of the saddle and into a splash. A slowly rolling wave tinted pink, then knifed abruptly by a triangle fin, showed the islanders' pelagic friends were on the job.

Teata, a *Piccard* crewman, short, dark and wiry, with hair gathered into a tail that fanned down his bare bony back like a kinky broom, emerged from a hatchway in the superstructure's side carrying a BAR and a bag of magazines. His disproportionately large bare feet slapping the deck, he ran forward to toss the twenty-pound rifle and equally heavy duffel to Kane.

Thankfully, Kane just had time to bend his knees slightly and brace. The double impact was like having a good-sized dog hit him in the middle of the chest, and he was damned if he was going to be shown up by a skinny-ass native who could barely weigh twice as much with his hair soaking wet—not to mention let himself get knocked ass over tea kettle, right off the ship and into the water.

Kiri snapped her head left and right, her own mass of hair whipping her about the shoulders. Fishing a heavy magazine out of the bag, which he'd dropped to the deck at his feet, Kane shot her a glance, somewhat surprised at her dithering.

"My ship," she said in a voice shot through with real pain. "I should go there—"

"Bullshit," Kane said, straightening. For emphasis he slammed a magazine home in the BAR's well. "You'll never get there through this shit. You told me your people are the best, and I think you know what you're talking about. They can handle themselves. Stay here and do what you can, keep your cute little son safe."

She shot him a look, and even in full battle mode with the adrenaline singing its death song in his veins, its sheer hateful raptor intensity rocked Kane momentarily onto his heels. This woman doesn't like to be ordered around, he thought. By anybody.

She set her square little jaw and nodded. As Kane

racked the stiff action with a bright metal clatter, she turned and began shouting in Polynesian, or whatever it was exactly her people spoke when they weren't speaking English. He understood not one syllable. But he figured she was bawling for a weapon.

Back about amidships, Grant was setting up shop on top of the waist-high hold cover behind the telescopic sight of a big Remington .338 Lapua bolt-action rifle with the bipod dropped. A quick implant call confirmed Brigid was at her battle station, belowdecks in the infirmary. She sounded guilty to be out of the action and at least nominally safe.

Kane had no time.

He heaved the heavy blaster to his shoulder, braced hard, sighted at a Jet Ski skimming past about fifty yards off the port beam. Just before he pulled the trigger he heard a scream of fury from the flying bridge.

What's up Domi's back now? he wondered, and fired.

"WHAT, YOU SPEAK NOT English all of a sudden?" the albino girl shrieked, her slight white body a straining knot of fury. The Cerberus contingent already knew full well from its Snail Cove operation that the islanders had a propensity to forget what was in effect their second native language when it they found it convenient to do so. "This is my spot! I saved your asses from up here last night."

One of Kiri's warriors, a long lanky man with streaky blond hair named Tailo, was hoisting a heavy belt of huge linked cartridges from a green steel box at the front of the flying bridge.

"You were firing from the rear of the bridge," Tailo pointed out. "We sure appreciate it. And now maybe you could sort of roam around the structure and shoot at targets of opportunity. But this mount is ours."

As was what was fastened to the pintle mount welded of lengths of steel pipe: a Browning M2HB .50-caliber machine gun. Tailo straightened with a grunt, holding the heavy ammo belt while another mostly naked male warrior fed it into the boxy receiver.

The weapon had never had the blue Mylar sheet that shrouded it from the virulently corrosive salt sea spray unwrapped from it during last night's attack. It was a relatively long-range weapon, and that assault had been of an up-close-and-personal variety. And while Domi's bullets had done minor cosmetic damage aft of the superstructure, the much heavier slugs the big Browning fired could've crippled vital systems—although they were much too small to attempt sinking a vessel of this size.

Domi bit her lip. She was never known for her patience, and her blood was up from the snarling motors and screams and gunfire of the Lemurian attack. Her reflex was to claim the prime shooting vantage despite the plan agreed to in advance.

But Tailo, perhaps with the diplomatic eloquence so common among his tribe, or maybe just touched with serendipity, had pointed out an alternative even more attractive to the Outland girl's predatory soul.

She grinned and nodded. From a rip of gunfire she knew Kane had already staked out a firing point to port, and it really pissed her off he'd gotten into action first. So she shifted clockwise to scan the sea to starboard.

It was good she did so—in more ways than one. A skimmer was riding a white foam mustache straight toward *Auguste Piccard* and no more than forty yards out. The light machine gun mounted in its snout flared as she raised the massive BAR.

Bullets sprayed the .50-caliber mount, sparking off its makeshift pintle. Tailo grunted softly and folded around a blood-jetting hole right beneath his breastbone; at its upward angle it had to have pulped his heart before blasting a bloody chunk of scapula out his back.

His fellow gun crew struggled to turn the heavy Ma Deuce to bear. But they couldn't swing it far enough without the gunner hanging in free space before the flying bridge—which would of course have the effect of levering the perforated barrel unbendably skyward.

But Domi had no such problem. She took a long forward-leaning stance, raised the big rifle and fired.

Domi's BAR made much noise and flashing. A line of geysers walked toward the charging surface craft. The Lemurian pilot had to turn his speeding craft to shift aim. Although it was a matter of only a few degrees to correct his fire from the heavy MG into Domi, that was easier said than done in the second or so he had.

Instead he opted to bank left away from the incoming bullet. In the impromptu game of chicken he and the slip of a girl away up on the much larger vessel's superstructure were playing, he lost.

The stake proved to be his life. An instant later she walked her burst right across his left thigh and his synthetic-clad torso. He spilled off to starboard. The craft wobbled far over. Then its heavily weighted keel pulled it back upright. With no hand on its throttle it slowed to a bobbing halt within twenty yards.

Injured though he was, the Lemurian swam with splashing urgency—for what, Domi couldn't see. Acting more on bloodlust than tactical sense—for clearly he posed no further threat, even if he weren't mortally hurt and bleeding to death—Domi drew down on him to finish him with another burst.

Suddenly the front part of him vanished under water. Flipper-tipped feet kicked with futile frenzy at the air. Then he was pulled from view by the unseen shark that had bitten deep into his head.

Domi shrugged, grinned. This was better than blasting the puke again. Way better. She started casting about for other targets.

Despite herself she winced when the BAR's immense cousin spoke up from the front of the flying bridge. Even well back away from the muzzle the blast struck her like a gale wind, and the noise was enough to threaten to pry the molecules of her slight body loose from one another.

Though she knew it was a bad idea to break her concentration on what really mattered—fighting her own fight—Domi looked around. The big fifty sent up geysers of seawater as tall as a ten-man outrigger canoe was long. She saw a skimmer simply vanish in eruptions of spray. When the burst ended, the light craft was sinking straight down, its leaded keel broken. Of its rider Domi saw no sign. He was chum, most likely.

Even before the monster machine-blaster weighed in, the skimmer jockeys were losing their taste for the fight. Domi saw several of the craft shear off to zip directly away from her and the fleet. They were getting ripped from all directions by high-power blasterfire that they no way expected from the near-naked low-tech islanders. The heavy weapons were a big part of the payment—and assistance—Cerberus was giving the Children of the Great Wave in exchange for their escort services, not to mention the treasure *Piccard* carried in her steel womb.

The recoil rocked Domi back as she fired at another, more distant target. The BAR fired a .30-06 cartridge, longer but of the same bore-size as the more "modern" .308, and about ten percent more powerful. Its mass helped suck up the forceful recoil. Domi found that shooting it the way she'd long since been taught to fire any high-powered rifle made it readily controllable, although of course if she fired a burst of any length the muzzle would kick skyward in a hell of a hurry.

Controlling all that blasting, bucking power and noise, she would keep the bad guys headed in the right direction—and score another kill or two if she could.

And then the catamaran right beside *Piccard* and scarcely two hundred yards away burst into flame with a whomp like a match hitting an open can of gasoline.

DOWN ON THE STARBOARD RAIL beside the superstructure, a man and a woman from *Piccard*'s crew cracked open a long narrow crate to unlimber another secret weapon. Through the orange flames and brown smoke of the burning catamaran, Kane could see an egg-shaped sea-craft about the size of a Sandcat crawling toward them, raising little more than a V-shaped hump of green wake.

Kane's lips skinned back from his teeth. "Come on," he gritted to the crew. If that big bastard decides to blast us with his laser, there won't be anything left of me but a last loud scream, he thought.

With a loud crack, a blue-green lance stabbed from the enemy craft. A louder but duller thunderclap answered from Kane's left, with a white flash and puff of smoke from the hull below his line of sight. He felt the blow through the soles of his boots as if a hundred-pound boulder had struck the vessel.

He turned his head, belatedly closing his eyes on a throbbing magenta spear of afterimage. Thankfully the big laser fired in pulses, not a continuous beam. From the Wave Children's description of the first attack, Philboyd—knowing what he was talking about, for a change—postulated that the Lemurians used a variety of chemical-electric laser, employing some kind of chemical capacitors to store charges between the shots, drawing on whatever power source the egg craft used. That was their first break.

The second was that the submersible, probably not thinking they could harm it, had chosen to ignore the crew on *Piccard*'s deck in favor of going right straight for structural damage. The Lemurians seemed to know the old freighter was carrying a very precious cargo, and were aiming to neutralize it. Then again, Kane thought, we already knew we were penetrated….

His vision still bisected by a pulsing pink line, Kane looked at the crew, stretching out his hand. But Kiri had stepped between him and them, taking their burden from them and swinging it onto her own right shoulder as if she knew what she were doing.

"Hey!" Kane exclaimed.

Without glancing at him, Kiri put her eye behind the optical sight. "It's my fleet, my fight," she said. "I need to get into it."

Before Kane could protest, another hammer blow made *Piccard*'s hull ring. Blinking at the new afterimage that crossed the old, fading one at a narrow angle, Kane said, "You better know what you're doing. We don't have much margin for error here—"

For answer Kiri pulled the trigger set in front of the pistol grip.

By good luck no one was passing behind the RPG-7 launcher as exhaust flame jetted out the back, although it bubbled white paint on the superstructure. By even better luck, the enemy craft was closing at the speed of a slow walk, straight at them: a zero-deflection shot. The fat, spindle-shaped warhead sprang toward it on a bright bead of white fire.

It struck against the bright panel of reflected sunlight that obviously indicated the forward viewport. It was no doubt made of thick armaglass or some equivalent. But the warheads from South America were an after-market upgrade to the venerable Soviet launcher: they used a far more effective shape-charge based upon that used in the Western European MILAN antitank launcher.

Whether or not the original rockets would've done the job, this one did. In spades. It went off with a vicious crack. Kane saw the cramped interior of the crew compartment lit up by a blue-white flash of fiendish intensity as incandescent copper sprayed its hapless occupants at supersonic speed.

Grinning like a wolf, he slapped Kiri's shoulder. "Great shot!"

Kiri had already stuck the empty launcher back at the techs to have it reloaded. "Don't sweat a follow-up shot," Kane said. He nodded toward the stricken enemy craft, which had already veered away to his left and come to a halt in the water. "That bastard's toast."

"But the others aren't," Kiri said as the female crew-person socketed a reload in place in the launcher's business end with a click.

Kane pulled his head back on his neck in surprise. "Damn straight. Not too many people have ever set me straight on something like that. How the hell come did you ever wind up as chief navigator or whatever, instead of war boss?"

She flashed him a grin as she took back the reloaded rocket-propelled grenade launcher. "Heredity," she said. "Not all our adherence to tradition is exactly functional."

A double crack like thunder on jolt, barely muffled by the mass of the superstructure, announced that two more rockets, fired from two different islander craft, had struck another submersible almost simultaneously. Cheers followed.

The cheering, from the whole fleet at once, only grew louder as three protracted bursts from the big Browning planted on the flying bridge, which seemed to make the whole ship rattle around Kane, proved that the egg craft weren't invulnerable to .50-caliber fire.

Then *Piccard*'s crew members were dancing around Kane and their fierce fleet mistress, pounding them on the backs. "They've had enough!" one shouted. "They're running!"

Kane looked around. It was true. Three of the ovoid craft vanished from view below the water even as he watched. The sons of bitches didn't seem to have much taste for a fight they might lose.

Or their CO was operating under orders to conserve scarce assets, he thought. Both were likely true—and worth knowing.

Then Kiri caught him in an embrace that made his

ribs creak, and planted a kiss on his bearded lips that made him, just for a moment, forget about the struggle for survival in a cold cruel world.

Chapter 12

Yellow flames leaped higher than a Samoan's head from the center of the cover of *Piccard*'s aft hold, bright against the star-sprayed black of the night Pacific sky. Kane, seated cross-legged on the deck beside the hold, felt uneasy about a big-ass fire on board, and an open one at that. Even though it had been built on a carefully arranged base of some kind of tile or fire brick before being set alight.

But their hosts had centuries of experience living at sea, sometimes out of sight of land for months at a time, so he gathered from their conversations. From what Baptiste said, some of their ancestors had millennia of practice. One thing was sure: they knew shitloads more about life a sea than he did, or with luck, ever would. So he kept his misgivings to himself and concentrated on listening.

Two figures stood flanking the fire. One was elderly, and projected a sense of infirmity, although his carriage was straight. This was Anui, the oldest crewmen in Kiri's flotilla. Like Kiri herself a navigator, he had always refused mastery of his own vessel.

He spoke in a voice that trembled under the weight of his years, yet he spoke right out clearly and proudly. Too bad, Kane thought, that he spoke in the Polynesian dialect these people used, of which neither Kane nor his three companions from Cerberus understood a syllable.

Kiri sat cross-legged to Kane's right. In the warm night she was stripped for ceremony, clad in nothing but a hand towel of a loincloth and a light sheen of sweat. Kane himself wore his camou pants with many cargo pockets and a khaki T-shirt.

The fleet mistress leaned her head toward Kane's. Her dense curls tickled his bare shoulder.

"They're telling the story of our people," she said, nodding at the ancient navigator and his counterpart across the fire. This was Reva, her own son, the fleet's youngest member, who stood so stiffly upright he seemed to be quivering with pride at his role in the ritual. Her voice was low and throaty. "The Children of the Great Wave. How we came to be, how we came to dwell where we do, how we came to dwell as we do."

The ritual for the day's dead was done. It had been brief: the Shark Tribe had a let-the-dead-bury-the-dead attitude, reflected by the fact that no sooner was one of their own confirmed to be lifeless and beyond resuscitation, than he or she was dumped immediately to feed the underwater carnivores who were their constant attendants—and allies.

"I thought you were all Polynesians."

A minute shake of the head. "We are now, in effect, but not always."

The butcher's bill had been stiff today: ten killed, eleven wounded, two of whom had died and one deemed unlikely to live out the night. Stiff for such a small and cohesive folk as the Wave Children, accustomed though they were to daily dangers from living on the breast of the cruel and uncertain Pacific Ocean; everybody knew everyone else well, and like or not was related.

But the casualties were light indeed for the kind of firepower the skimmers and their egg-shaped bigger brothers had been able to bring to bear. Three vessels had been lost, burned, all lit off by egg-craft lasers. But their crews had mostly survived. The islanders swam like fish, and there was definitely something to be said for having sharks on your side when you had to dive from a hopelessly flaming vessel….

Kiri looked back at the speaker. He was really getting into his storytelling now, making shapes and motions with his hands in the air. "We were once many peoples, he's saying," Kiri said. "All the peoples of the Pacific Rim—Polynesian, Japanese, Chinese, Malay, American, Australian. White, yellow, Indian, black. All that we had in common were that we were either at sea or swept out to sea by the great tsunamis that followed the big war. And that we survived."

Reva took over. He spoke in a high, clear voice. After a slight stutter or two, his narrative flowed smooth as ocean current.

Kane saw his translator smile. She really loves that

kid, he thought. Not that that was unusual—at least not in the Outlands, where there was nothing except the harsh dictates of survival to restrain human emotions and the free display thereof. It was just a curious contrast, the tenderness this fierce woman warrior displayed toward her son, and the almost furious intensity she brought to most other areas in life.

To Kane's right sat Brigid, her head tipped to one side, her face slightly pinched with concentration. He wondered if her curiosity, inborn and highly trained, was overcoming her natural reserve to the point she would eavesdrop on the translation Kiri was performing for Kane. He guessed not. Beyond her sat Grant, then Domi. Grant had his long chin sunk to his breastbone; veteran campaigner that he was, Kane guessed he was sleeping with his eyes open. Domi sat cross-legged, leaning forward, with firelight turning her eyes the wet red of fresh blood.

"—came together, gradually finding one another as the spirits directed," Kiri was saying. "Though times were hard, our mothers and fathers found ways. Those who lived closest to nature taught the rest how to live, how to win food from the sea, how to survive storms, how to obtain fresh water in the middle of the ocean."

The oldie took over again. "Particular honor is given to those of our forebears who called themselves tech-nomads. They combined wisdom of native lore with the highest technology of the ancients. They provided us both remarkable tools of survival and services and goods to trade, once such things became possible again, after the Long Night."

Brigid caught Kane's eye past Kiri. The erstwhile archivist was listening openly now. No doubt the English word "technomads" had made her perk up her ears. There was mention of their landborne variant in the Cerberus database; although secret files in baronial records claimed they were wiped out during the Program of Unification, both Brigid and Lakesh had expressed doubts that that was true. They were a formidable and resourceful people with a demonstrated knack for both survival and stealth.

It'd explain a whole hell of a lot about these people, Kane thought. Not least the existence of this ship, not to mention how a Wave Children tribe happened to have it stashed away in some island harbor—and its cargo.

The story continued, alternating tellers: how the people survived the seemingly endless years of winter, and the centuries of strife and discord that followed. The sea had been a harsh place at first: most of those who had somehow been washed alive from the land, some clinging to bits of flotsam, some makeshift rafts, others craft washed from marinas and harbors, had died within weeks even if, in the case of those driftwood-clingers and solo boaters, they managed to come together or be rescued by larger groups with more seaworthy craft. And of course no one could ever count the lonely deaths of those who had survived the nukecaust and the quakes and seismic sea waves, only to die of exposure or thirst—or the omnipresent sharks.

Sharks, rats, roaches and hybrids, Kane thought. They're the organisms that profited from the nukecaust.

In time a new people arose. Because Polynesians of various sorts formed the backbone of almost every surviving group—Tahitians, Samoans, Hawaiians—the culture derived most strongly from the peoples of Oceania. Because English was the lingua franca of the world before the nukecaust, it became their second "first language."

So it was explained, by the white-beard and proud Reva in turn. By the end Kiri openly translated for Brigid, as well as Kane, and a crewman was doing the same for Grant and Domi, although neither showed much interest.

"The rest is just a litany of our victories and defeats," Kiri said in time, smiling.

"Defeats as well?" Brigid asked seriously.

"Yes. We learn from them. Besides, it helps to remind us that, in the end, the Children of the Great Wave have always endured no matter what disasters and privations overtook us. And we always shall."

The circle of listeners crowded onto the decks of *Auguste Piccard* began to break up into knots of quiet conversation. They'd listened with rapt attention to the story of their origins and the initial struggles. The rest seemed of less vital import to them.

Past Kiri's head Brigid's eyes caught Kane's. Emerald highlights from the firelight danced deep within them. Though her expression was as carefully neutral as a seasoned archivist could make it, he read her thoughts clear enough.

Will they survive their involvement with us, though, she was wondering, and the terrible events we've embroiled them in?

Kane shrugged. Events seem to have caught up with them all on their own, he thought. And anyway, no one gets out of this world alive.

Still, looking from Kiri's strong-featured beauty to her son, now finished with his oratory and talking animatedly with various crew members who had clambered up onto the hatch cover by the fire, he couldn't help feeling just a pang that they and many more of their vibrant life-loving nomad folk might just be leaving the world a long ways ahead of schedule, as a result of having their lifelines cross those of Kane and his companions.

BODIES DANCED, orange where they faced the fire, now replenished, almost blank shadows where they faced the ocean of night that surrounded them. The Wave Children feasted, drank and celebrated: their victories, their survival and the lives of those who had gone down to join the sharks that day.

The Cerberus contingent already knew the islanders made their own wine and beer, some from palms or coconuts, some from God knew what. It was definitely an acquired taste, and one Kane, who'd never become an avid drinker, wasn't in an hurry to acquire, although he'd choke down what he had to to make nice with the allies like a good soldier. It turned out they also had distillation—a whole lot less surprising, since he'd learned of their technomad connection—and produced some kind of clear evil fluid that went down the throat like napalm and burst in the stomach like a city-buster nuke. The taste suggested paint thinner and corrosive sublimates.

After a few shots of it, it actually wasn't bad. By which, Kane thought, I guess I'm drunk.

Drunk and dancing and altogether too conscious of the splendid body of Kiri, naked or as near as made no nevermind. The music was a blend of drums and wailing synthesizer, played by an ensemble collected from across the fleet and gathered up at the aft of the superstructure. It rang discordant in Kane's ears, not altogether pleasant. But the pulsing rhythm had got inside his bones, and was driving his heartbeat.

"So we had more to offer you than you thought," Kiri said, leaning close to his ear. She was tall enough to do it. Her right breast brushed across his bare right biceps. Her nipple felt firm as a finger dragged across his skin. He lost track of his Cerberus companions; at the moment he just reckoned they could look the hell out for themselves.

"That's true," Kane said. "I just hope we're not bringing you more trouble in exchange for your help."

Hearts and minds, he thought. It occurred to them, late and fuzzily, that it might not be the brightest idea he'd ever had to try to talk the commander of their escort out of helping them.

Especially since, if Kiri's people pulled out now, the

mission he and his companions were undertaking for Cerberus was literally dead in the water.

But the warrior woman only laughed. "The trouble had already found us," she said. "The death worshipers, the fish devils. Now the Lemurians. You think we imagine it's all coincidental?"

She shook her head. Her hair momentarily veiled, then unveiled her face. "And the dreams. Many of my people report their nights are made hideous by whispered promises and threats. And some have heeded them…."

She reached to touch his cheek with her fingertips. "Great forces are on the move in this world of ours. Terrible forces. I believe they had already caught us before we got involved with you."

"I think you're right," Kane said. He was glad to be able to speak candidly. He also started feeling more sober than he really wanted to, all things considered.

"Tomorrow you should reach your goal," Kiri said.

"That's true." Or at least, late the next morning they were projected to reach the coordinates Lakesh had relayed to them from his mystery pen pals. "At least, that's the plan. But I get a feeling right here—" he touched himself over the solar plexus with three fingers of his left hand "—that the hardest part of our journey begins when we say goodbye to you people."

She flashed her teeth at him. They gleamed bright in the firelight, against her darkly tanned face. "But there's still journey to go before then," she said. "Our enemies may not leave us in peace to its end."

Kane grunted. "Now, that's some positive thinking."

She laughed. Stopping, she swept her hair back from her face with both hands. Her eyes were like dark suns as they caught and held Kane's.

"I call it realistic," she said. Although she did not speak loudly, Kane heard her clearly above the wail and skirling of the music, the stamping of feet, voices raised in conversation and laughter. It was as if she somehow projected her words directly to his ears. "Our life out here upon the open sea has a way of keeping our outlook that way. It's a good life, especially from what I've seen of the rest of the world. Though death is always near."

"It's always near for all of us," Kane said. "But I guess there're times in history when most people have the luxury to forget about that."

She stepped forward. Her breasts compressed themselves between her ribs and his. Her nipples prodded him like thumb tips. He could feel the heat from her body as from sun-heated metal.

"That's right," she said, slipping her hands behind his neck. She drew his head forward. He didn't much resist.

"Kane," she said. "A good name for a man. We have a god named that. He is a god of war—and masculinity."

"Is that a fact?" His voice rasped his throat.

"And because we both might die tomorrow," she whispered into his ear, "shouldn't we make the most of this moment right now?"

His brain wasn't alcohol-fogged enough to call that airtight reasoning. But he didn't feel like expending the mental effort to refute it. Fact was, he didn't feel like refuting it at all.

He took her waist in his hands. She wasn't particularly narrow waisted, although the breadth of her shoulders and the fullness of her hips gave that impression. It was like taking hold of a hardwood statue.

"You sure about that, lady?"

She pulled his head down toward her. Her strength surprised him. Their lips met. Her tongue probed deep in his mouth. It burned like a wet flame.

She broke the contact. Taking him firmly by the hand, she led him forward, toward the hatch to his cabin belowdecks.

Her hips rolled like the sea. He followed without resistance.

Chapter 13

They were down in the echoing womb of the bay at the root of the ship when the Klaxon sounded.

The bay lay at the odd squared-off stern of the ship. The deep thrum of the engines purred from the other side of the forward bulkhead, lacking any pulsations that would indicate that they were out of tune. They had been tended with compulsive, almost reverential care for centuries, first by the *Auguste Piccard*'s original crew, then by their descendents.

Now, as far as any of the Wave Children knew, the ship and its cargo were about to be used for their original purpose for the first time since the nukecaust.

Kane looked around. He and Grant, who was in the pilot's seat inside the single compartment of the curious little craft within *Piccard*'s hold, were both kitted out in their shadow suits. Domi and Brigid, eyes wide in alarm, wore wet suits, Domi's yellow and black, Brigid's green and black.

Kane cursed. In the manner of communicants following holy ritual, the *Piccard*'s technicians continued their work of preparation. They weren't fighters; their abstruse and particular knowledge had been passed down father to daughter and mother to son and zealously guarded by their warrior kin. To lose that lore would mean in effect the loss of the vessel and what it carried. Neither meant a thing without it.

"Stay here," he directed his companions. "I'll see what's going on. You keep getting this damn thing ready. I have a feeling in my gut we may need to de-ass this tub in one hell of a hurry."

The others acknowledged. He couldn't see Grant's face, but he knew without question that the big man was giving him a look. There wasn't any good reason for Kane to go above. The Wave Children were already on watch and as well armed as they were going to be; the Sin Eater strapped to Kane's forearm wasn't going to mean diddly-squat in a sea battle. And they already had all the RPG launchers divvied out and good to go.

"Because I'm the point man," Kane called in answer to the unasked question as he raced along the catwalk forward to the steel ladder. "I've got to know what the hell's going on!"

A SQUALL WAS BLOWING IN. The little fleet was bearing straight into the teeth of the wind. The escort vessels all had sails tightly furled and were either under power from their mills or under tow from sister craft with engines.

As Kane burst out of the starboard hatch onto the deck, a smell of wet, salt and burned propellant hit him in the face like a dead mackerel. Right ahead of him, beyond the rail, a sea skimmer splashed through a sharp wind-driven chop not twenty-five yards away, cutting grayish scud off the wave tops as it moved from the rear of the fleet to the front. Another twenty or thirty yards beyond that, Kiri herself stood on the port deck of her trimaran's central hull, waving a longblaster over her head in obvious signal to her own crew to hold their fire. Even at this distance Kane recognized either an M-14 or an M1A, in either case a hefty chunk of iron.

Oh, well, he knew she had no problem with upper-body strength. His ribs ached to prove it.

A loud snarl ripped from Kane's right. A *Piccard* crew member had opened up with a BAR from near the stern. Kane nodded with appreciation of the crew's professionalism; the crew was concerned about crossfiring their fellows. By firing at a downward and forward angle, the BAR gunner was minimizing the risk of splintering the *Great Sky Reef*'s laminated-wood hull with her .30-caliber slugs.

Despite the fact that Kiri's hard-core fighters had long since proved they knew their trade, Kane watched the action through the optical sights of the Sin Eater, which had magically appeared in his extended hand.

A line of spouts cut transversely across the skimmer's wake its own hull length behind. A faint red patch appeared in the middle of the indigo-clad back as Kane took up half the slack of the trigger, activating his laser sight.

A second line of water jets cut right to left directly across the swift craft's course. The *Piccard* crew member had led her target perfectly. The skimmer rider flailed his limbs in a spastic dance as 180-grain slugs sleeted through him like free neutrons. From the uncontrolled violence of his reaction Kane guessed the bullets had smashed some vertebrae and severed the spinal cord.

He lowered his handblaster and looked around to take in the full tactical situation. He felt a little sheepish. It'd been stupid to get locked in the glass onto a single target as insignificant as a single rider.

Overall the situation was…confused. Like any battle. The sky had gone pigeon-gray overhead. In this light the smoke from the fleet's gunpowder weapons hung in a greenish-brownish haze layer at about the level of Kane's boots.

Kane heard the door slam crack of ionized air as big lasers stabbed from egg craft, and the sharper, nastier crack of RPG rounds going off. A dogfight swirled around the sprawled-out fleet. Several columns of black smoke that abruptly trailed away down the wind about thirty yards overhead marked the pyres of islander ships. Whatever motive force the Lemurians craft used, it didn't involve burning fuel; anyway, their craft didn't burn when destroyed, if you didn't count minor fires inside the egg crafts' cabins sparked off by shaped charges.

Forward and to the right of *Piccard*'s course Kane saw a commotion in the water. Shapes were leaping from the water, gray in the dwindling light. Another form, larger, just broke the surface, white belly turned toward Kane. It was a shark, huge, if not half big enough to be Old Grandfather. The other shapes were dolphins, ramming it with their beaks. Apparently the Lemurians had brought their sea-mammal pals to the party.

Fleetingly, Kane wondered where Reva was. Presumably inside whatever cover the main cabin of *Great Sky Reef* offered. Even for a kid whose greatest joy in life was to swim with sharks, this wasn't the day for it.

The dolphins liked to play with their prey. At least the ones Lemuriaville used. The Wave Children had regaled their mainland guests with tales of how they would ram high-speed into a seal, or a lesser dolphin—or a hapless islander—and toss them high out of the water. They'd been known to toss a victim like that twenty minutes or more....

Kane had always thought well of dolphins, on the rare occasions he thought of them at all. But that image made his flesh creep. Better to be decently bitten in two by a great white, he reckoned.

Cyan flashed. A crash from overhead made Kane duck. His ears rang from the noise. Something stung the back of his neck and the back of his left hand. He looked up to see the last of the shower of yellow sparks bursting from a hole a big laser had made in the flying bridge.

On the weather deck people pointed and shouted excitedly. He looked away where they indicated, off the starboard beam. He could make out an egg shape perhaps a three hundred yards beyond Kiri's vessel. He thought that was what they were fussing about, understandably enough.

Then he noticed a couple of lines of dirty white, extending along the uneasy ocean surface to converge on a low, dark, humped shape perhaps another two to three hundreds yards farther out. The nearer ends of the lines seemed to be drawing themselves right toward *Piccard*.

Kane frowned at them curiously. His mind couldn't quite make sense of them.

Until a crewman grabbed his arm and shouted, "Wakes in the water!"

Kane looked at him. "Huh?"

"Torpedoes!" the man shouted. "Grab on to something, fast."

Kane had stepped up toward the water. The two wakes streaked under *Great Sky Reef* at a slight forward angle. Kane started to run toward the hatchway, shouting a radio warning to his friends below.

One torpedo passed just ahead of *Piccard*'s bow. Set to strike the deep-drawing freighter's hull, it would pass through the rest of the skirmish harmlessly. In fact it was unlikely the underwater missiles could be set to run shallow enough to strike the high-riding catamarans and outriggers, even Kiri's larger flagship.

The other fish slammed into the ship about five yards back from the bow—no more than ten yards ahead of where Kane was. The impact rocked the ship and slammed Kane hard against the steel side of the superstructure. Then a mountain of spray slopped over the side, knocked Kane to the deck, carried him outward. It would've washed him overboard but for the gunwales.

His ears were really ringing now. Over it he could hear shouts and screams. He realized one voice was inside his skull.

"Torpedo, Baptiste!" he shouted over his Commtact. "We're hit."

"I could tell," came the cool, dry response over his implant.

"Tell the crew to start lowering the ramp," Kane said. "Grant, get ready to roll. This pig may be about to sink beneath us!"

WITHIN THE GANGWAYS the *Piccard* was a hell of smoke and noise and confusion. Hurtling bodies bounced blindly off Kane as he tried to make his way aft to the launch bay. The islander crew, normally so cool and efficient in action, seemed seized by panic.

Kane understood. It was hard for him to keep it together himself. Moving toward the stern was a climb uphill; the ship was already well down by the bows. Loud bangs echoed through the hull. They weren't secondary explosions; most of the RPG launcher reloads they'd taken aboard were up on deck where they were busily being directed at the attacking Lemurians, and anyway no munitions had been stowed forward where the torpedo had hit.

The damn ship's breaking up around me, Kane knew. He felt a sense of powerlessness that threatened to powder his bones. The sinking *Piccard* might be about to take him and his friends to the bottom of the Pacific, and there wasn't a thing he could do about it.

Except get them all out before the ship went down. Nut up, he told himself harshly. It's not like you to go flying out the window like this. It was no excuse that he hadn't had much sleep last night, what with the extra-curricular activity—and the dreams.

He most especially didn't want to think of the dreams right now. Shockingly vivid sensations of being crushed to death in the black ocean depths were not very help-ful to have in his mind.

He burst through the final hatch. As he was clatter-ing down the metal steps, another explosion shook *Piccard* like a terrier with a rat.

He was flung forward onto the metal ways that ran beside the berth where the little craft was secured. The hull rang like a bell, then began to boom and rumble as it began breaking up in earnest. The world was a roar of inrushing water.

Water lapped over at him, wetting his hand as he sprawled facedown and causing cool sensations through the sleeve of his shadow suit. At first he thought this compartment had been breached, as well. Then he re-alized it had been deliberately partially flooded by the techs, to provide flotation for the craft.

The upper hatch yawned open. Brigid stood out of it, shouting and beckoning to him. He picked himself up. Four or five techs were present, a couple up on top of the little strangely shaped craft itself making final ad-justments and decoupling cables. Others were doing things on the dock. They looked at him with faces gray beneath their natural dark complexions and deep water tans. He realized that, by sticking to their posts to help him and his companions get free to continue their mission, they might have doomed themselves.

"We're opening the ramp," shouted Miracuse, the chief tech for the small craft, who had a sheaf of iron-gray hair sticking out behind his head and wore a white lab coat over a pair of Bermuda shorts.

As he spoke, the words were almost drowned out by a colossal squealing. Piston-driven rams began to force open the ship's flat stern, which was hinged at the bottom. Water jetted in as from giant fire hoses, knocking technicians sprawling against one another and flying like bottles off a shelf.

If the ship were operating normally, only the bottom of the bay would be submerged, so that the little craft *Piccard* had been extensively modified to carry could have positive buoyancy to launch. The larger vessel was balanced in such a way that it wouldn't sink or even settle at the stern despite the inrush of seawater, Kane knew from the crew's lectures. He had no idea how, nor interest in finding out. As always, if he needed to know, he'd just ask Baptiste.

But nothing was normal now. The whole vessel had settled well in the water. With a nasty flash of fear Kane realized they could already be plummeting toward the bottom, to be crushed by the awful weight of seawater. He stamped hard on the flare of emotion, grinding it like an ember beneath a heel.

And no—he saw gray daylight at the top of the opening. Motors whined protest as they drove open the ramp against the pressure of vastly more water than they were designed to move. But gradually the opening widened.

The chamber flooded for real. Kane was caught up by a surge of chill gray water, scummed with foam like the ghosts of bubbles. He was banged against the hull of the submersible, then against the inner hull of doomed *Piccard* herself.

"Grant," he had the presence of mind to shout as he grabbed hold of some kind of armored cable to keep himself from being washed to the front of the bay by the inrushing torrent. "Get her ready to go!"

"I'm on it!" Grant shouted back through his communicator. "As long as they get the damn door open. Now you get your ass on board!"

"Affirmative!"

Water surged as the little oblong craft's twin propellers began to agitate water through their armored ducts. It obligingly moved forward at less than a crawl. Whatever connections had held it fixed snugly in *Piccard*'s steel womb had been cast loose.

Kane saw technicians bobbing in the water around him. Their task done, they were looking to swim out of the sinking expedition ship as soon as the rushing seawater calmed enough to let them do it. They and the Cerberus operatives had a wisp-thin advantage: the ship had leveled somewhat when the sea began to pour in aft, but now the bow was angling downward again, so that the water was far higher at the front of the bay than the rear, and their natural buoyancy would help them to float out of the hull.

The bad news was, the ship was obviously about to start her long dive to the bottom, almost fifteen hundred fathoms below. Once started it would be a smooth and rapid plunge—from which there could be no escape.

Kane splashed toward the small craft as it chugged toward the opening, which now diminished again as the ship continued to settle. He hoped fleetingly that the ramp was open far enough to let them out, but what would happen, now, would happen. Domi and Brigid both stood on the submersible's curved upper surface, reaching for him as he swam frantically toward them.

And something like a finned torpedo shot in through the open stern, just submerged, to strike him in the ribs like a piledriver.

Chapter 14

Blackness exploded behind Kane's eyes. For a moment he was back in the dream, being drawn into an abyss of infinite night by tentacles that were somehow blacker than that ultimate darkness.

Then his head broke the surface of the water he was unaware of having been driven under, and he sucked a great convulsive gasp of air into his lungs. The whole left side of his chest pounded with white flashes of pain to the beating of his heart, and inhaling was like pressing his body to a white-hot iron plate. But the cold, salty, smoke-tainted air tasted sweeter than anything he had ever known in his life.

Something bashed him in the center of the chest. This wasn't a sharp, savage blow like the first. It was more like being hit in the chest with a medicine ball. Granted, one fired out of a muzzle-loading cannon....

Despite the resistance of the water, he was knocked back into the hull of the submersible with enough force to kick the breath he had just drawn out of his lungs again. His head cracked painfully against the metal-clad ceramic hull of the craft, evoking a spray of scarlet sparks through his brain.

He shook his head to clear it of residual flames, and to clear his mouth and nose of the water that had struck him in the face. He was aware of a great gray shape stirring in the water before him. His reflex thought was of alarm: *shark!*

Then, treading the rapidly rising water, he thought, Wait a minute. Sharks are the good guys here.

He became aware of Domi screaming, "Dolphin!" In the villes they were taught almost to revere dolphins as examples of sublime natural intelligence, blessedly free of acquisitiveness and other human vices. Outlander born and bred as she was, Domi was free of any such prejudices. To her the dolphin was just another wild animal attacking, hence an enemy.

Meanwhile Brigid shouted for Kane to take her hand. He turned and flopped upward with his arm. She stretched her hand to grab it.

The bottle-nosed shape wedged itself between him and the submersible, knocking him back into the water. He thrashed on his back, submerging briefly, then surfacing again with another shake of his head. Brigid overbalanced; only Domi throwing her surprisingly strong arms around the larger woman's waist prevented her from pitching in headfirst with the floundering Kane.

The bay was half full with water and more. The daylight at the top of the opening dwindled rapidly to a sliver. That's my lifeline, Kane thought. If it vanished, the submersible and his friends could still escape—provided they had sealed themselves inside, leaving him literally to sink or swim with the *Piccard.*

"Fuck this!" he exclaimed. He punched his right hand out of the water, forming it into a half fist. The Sin Eater slammed into it.

A smooth silver hoop appeared in the water between him and the submersible; the creature was rolling through the water without breaking the surface tension. Bending his wrist, Kane triggered a burst into the slick gray hide.

The dolphin emitted a piercing scream through its blowhole, spraying the women atop the submersible with water. It dived. The surface was too roiled for Kane to see to any depth beneath it. He didn't much care; all that mattered to him was getting the hell out of the water and into the submersible before he was entombed in the bay with his little aquatic playmate.

He splashed back toward the craft. Again the dolphin struck him, this time from below. The great dome of its skull hit him in the belly—missing both groin and solar plexus. The beast had outsmarted itself this time. It flung Kane upward out of the water to land on the upward curve of the submersible's white-painted hull with a thud.

He didn't feel as if he'd fallen there from more than two or three stories. He was almost overwhelmed by a temptation to just lie there and rest a spell with his cheek pressed against the almost sensually smooth solid surface.

By sheer force of will—or cussedness—he roused himself and began to claw his way up the curve to the flat top of the hull.

Something seized his right foot. The sudden stop caused him to plant his left cheek against the submersible's metal hide. He looked down to see his foot enfolded by the dolphin's triumphant grin.

With a savage curse he thrust the Sin Eater down the right side of his body and triggered a triburst. An impact slammed the outside of his ankle. He'd clipped himself with one bullet; his flexible armor kept it from penetrating, as it kept the muzzle flash from burning his thigh. It might not have prevented the high-velocity slug from chipping the bone; he didn't have time to care.

The big dolphin head vanished into the seething water. Kane had the impression the thing had released his leg a moment before he fired. His bullets kicked up an impressive spray of water. But he knew from experience that handblaster bullets wouldn't penetrate much water and that confounded monster could maneuver underwater with demon speed.

A hand grabbed the hair on top of his head and yanked. The roots seemed to take fire; in his current state he was almost afraid his head would split like a rotten gourd. But it was enough of an assist to allow him to half spring half crawl to a sprawling, winded heap on top of the submersible's sail.

Given the brusque efficiency of the assist, he wasn't surprised when his eyes opened to see Domi leaning over him.

Muted thunder rumbled up through the submersible's hull. A huge gout of water erupted up toward the ceiling, whose light fixtures would have endangered Kane's head had he been able to stand upright. A scream rose out of the water with the spray, shrill, ear-burstingly loud before it vanished into the supersonic.

Domi stooped to grab Kane under the armpits. He forced himself up to all fours. As he did so, he saw Brigid, hand outstretched, tears streaming down her cheeks.

"Grens" was Domi's comment.

Without further delay Kane slithered forward and down the open top hatch. He tumbled into the cramped interior. A heartbeat later, the two women landed on top of him, driving the breath out of him yet again.

Under other circumstances, he might've enjoyed it.

COMMANDER ZENO NODDED with satisfaction as he watched the stricken ship sink below the waves. He wasn't looking through anything as crude as a periscope; rather, he sat in the small bridge of his submarine cruiser watching on a monitor the images gathered by a fiber-optic input at the end of an invisibly thin tendril extruded above the surface. He had chosen to submerge *Nautilus* almost immediately after launching his torpedoes; he didn't believe the shaped-charge warheads of the barbarian rocket launchers would penetrate the pressure hull of his larger craft as it did his hunter-killers, but he didn't choose to put it to the test. Even a slight compromise, the slightest alteration of the crystalline structure of the polymerized-ceramic spinning of its hull, could spell doom for the vessel and its occupants as it dived deep.

Zeno was far from a coward. He had proved his courage in countless actions not just with the island barbarians but with the forces of the barons of the surface villes. As well, he had taken part in the suppression of riots in the Bilge, and fought mutinies among the technicians and technocrats of the great dome, including a mad conspiracy to supplant Baron Lemuria himself. His face and limbs bore scars to attest his mettle.

Nor was he what would have once been called cautious—a career-ending insult among surface navies of the days of fighting sail, as he knew from studies of the history of naval warfare, which had fascinated him since his earliest days as a cadet of the Deep Wardens. But no man survived so many battles without also being judicious. He would sacrifice himself without hesitation to serve Lemuriaville and his baron. But he wouldn't risk his highly trained crew, his compact but powerful ship nor himself—perhaps the most valuable asset of them all—without cause.

"Dispatch two hunter-killers," he ordered the aide who stood behind his chair of command. He referred to the smaller egg-shaped submersibles, of which *Nautilus* carried eight clamped to her hull like remoras. "We want to insure no rats escaped the sinking ship."

He regretted not being able to take captives. Lemurian intelligence reported that mysterious mainlanders were working with the barbarians, possibly even the semifabulous baron blasters of whom rumors persisting over the past several years claimed had been causing the North American baronies such woes. But Zeno would've liked simply to talk to the crew and technicians who maintained the ship, a wonderful relic of a long-dead time.

But his own superiors had ordained a degree of caution he found inordinate. He suspected they feared incurring some kind of strike from the transformed overlords if they tarried overlong near the surface. The first garbled rumors of the strange transformation had induced a state of panic in the higher ranks of the domed submarine ville, and while it had subsided to a sort of background like static, it persisted and spiked from time to time. More frequently, he reflected, of late...

And here came a blinking cursor yellow at the upper right corner of his monitor. He barely had time to invoke the privacy screen, a software-driven unit that would project sound waves to interfere with and cancel any sounds emanating from the commander's vicinity.

He couldn't prevent the visage of Marshal Bennett appearing on his screen. "Belay that order, Zeno!" the bald man snapped. His mouth was like a trap, and sweat gleamed on the curve of his skull that sprouted like a pallid, fleshy-stalked mushroom from the indigo collar of his tunic.

"Marshal," he said, and it took all his years of steeling his self-discipline to keep his tone level, "I deem it wise to insure that we have made a clean sweep."

"Have you let wax build up in your ears, Zeno? I have given you an order. I need not explain myself, but in view of your lengthy service and the efficiency with which you have carried out your orders today, I shall say this—you can see as well as I that the ship has sunk."

Zeno allowed himself to nod. Inwardly he seethed that this desk admiral should monitor his actions constantly, peering over his shoulder in real time.

A grayish-yellow sea slug of a tongue stole forth to moisten the image's near-invisible lips. Is he fearful? Zeno thought in wonder.

"We're at war, Zeno," the marshal said. "We must conserve all our resources. More lies at stake here than you can possibly imagine! Now comply."

Zeno had already passed the order for the hunter-killers to stand down. "It is done, Marshal."

"Bennett out!" The viewscreen returned to a vision of the surface, now dark and lashed with rain. Under the savages' unexpectedly heavy and effective firepower the scout skimmers had already retreated and submerged to be recovered by a pair of submarine tender-carriers that accompanied *Nautilus*. The hunter-killers had pulled back beyond the antitank grenade launchers' effective range, though not the handful of heavy machine guns scattered among the surface-dweller fleet. These had sufficed to disable one egg craft already; what protected the Lemurian craft now was near invisibility in the rising waves.

They were likewise beyond effective in-air range of their own powerful lasers. The beams lost focus quickly, especially in the dense, humid, spray-laden air.

He permitted himself the slightest of frowns. Was there more at stake than he could imagine?

He had a capacious imagination—as vital an asset in a field commander as it was detriment to a grunt warden. Yet he could imagine no stake higher than the safety of their fragile bubble of life, under constant assault from unimaginable pressures, as well as vulnerable to a myriad of threats from within and without. Only the terrible exigency, the risks sheer daily existence posed to Lemuria, justified within Zeno's mind many, many of the actions he had been compelled to order, or undertake with his own hand, as a Warden of the Deep.

Surely Bennett knew all this. Or did he just talk to reassure himself? Zeno had long understood that his superior had gained and held his position far more upon the basis of his skill at intrigues among the dome's power structures than any real gift of command.

As if to confirm this, Bennett's face reappeared. "You are in a dangerous territory, Zeno. Best not to linger there too long."

Zeno clamped his mouth to keep his bearded lips from sneering. Was it possible that the Marshal of the Deep had listened to the common submariners' superstitions about the demons who dwelt near the pipelike fields of deep-sea vents? It scarcely seemed possible—

if only because Bennett was no man to pay much attention to the muttering of proles.

Zeno felt a strange flutter in his stomach. Something rotted within the dome; he seemed to smell the decay even here in his own bridge.

So he fell back upon the formula dinned into him since boyhood: "I hear. I obey."

He touched himself over the heart with three fingers of his right hand. Bennett's bald head nodded jerkily. "Excellent, Commander. Bennett out!"

The image of the tuberlike head again collapsed upon itself, vanished. The surface was now lashed by the fury of a full-dress Pacific storm. The barbarians' canoes were dispersing, running before the wind in their cowardly fashion. Sadly, he knew from long observation they were unlikely to suffer more than minor damage to rigging, no matter how fiercely the storm winds blew. One thing the savages knew was life upon the uncertain bosom of the sea.

It doesn't matter, he told himself. When the time comes, we will sweep that litter from the surface of the sea. And that time is coming soon.

And in the meantime...

"Ensign," he said without looking at the man who hovered behind his left shoulder, "order out two of the hunter-killers to make a sweep below the surface where the enemy ship went down. Then shape course for our squadron back to base."

That eased Zeno's feelings. He had heard and he did

obey. But he would also obey his own conception of his duty to dome and baron—and his own sense of thoroughness.

Chapter 15

A metallic scrape raised the hair on the backs of the Cerberus operatives' necks as if it had sent current through their bodies. As it escaped *Piccard*'s womb the submersible had kissed the doomed ship's hull. Then they were falling free, amid rumblings and groans and startling cracks as the larger vessel surrendered to the implacable force of the ocean.

For what seemed an eternity the Deep Sea Vehicle *Orpheus* plunged toward the bottom of the Pacific fifteen hundred fathoms below. With his stomach trying to crowd its way past his clamped jaws Kane got himself sorted out from Brigid and Domi. It was a demanding job; the cabin was cramped and full of protrusions and the little craft rocked like a thrill ride. All three collected scrapes and bruises.

In the dim red illumination Kane could make out an empty seat forward, beside Grant. He struggled into it.

As he did, the craft settled finally onto an even keel. "Got the bitch under control," Grant said in a matter-of-fact tone. The way sweat streamed down his carven-mahogany features belied his apparent calm.

Unlike the Lemurian egg craft the DSV had but a single narrow circular viewport forward. Grant was hunched toward it, peering into a tunnel of blue-white light driven through darkness by the submersible's spotlight. Rather than try to crane to peer through the port himself, possibly distracting the man who only held all their lives in his large, strong hands, Kane settled into the role of instrument officer, trying to read the bewildering array of readouts and general blinky lights that seemed to occupy every square inch of the vessel's interior except the deck underfoot.

It was a role he was intimately familiar with from Deathbird days, when Grant piloted and he sat down in the dropped snout of the attack chopper watching the instruments and looking for things to shoot. And also shooting them, of course. Here and now he couldn't make sense of much of the information being conveyed. He could track what was necessary to keep them alive and headed in the right direction—he fervently hoped.

Vibration enveloped them. It grew to a rumble that shook the little craft.

"What the fuck's that?" Domi asked. "A tornado?"

"Sounds like a big arty shell passing overhead," Grant said, staring intently forward with his hands clamped on the yoke so hard his knuckles were pale yellow. "Mebbe a whole damn barrage."

Kane's gaze flicked around. There was just the one window to look out of. But the little beast had video cameras mounted all over its hull so that they could be remotely swiveled to view the entire sphere of space surrounding the craft. It also had multiple monitors so he could instantly look in several directions at once.

Including straight back. He checked their six and let out a yelp. "Holy shit! It's *Piccard!*"

"Doing what?" Brigid asked. "Chasing us?"

"Yes!"

Lights within its launch bay still burning yellow, lighting the opening up like a maw, the sinking hulk closed in upon the tiny submersible. The bizarre sight reminded Kane of pictures he had seen of deep-sea angler fish, the kind that drew its prey in with luminescent lures. Two screws set at the bottom corners of the extensively modified hull still churned gamely but with definitive futility as if trying to drive upward the ship's mass plus an extra couple hundred tons of water that had forced most of the buoyancy-providing air out of the steel bubble, her hull.

WITH ITS TUB-SHAPED TITANIUM hull and fiberglass skin, the *Orpheus* looked to the eyes of Kane and Grant more like an appliance than a craft: possibly an old-fashioned clothes dryer. The kind with the round window in the front to watch your load go round and round.

The DSV had been built in the mid-1990s with funding and significant design input from a megalomaniacal movie director and producer with an obsession for making movies about great disasters. He had a particular fetish for shipwrecks. When his last few movies—

and accordingly his career—emulated his favorite subject matter, the vessel was taken over by his frequent collaborators, the Mauna Loa Oceanographic Institute in Hawaii.

Shortly thereafter the Archon Directorate, with more than a little help from Murphy, produced the greatest disaster extravaganza in known human history.

By chance *Auguste Piccard* and her original crew had been anchored off Pohnpei—known generally in North America as Ponape—conducting surveys of curious underwater structures in the waters off the island when the balloon went up. Knowing what to expect from the first panicked satellite news reports of the Third World War, the crew had hastily packed aboard as many of the islanders and their livestock as the converted freighter—fortunately a bit oversized for its nominal mission and crew—and lashed on all the vessels for tow that they could find room to bend cables for. Then they ran for the middle of the deep blue sea as fast as the twin screws of her chopped-off stern could drive them.

Being sea scientists the crew knew full well that in any sort of catastrophic seismic sea event the safest place to be, other than around, say, the Rocky Mountains, was open water.

The crew of *Piccard* realized the greatest danger was not the wave itself, but like any fall from a great height, the landing. If the waves carried her inland she might scrape her hull to shreds on outcrops or even buildings. More likely she would be carried inland to be dumped when the wave subsided, stranded at best, or swamped and smashed to flinders if she were too near the leading edge of the impulse when a landmass striking its base made it break like mile-high surf.

According to the oral traditions, *Piccard*'s crew had estimated that they were driven back straight over Ponape itself, and when at last the fury of the rolling overpressure was spent, they rode the watery elevator back down to an imperceptibly gentle return to the restored surface of the sea. So they survived.

For the moment.

There were unimaginable storms and upheavals; and of course, the advent of the long cold and dark. But the sea remained an abundant source of nourishment for those who knew how to exploit it, and they were sheltered from many of the worst killers that winnowed the hapless wretches on land, such as a brutal Hobbesian battle for dwindling resources of food and the increasingly vital fuel; and the most enthusiastic Horseman of any Apocalypse, Pestilence.

As for fuel, the diesel in *Piccard*'s great storage tanks had inevitably been used up; her engines and generators had fallen silent for over a generation, during which time the ship simply floated where the currents took her. By that point it had already become a sort of free-floating island itself, home base to a fleet of small, or smaller, watercraft. When scavenging and trade had restored a trickle of fuel to the ship, *Piccard* made her way to an island, one of thousands of new

ones that formed in the final cataclysm of the twenti-
eth century.

Most neonate islands were seamount tops that had
thrust heads above water in the remarkable seismic orgy
following the war, which continued in diminished extent to the present day. Others resulted from actual buck-
ling of the crust—the same sort of event that had
rendered the highly comprehensive nukecaust survey
maps of the Pacific floor useless fictions, histories that
might as well have come from an alternate dimension
for all the good they did in the here and now.

In time some of the Wave Children, including *Piccard*'s Grouper Tribe, moved their main bases back to
land. The ship herself was retired. The islanders had little need for the cargo capacity they could have acquired
by converting her back to a freighter; the realities of the
postnukecaust world ideally suited the highly decentral-
ized small-craft trade they preferred.

But instead of rusting at anchor, an abandoned hulk,
she became a sort of temple, maintained by descendants
of the original crew. They fabricated certain metal trade
items in the ship's small but elaborately equipped internal machine shops. Most of all they served as a school
of advanced knowledge for the best and brightest of
their children. Kiri herself had trained there, as had her
deadly rival, the handsome if occupationally misplaced
war chief Tupolu.

So by chance—or as Lakesh was wont to hint sometimes, by some nonchance movement of the chronon

flow, which Kane's and Brigid's skeptical minds discounted but their jump dreams tended vividly to confirm—the Wave Children found in their great need precisely that which their most likely allies most had need of.

And here were the Cerberus quartet, plunging toward the bottom of the Pacific. And here came *Piccard* herself, doomed by their actions, pursuing them with mouth agape like a giant predator fish—or like some nemesis intent upon avenging itself by entombing them within its belly forever, their ghosts to replace her vanished crew....

KANE WATCHED THE MONSTER with its eerily glowing maw grow larger. He hoped he could estimate its relative distance from the screen image. He needed to be stone certain of the course it was following to the bottom.

"Got it!" he exclaimed. "Grant—break left! Do it now!"

Kane braced himself for what he was sure would be a painfully slow roll into a bank to port. He hoped it wasn't too late. But he was damned if he'd steer Grant into a collision with the diving behemoth.

Instead, slowly and sluggishly, he felt the craft move to the left without rolling. *Orpheus* had movable ducted-fan thrusters; instead of needing to bank to turn, it could dodge sideways like a Harrier jet. Grant, consummate pilot that he was, knew that was their best bet.

Like a dying whale, or an ancient steam locomotive,

Piccard hurtled past in a mountain of sound: rushing, roaring, groans and bangs and the imagined screams of trapped and dying crew. Kane hoped they were imagined, as he sat watching the monitors from the starboard vid inputs as the beast rushed by. Not that there was much to see: a sliding gray-black cliff, then a plenum of bubbles as if they had been teleported to an alternate-reality casement in which quantum foam was visible on the macro scale.

Kane had heard stories of the suction of a big sinking ship sucking objects nearby, swimmers or even lesser craft, down with it. Instead the wave of *Piccard*'s passage buffeted them aside like a gentle tail-push from the mother of all whales. The little sub wallowed like a pig in a trough. Grant, getting the feel for the controls for real after hours in the computer simulator aboard the stricken *Piccard,* gentled her back level.

Then the mother ship was visible in Grant's forward port, its round bow and superstructure growing smaller and fainter in the spotlight glare. Kane grabbed reflexively for handholds again, his gut convinced that they were rocketing upward away from it.

Then the sea swallowed it. But for a trail of bubbles it was gone as if it had never been.

Kane let a breath explode from him. The killing muscular tension went with it, all in one long whoosh, leaving him so utterly spent that it was a wonder to him his cell walls hadn't just slumped and let go, too. He could not have stirred a micron had they all been abruptly jumped back to Manitius in the Moon, into the midst of a pack of ravening carnobots.

Then he felt an insistent tapping on the mass of undifferentiated protoplasm that had been his well-muscled right shoulder. "That was fun!" Domi said brightly. "Do it again."

Kane groaned. He prayed that some cosmic god would prove its existence, and indeed benevolence, by striking her dead. Or at least dumb.

"Only this time," she said, eyes glittering like blood rubies, "I drive."

"When Hell freezes," Grant rumbled, shaking his big powerful body as if emerging from a sauna.

"Happened," Domi said. "Called it skydark."

"Okay. Then when they pave Hell for a skating rink. As in, no, never under no circumstances."

She sat back and folded her arms in a showy sulk. "You never let me have any fun."

"For Christ's sake. Put a *sock* in it, girl."

Over the few days of their sail to this mysterious spot in the open ocean Grant and Kane had familiarized themselves thoroughly with all phases of the DSV's operation. They had also gotten the two women checked out on the systems, although neither was as sure-handed as the former Deathbird jockeys. And nobody sane was eager to allow Domi scope, much as she loved to drive any form of conveyance.

Brigid had gotten oriented and was reading instruments as she had also trained to do. Oddly, she was most in her element of all of them. After all, though not a technician, she had trained her whole life to work with computers. And information was her life: accessing, absorbing, evaluating. She was more accustomed to facts expressed in words than numbers. But the task of monitoring information about their location and course—functionally undersea navigation—required neither a mathematician nor an accountant.

Preskydark militaries, at least the U.S. Navy, had possessed means of communicating with their submarines no matter how deeply submerged, real time, all the time—a fact they'd lied about as blandly and blatantly as they did the resolution of the surveillance images their satellites captured. As Brigid knew from her research into the late-twentieth-century United States, the Department of Defense had routinely released photographs and communiqués that rendered their official estimates of their technical capabilities ridiculous. Then they labeled those who pointed out such inconsistencies as "conspiracy theorists"—when they deigned to respond at all.

Orpheus possessed no such communications, however. In the past she had kept in touch with the mother ship by means of a physical cable played out from a spool in her stern among the ducted-fan thrusters. That had never been connected this time—which was fortunate, since it would only have served to drag them down with Piccard to her final rest in the soft, silty gray bottom muck. It meant, though, that they had no access to position hacks from satellites controlled by Lakesh in Cerberus. However, they had a good inertial guidance system, which should be robust enough not to have been discombobulated by the gymnastics the little ship underwent escaping her mother.

As soon as she had sorted herself into her seat, knees bumping Domi's in the constricted space, Brigid was absorbed into the data flow. She looked up briefly when it appeared *Piccard* might engulf them and bear them down with it, to lie inescapably entombed until they suffocated. When the sinking ship and its danger had passed, she went back to her readouts.

She was nodding in satisfaction, having confirmed that they were on the proper bearing and angle of descent to make the next waypoint Lakesh's mysterious communicants had given them to report it as fact. Then she frowned.

Although Kane was in charge of monitoring their immediate environment, he was literally out of his depth here. This wasn't a Deathbird or Manta, and a few days' lectures and simulator work could not complete a transition to perfect comfort in this alien environment. It was the corner of one of her emerald-green eyes that caught a flicker on a screen to Kane's left elbow.

"Isn't that our long-wave radar," she said aloud, "showing a couple of returns from behind us?"

As the words left her mouth, a ringing scream pealed through the hull.

Chapter 16

Rain lashed the fleet. But the enemy no longer did.

Waverunner lay alongside *Great Sky Reef,* obedient to the fleet mistress's command.

"Don't make me leave, Mommy."

Kiri Far-Seer caught her son to her and hoisted him off the deck. "You have been brave and more than brave," she said, and kissed his golden cheek. "But the time has come for you to leave."

"But I want to stay with the fleet!"

She tousled his hair. "Someday soon you'll be grown. Then you can stay." He's been here too long already, she thought with a grimness she didn't permit her face to show. He's seen too much danger. What would I do, were anything to happen to my son, my treasure?

"You go in *Waverunner* with Meherio," she said. "Help her guard and tend the wounded. Our battle here is ended." For the moment. "I am not sending you out of danger, but on a very important assignment."

He pressed his lips shut for a moment. But then he nodded. For he was the fleet mistress's son, and would one day, spirits willing, take over as fleet master himself.

"I'll help her, Mommy."

She kissed him one last time, then leaned over to hand him down to *Waverunner*'s boatswain.

DOMI JUMPED like a startled cat. "What's that?"

"Sonar," Grant said grimly. "We've been pinged. Big time."

The sound stopped, then it pulsed again, twice more.

"Who could be doing it?" the albino girl asked.

"You a bit slow today?" Kane asked. He was working his board now, refining the computer-enhanced image of their radar returns, checking outputs from other sensors. "The bad guys. Who the hell else?"

He was feeling pissy because the tactical situation was his responsibility, and Baptiste, of all people, had caught the vital data before he did. He was still the point man. It was his responsibility!

"Must be a pair of those damn egg ships on our ass," Grant said.

Brigid raised her head in alarm. "They have lasers. What do we do if they shoot at us?"

"Die a lot," Grant said.

"Do lasers work underwater?" Domi asked.

"Blue-green ones do, according to reports I read," Brigid said. Relating historical fact comforted her, as it always did. Life had been a constant low-level threat in the Enclaves, the only variance being the odd spike of mortal peril. One terrific advantage of being a fugitive exile was that she and her friends were well-armed and

more than willing to fight back, whereas in the Cobaltville Enclaves resistance of any sort had seemed impossibly useless.

"If they don't, they'll have something that does,"
Kane said. "The question is, why haven't they zapped
us already? This tubby bitch has the dogfighting characteristics of an oil rig."

"How about our weps?" Domi asked earnestly.

Everybody turned to look at her. Except Grant, and
his big shoulders, already tense with concentration,
flexed with the effort it took him not to turn away from
his porthole and screens.

"Those would be our side arms," Kane said, speaking as he would to a simple child, "plus knives and a few
grens in our packs." Fortunately these had already been
placed inboard when the balloon went up and *Piccard*
down. "None of which do dick for us in our current
happy situation."

"What about our big blasters on this ship? Rockets,
lasers, machine guns?"

"It's a boat, Domi," Brigid corrected mechanically.

"Domi, it's an exploration vehicle," Kane said. "It
doesn't *have* weps. Some rich movie nutcake made it
so he could poke around the staterooms of sunken ocean
liners." Which struck Kane, suddenly, as an exceptional
creepy form of voyeurism, somehow.

"What can we do?" Brigid asked.

Grant shrugged. "I'm open to suggestion. I'm no
naval architect, but I'm smart enough to know those

eggs are built to move fast and fight hard below the water, as well as on top of it, just by looking at them. This thing's designed to go down deep and come back up. Not much else at all."

"Could we go so deep the pressure'll crush them?" Domi asked.

"Probably," Kane said. "The Wave Children even told us there's a deep trench that runs not far from here."

The Wave Children had done some rough and ready soundings, but either they'd lacked the equipment or the inclination to do an exhaustive survey. Or at least the ones Kiri contacted had—but they were a pretty cohesive bunch, for a people scattered all to hell over millions of hectares of ocean. Kane had the impression preskydark satellites had once possessed the capability to map the sea-bed from orbit. Either the ones that did had been wasted—or just wore out over two centuries—or Lakesh was unable to access them. Or he was and hadn't bothered to pass that possibly bone-vital information on to his ace operatives.

Kane didn't think Lakesh would withhold from them data that could prove utterly necessary for the completion of their mission. Quite.

This time, anyway.

"Question being," Grant said, "will they even let us get that far? I was them, I'd just go ahead and chill us once we showed signs of being able to escape down past their crush depth."

"Which again begs the question," Kane said, "why they haven't fried us already."

"They want to see where we go," Domi said.

Kane glanced back, nodded his head slightly. "Great."

Grant glanced at him. "So what do we do, point man?"

Kane shrugged. "Go there." He grinned and touched his brow with a forefinger. "Hey. Classic one-percenter. Right?"

"Beyond one-percenter," Grant grunted. "Way beyond."

BACK IN KANE'S boyhood days in Cobaltville, they'd been taught the world's oceans were just a big blue bowl of life. Since the pollution bled into them over careless decades had broken down, they were now mostly pure, unsullied by the evil, irresponsible hand of humankind, which despoiled all it touched.

As usual the truth was not so simple. All Kane and his companions had been able to learn about the Lemurians was that they were there, and while Cerberus had never had an inkling of their presence—at least, that Lakesh had seen fit to share—and that the various Pacific tribes had started brushing up against them within a generation or so after the sky cleared and the surface warmed again from skydark.

Not even the islanders had any clear idea where Lemuriaville lay. They had analyzed their pattern of contacts over decades, and decided the dome had to lie within about five hundred miles of where *Orpheus* was right now. Big help.

But back to the juicy, unsullied pelagic biosphere…
the fact was, it was a shell, and a fairly shallow one: no
more than about six hundred fathoms deep. Beneath
that was what somebody called the Great Desert, a zone
of lifeless water.

Until one reached the bottom. There deep-explora-
tion vessels such as this one had discovered something
very unexpected indeed.

"WHAT THOSE?" Domi asked, pointing to a monitor that
showed the view ahead. Grant kept his nose in the porthole, trusting the view his own eyes gave him, glancing
aside mainly to check the readouts that helped him keep
in touch with the health and status—body and soul—of
the ungainly craft he piloted.

Despite that, the view on the screen was far clearer
than that through the actual port. The craft's software-
enhanced video imaging from the external cams used
thermal and other inputs from beyond the range of
human vision. Maybe even radar—Kane wasn't sure.
There had been only so much he could absorb about
how the beast worked in the past few days, and he had
concentrated pretty exclusively on getting down cold as
much as he could concerning keeping the vessel alive
and performing its job—which to them was transport,
after all, not exploration.

So it was to the screen that Kane looked to answer
Domi's question. He frowned. They were nearing the
seabed here, and ahead rose a forest of strange spires,

looking for all the world like wind-carved spires from the vast Red Sands desert of Central Asia.

"Black smokers!" Brigid exclaimed.

The screen showed the odd forest of what looked like irregular stone towers. Dense black clouds boiled from the tops of them like chimneys.

"Deep-sea volcanic vents," Brigid said. "The towers are built from minerals carried up molten from the magma, freezing in place on contact with the water."

"Cold down here, people," Kane said, checking a readout. "Mortal cold." Although the hottest day in the midst of a Death Valley summer was frigid, compared to the heat of molten stone. "But the temperature's rising. Gone up a good ten degrees."

"Heat from the vents," Brigid explained.

"Something's moving," Domi said.

"Not possible," Grant said.

"Yes." Brigid reached out to a keyboard, punched buttons. The view shifted and expanded as she altered the aim of the forward-looking cam and adjusted the screen's magnification.

Around and between the bases of the vent towers— smokestacks, Kane couldn't help thinking of them— grew what looked like underbrush. White growths branched upward from the seafloor. From them protruded fleshy red projections that waved slightly but perceptibly. Among them, things stirred, too small to be resolved even with the aid of the real-time enhancing software at this distance.

"Giant tubeworms," Brigid explained. "They have no digestive system—no mouth, no gut, no anus."

"Bummer," Domi said. "Can't eat, lousy sex life. Triple boring."

"How do they live at all?" Kane asked.

"A whole ecosystem exists down here," Brigid said, "based upon bacteria that live in colonies around and even in the vents. They're called chemoautotrophic. It means they synthesize their own food from chemicals and heat, the way photosynthetic plants use light plus chemical nutrients."

"They live *in* those hell chimneys?" Kane asked. "The temperature—"

Brigid nodded. "Furnace heat. Crushing temperatures. Hydrogen sulfide that would kill us in a single breath. They thrive on it. They use the earth's heat instead of sunlight."

She gestured toward the screens. "Before the nukecaust, nobody was close to fully understanding this environment. Those worms seem to have colonies of the vent-form bacteria living inside them in a symbiotic relationship. They get energy from them somehow."

"What do the bacteria get?" Domi wanted to know.

Brigid shrugged.

"That's an impressive mystery," Grant said, "if Brigid doesn't even have words for it."

Kane was shaking his head. "All that heat and pressure and sulfur—isn't that what Venus is supposed to be like?" he asked.

"Oh, yes." Brigid's eyes gleamed like green lamps with enthusiasm. "Although surface conditions on Venus might actually be too mild for these vent-form microorganisms to thrive. They are in effect alien life-forms, like nothing else on Earth."

"That we know of," Kane said. "Damn."

"Why the hell has Lakesh got us down here?" Grant demanded. "Nothing intelligent lives down here, that's triple sure."

"We…do," a strange, shrill voice said from behind them.

The four turned.

Standing before the instrument stack of the after bulkhead was a three-foot-tall humanoid mouse wearing shorts with suspenders, smiling at them with hideous inhuman glee.

Chapter 17

"Commander Zeno," the communicator said. "Our target prepares to enter the field of volcanic seabed vents located in sector Neptune Neptune 523."

Seated in his command chair on the *Nautilus*'s bridge, Zeno nodded judiciously. He knew the NN523 area. He had operated in this sector before.

"Very well, Seawasp Leader." He was about to utter the orders to continue shadowing the submersible when a yellow cursor blinked to life in the upper right of his central screen, imperiously demanding attention. With a tightening of his black-bearded jaw he clicked to accept the call.

It was Bennett's face, seemingly even redder and more sweat flushed than previously. "Destroy them!" the marshal said without preamble.

"Marshal—?"

"You question my orders? Do you forget yourself?" He barked like a bull elephant seal at a rival in the rut.

With effort Zeno commanded himself. "Marshal, I ask, destroy whom?" Only an iron will kept him from adding the insubordinate query, *our hunter-killers?*

"There are enemies above and below our task force."

"The escaping submersible! It must be destroyed at once. Do not waste any more time, Zeno. I warn you!"

"It will be done, sir," Zeno said tautly.

The florid face nodded and vanished.

He's scared, the commander thought. I can smell his fear from three hundred miles away.

What can possibly scare the masters of the greatest power in the Pacific?

It was perhaps not his affair. His, after all, was to obey, like the lowliest warden cadet. Yet the task he had devoted his life to was insuring the safety of the dome and the power structure that kept at bay the anarchy that racked most of the surface world.

Whatever threatens us, he thought, I should know of it. Do my masters not trust me?

There was, he realized with a shock like an ice-water enema, a second alternative. One that pleased him far, far less.

He moved to order the hunter-killers to reify the latter halves of their names.

"IT WAS NOT WORTH IT," the war leader said from the deck of his catamaran, *Mako*. "Whatever we have received in exchange, it wasn't worth the cost to us."

The storm had passed like the battle. The fleet wallowed beneath a gray sky in crepuscular light. The gray ceiling was as much smoke from burning vessels as remnant cloud. The stink of burned wood, petroleum fractions and the barbecue aroma of burned crewfolk was so tangible that Kiri felt she might mold it with her fingers.

Or was it that she longed to wrap her strong fingers around her rival's throat and choke the life from him?

The flames that had gutted *Mako*'s cabin had mostly been doused. His dead crew—half their number, courtesy of repeated rakings with skimmer-fired machine guns, and two blasts from egg-craft laser cannon—had been tipped over the bullet-chewed gunwales to feed their kin, the sharks. Their brothers and sisters of the sea were hard-pressed to give the dead their final benediction, subsuming the flesh of the dead into their own, for even the mighty appetites of the school of sharks that attended the Wave Children's flotilla were challenged by the feast they'd been served this day.

"We won, didn't we?" Kiri said. "We drove the bastards off, fed many to our shark kin, wrecked half a dozen of their egg ships and emptied the saddles of a good fourteen skimmers." The sharks' teeth, of course, guaranteed that any skimmer rider who lost his seat, even if unwounded, lost his life, as well. Sadly, the Lemurians' dolphin allies had killed at least a dozen of the Wave Children's unshipped survivors, battering them unconscious or dead with their beaks, tossing them, or simply driving them deep to drown.

"What's more," she continued, pitching her voice to carry across the lessening storm chop to the other vessels pitching near, "we won our aim—Wavestrider from *Piccard* says he saw the deep-submersible launch safely from her bay and begin to descend under power, before he himself swam out and to the surface."

The mainlanders would be astonished any of our folk got out of the bay, she thought. They still don't know how resilient we are. Her heart swelled with fierce pride.

But Tupolu shook his head. The skin of his face, normally taut and tan, now showed ash pallor and hung loose on the strong bone structure. He had lost good friends, kinfolk, shipmates of many moon cycles' sailing. Her heart almost went out to him.

Almost.

"Another such victory," he said, "and we Children of the Great Wave shall persist only in the songs of our ocean-borne cousins. Even with the mainlanders' wonder weapons, we cannot long resist the undersea marauders. Remember how they might have decapitated us at a stroke when they delivered their ultimatum to the faces of our whole council!"

"But they did not," she reminded him. "They are fallible."

"Perhaps the fleet mistress trusts them to blunder quicker than we die," he said. "That's no race I can see we win."

"Then begone," she said crisply. "Your ship is wounded. No one could say she did not fight well." Although I won't say you did. "Take her back to our season home and heal her hurts. We shall continue to patrol in case our allies have further need of our help."

"Shall I escort the other badly damaged craft?"

"Just go."

Tupolu stared at her. She could see the emotions war behind his weary, still handsome features. She had done him dishonor in front of the flotilla. Yet he would not challenge her here and now, in the face of the enemy. Most likely for fear of dividing the folk in their danger and to their greater peril, she grudgingly admitted to herself, as she would have preferred to blame his faintness of heart. And his craft in truth would survive no further attack.

"I obey your lawful command," he said at length, his own voice now ringing to match hers. "But do not deceive yourself that this matter is concluded."

She turned away. From behind she heard him order his boatswain to fire up the small solar-battery-powered electric motor to begin the crawl to the Wave Children's temporary island base.

Oh, yes it is, she thought. Or nearly so.

KANE JUMPED. "Holy shit!"

The creature had a big rounded head, small body, big hands and feet. The features had been anthropomorphized until they were marginally more human than rodent.

"It's a hologram cartoon," Grant said. As if it made sense.

"What in hell's it doing in our ship?" Kane asked.

The figure did a happy little dance. Kane felt an overwhelming urge to throttle it. He only held back before he knew its neck had no substance, and if it even drew breath, it did so somewhere well beyond his reach.

"Guide…you. You passed test first. Guide now. Guide." He nodded and smiled as if he'd delivered some great gift or cosmic revelation. "All happy. Happy!"

"Tell me," Grant said slowly, "that's not why we just ran the gauntlet through Hell to the bottom of the deep blue sea."

"Hosed again," Domi said cheerfully. "What's new about that?"

"Hosed worse than we thought," Kane said, after glancing back at his instruments and doing a double take. "Those bastards shadowing us have just sped up and are closing with us. Firing pass, or I never strafed a slag-jacker raiding party."

"Why haven't they destroyed us already?" asked Brigid, always practical.

"Limited range or accuracy of their underwater weps, mebbe," Kane said. "Mebbe they're just closing in for a good gun-camera shot of us imploding."

"What can we do about it?" she asked.

Grant plied the controls in an attempt to take evasive action. With glacial slowness *Orpheus* skidded sideways. Even if he wasn't accustomed to the whippet responsiveness of a Deathbird, the DSV would have responded with dead-hopeless slowness. It had the handling characteristics and agility of the household appliance it resembled.

He shrugged. "Learn to breathe water. Real *hard* water."

"Not so, not so, no-no!" caroled the cartoon-mouse hologram from the rear. The others looked back; they'd forgotten about their new passenger, what with the imminent threat of death.

"No worries," it said with obscene brightness, "no fear. Safety's here. Straight ahead steer."

Before them rose an undersea cliff, right on the far side of the field of irregular rock chimneys streaming plumes of black pseudosmoke. Or maybe it was real smoke; Kane realized he had no idea.

"Driving into the side of a seamount will help how?" he asked.

But the cartoon creature had shut up. Right when it may have imparted something resembling useful information.

"They've formed up abreast and are closing," Kane reported from his sonar. "Won't be long now."

He worked the controls serving the aft-mounted vidcam. The pursuers were clearly visible in the computer-enhanced picture. They themselves showed no lights but a faint amber gleam through their front view panels.

"This," Kane muttered, "is it."

Chapter 18

Two things happened.

The two egg craft collapsed. Without any visible cause they simply vanished into twin boils of bubbles, shot through with a few brief bright blue flashes.

And a black hole opened in the sheer gray cliff before them.

"What the fuck," Kane said, "over?"

In the monitor showing the aft view, two fisted clumps sank toward the ocean floor, just beyond the first of the smoking towers. They resembled nothing so much as crumpled wads of aluminum foil. It seemed hardly possible that a moment before they had been sleek impervious vessels crewed by living, breathing human beings. Who were now mere organic paste, food for the strange eyeless white forms that seethed and surged among the towers surrounding *Orpheus*.

He glanced back to their cartoon-mouse companion. And saw a bank of consoles blinking green-and-red lights at him like tiny idiot eyes.

"Gone," he said. "Son of a bitch."

"Just like the vanishing hitchhiker," Brigid said.

Kane fixed her with a glare. "What's that, Baptiste?"

"Nothing. Later."

Grant steered the ship toward what Kane fervently hoped was a cave, and not just a patch of black rock that had been mysteriously hidden until seconds ago.

"Are you sure it's safe?" Brigid asked anxiously.

"No," Grant said. "What exactly have we done today that *was* safe?"

"Or the day before," Kane murmured. "Hell. *Ever.*" Because if they had learned one thing in the past few years, it was that safety dwelt nowhere in this world. Least of all, perhaps, in the cloistered illusions that were the nine baronies and their Enclaves.

They entered the hole. In dead darkness there was a strange sense of floating, not in dense, frigid salt water, but in an infinity of time and space.

Then it seemed they settled into stillness, as if held in place.

Light flooded in through the viewport. It was white with undertones of yellow and green and an uneasy edge to it that reminded Kane somehow of fluorescents. Outside it illuminated what looked like a curving surface of smooth, shiny gray stone.

"Kane," said Brigid. Her voice sounded as if it was speaking past a hand clamped over it. He turned.

"The aft-watching monitor," she said, and it was a token that all was not right with her that she spoke an incomplete sentence. "The hole we entered by."

"What about it?" Kane said, squinting at the small image.

"It's gone."

Everybody turned then—including Grant, who had nothing more to do; the craft did not respond to his inputs and seemed immovably held by something. The rear view showed about the same thing the first did: a blank gray surface, subtly striated, with slight hints of sparkle to it. It was so polished it looked wet, although something about its appearance told Kane it was as dry as the middle of Death Valley in July even though, not half a minute before, the chamber had been filled with seawater.

"How do we get out?" Domi asked, ruby eyes wide. Her feral instincts did not favor being penned; she was a wild one in truth.

"Whoever let us in lets us out," Grant said. "Or they don't."

"And there you have it," Kane said. "Let's pop the hatch and check out our swell new home."

As KANE SUSPECTED, the inside of the stone bubble was as dry as outer space.

Standing on the flat upper surface—it was way too small to qualify as a deck in Kane's mind—he just shook his head.

Brigid stood leaning way over, peering down. "Fascinating," she said. "It's almost as if concrete has been poured around *Orpheus*'s hull."

"Mighty quick-drying concrete," said Grant. Only his head was visible through the hatch. The big man seemed to be reluctant to emerge from the confines of the submersible into this strange and seemingly impossible new reality.

Domi jumped down to the gray platform that embraced and surrounded the vehicle. Then she looked up at her companions.

"What're you waiting for?" she demanded. "You're not freaked out by a little weirdness, are you? After what we've been through, we get weirder than this with our breakfast food."

"Mebbe not weirder than this," Kane said, looking around. The smooth walls formed a hemispheric bubble that approached no closer than two to three yards to the submersible at its closest. It was a small, confined space, but did not feel cramped.

Nonetheless it was hard for Kane to suppress a slight claustrophobic thrill. He felt a crushing awareness of the enormous mass of water over their heads. Not to mention the fact—

"How do we leave this chamber?" Brigid asked.

"Gotta be a way," Grant said. He still hadn't emerged from the ship. "If that damn cartoon mouse wanted us chilled, it could've just let those bastard Lemurians finish the job."

"Mebbe it's got a sense of humor," Kane said.

"Mebbe we should just use the door," Domi said.

"What door?" Kane asked.

She gestured with a ghost-colored hand. "That one," she answered.

Kane looked. Behind him a doorway stood open into the slick stone wall. It looked very normal, complete with a hatch of what seemed some matte off-white synthetic material.

"I'd swear that wasn't there a minute ago," Grant said.

Domi shrugged. "What difference? It's there now."

"Domi," Brigid said, her voice displaying as much strain as her taut, pale face, "another person might wonder how—"

The slight albino woman shrugged again. "Not obvious? We've come to visit aliens. What else could it be?"

The other three passed a look around.

"What else indeed?" Kane said.

Grant boosted himself out of the hatch to crouch a moment like a panther about to spring from *Orpheus*'s upper surface. "You through the door first, point man?" he asked.

Kane nodded and entered the black passageway. It was circular, as if just fresh bored through the rock. The curved floor made it difficult to walk.

Behind them the entranceway from the bubble containing *Orpheus* sealed, plunging the tunnel into blackness.

"You know," Grant's voice said from right behind Kane, "there can't be a lot of places darker than a sealed tunnel through a mountain eight hundred yards underwater."

"Yeah." Kane dug into the pack for a Nighthawk microlight.

A golden glow filled the tunnel. Well, it didn't *fill* it exactly, Kane saw; it just crowded the inky blackness to either end, where it seemed congealed into something solid. A sphere of gold radiance floated at waist height two yards ahead.

"Cool," Domi said. She started toward it.

"Domi, be careful—"

The light retreated before her like mercury from a fingertip. "See? It's here to show us the way," Domi said over her shoulder.

"If this shit doesn't let up," Grant said, "I'll start believing in Domi's triple-fused notion there's aliens down here."

"Doesn't make a bit of sense," Kane said. "Just more sense than any other explanation I can think of. Baptiste? How about it? You're the big brain here."

"I don't have any more information than you do, Kane." Surprisingly, she didn't sound annoyed when she said it, but mostly perplexed. "Lakesh and I hypothesized our mystery correspondents might be aliens before we ever left Cerberus. Now that we're here, it does seem hard to believe. But it would explain a great deal."

"Come on, you guys," Domi called. "It's not like we've never run into aliens before."

The golden globe came to the blank stone face of the tunnel's far end. It passed through. As its radiance died, plunging the passageway back into ultimate darkness, Kane saw Domi walking forward without hesitation.

Light poured in. It struck Kane's eyes with such impact that he pulled his head back, blinking away great purple-and-cyan globes of afterimage. The wall blocking the end of the tunnel had disappeared.

"How do they do that?" Kane asked.

"I don't know," Grant growled, "but it's starting to piss me off."

Domi stood awaiting them in the middle of a rectangular chamber. Its walls were off white, just short of dingy gray. They seemed textured, unlike the interior walls of *Orpheus*'s resting place, which seemed polished.

The others entered. Grant came through the opening last. Kane was already turning as he did, but he still missed the disappearance of the hole that had admitted them into this chamber. He looked at the bigger man and shrugged.

"At least this room has a door," Grant said.

Past Domi lay a door opening of conventional size and shape. It seemed to open on a semidark corridor, illuminated by a yellow glow strip running at about the height of Domi's narrow waist.

"Hel-lo, friends," a voice squeaked. "Well. Come."

Everybody turned. Through accident or intent it had managed to materialize where no one was looking: in the corner to the near-right of where they had come through into this antechamber or whatever it was.

"Great," Grant said. "Now it's a cartoon duck."

It was, stylized in much the same way the mouse in the sub had been. It was about three feet tall, wore a pinafore that left its brown-feathered butt bare and had what appeared to be a wig of startling yellow hair with pigtails on its head.

"Now, that's one of the scarier things I've ever seen," Kane said.

"So are you the same as the first one?" Grant asked.

"I am. A representation of. Pyrites," it said, in its near-stuttering way. "Before. Your guide was. A visualization. Of Rich-in-Sulfur."

"Can we have the mouse back?" Domi asked. "It didn't have a speech impediment."

"Domi!" Brigid said.

"Pleased to meet you, Pyrites," Kane said loudly, in hopes of overriding Domi saying something even less diplomatic. Although the damn thing didn't seem to respond to the commentary. "Ah, what exactly are you?"

"Smooth, Mr. Diplomacy," Grant murmured.

Kane shrugged. "Okay. I suck. But I don't think this thing's what you call sensitive."

"No," it said. "I am a computer-generated composite of images believed to be soothing to the primary surface sophont-form." It still stuttered, but Kane's mind had started to edit out the hesitation-waltz bits. "I am— we are—colony. Colony life. Colony. Collective—"

"Christ, it's stuck," Grant said.

"You are a colony entity?" Brigid asked.

"Yes."

"Colony of what?" asked Kane.

The holographic duck nodded its head several times

sagely. Then it waddled past Domi and into the passage leading out of the antechamber. The humans followed dubiously.

The passage was not straight, but undulated slightly, so that it was impossible to see to the end. The duck walked ahead of them without looking back or speaking.

"Not a very smooth projection," Kane murmured to Grant. "Notice how it keeps flickering every few yards."

"Yeah," Grant said. "What good does that do us?"

"It shows our hosts aren't infallible."

Grant rolled his eyes to the ceiling. It was a very normal appearing ceiling, light colored and appearing textured like acoustic tile in the dim light of the glow strips.

"We're under eight hundred yards of water," the big man said, "with nothing but our hosts' technology keeping it from landing on us and smashing us into goo. And you think it's *encouraging* that their tech glitches?"

Kane shrugged. "Okay. So mebbe it wasn't one of my better ideas."

The passage ahead widened into another room similar to the one they'd left. The duck walked into it without speaking or glancing back. The four humans hesitated, then followed.

A closed door stood to their right. A low red settee sat along the wall to their left.

Rising from it, clad in an orange jumpsuit that clashed so horribly with the settee that Kane was aware of it, was the extreme and cadaver-pale length of Gilgamesh Bates.

Chapter 19

"Welcome."

The mogul laughed into the muzzles of Kane's and Grant's Sin Eaters. But he blinked and held up a hand like a hairless white spider.

"Ease off your triggers, my friends," he said. "I trust you not to fire accidentally. But your laser target designators are blinding me."

Two red dots converged on the bridge of his long nose, almost coinciding into one. It meant the two former Magistrates had each taken up half the trigger slack. The tiniest further pressure and twin tribursts would vaporize Bates's long bean-shaped head.

Not a bad idea, Kane thought. But he relaxed his forefinger and let the perforated muzzle shroud of his handblaster tip toward the ceiling.

"Why aren't we chilling him?" Grant grated at him sideways.

"Because with him it makes five of us humans alone down here at the bottom of all that water," Kane said, "and we're still way outnumbered. Besides, our hosts may have a reason for having the son of a bitch here. If we peel open his head for him, they might take exception."

"As I thought, Mr. Kane," Bates said, smiling with horsy yellow teeth, "you show unexpected depths. Besides, I assure you I bear you nothing but friendship, at least in the course of this present emergency."

"Which emergency is that, Bates?" Grant asked. "The overlords?"

"One favor, big man," Bates said to him. "If you're going to kill me, do it with intent. Not suspense."

With a snarl Grant let his Sin Eater slam back into its holster on his shadow-armored forearm.

"As for the overlords," Bates said, "they're old news."

He shook his head. It looked more peculiar than usual: his reddish-orange hair had grown long, showing a tendency to curl and bush out, and he had begun a full if unkempt beard, pink banded with stripes of white on either side of his chin, which was on its way to Old Testament patriarch territory.

"If not the Annunaki," Kane asked, "then who?"

"Leviathan."

"Leviathan?" Kane echoed, incredulous. "What the hell is Leviathan?"

"An ancient mythological sea creature," Brigid said. "Sometimes identified with the kraken or giant squid. Thomas Hobbes used it as a metaphor for state power...."

She trailed off because Bates's big white hands were applauding with apparent lack of irony. "Splendid, Ms. Baptiste. Splendid. You are most erudite. Yet please permit me to assure you there is nothing either metaphorical or symbolic about our Leviathan. It—*he*—is altogether real."

"A giant squid?" Grant said.

"Ah, no. A giant spiral nautilus, it would appear. And rather than representing the all-powerful state, it may be the force that has lain behind all states throughout human history. But let's let our hosts explain, shall we?"

He waved a hand. He couldn't have been more gracious had he been maître d' at some tony twentieth-century restaurant.

The door that had been closed stood open; the entry through which the four had entered this chamber still existed, as well, much to Kane's unspoken relief. Through the newly opened portal he could see their two cartoon-animal guides, the big-headed mouse from the submersible and the stuttery blond-wigged mallard.

Between the holograms stood a third, looming over both to about Kane's height, a beautiful long-haired white cat with big pale green eyes with just a hint of blue. It was the most natural of the three, meaning it looked least like a cartoon and also more like an actual animal instead of an anthropomorphized character design vaguely based upon an animal. But it was still a cat that stood upright, wore green silk cavalier dress, had hands with thumbs—

And spoke: "Welcome, surface persons. I am the Old Tower. You are Kane, Grant, Brigid Baptiste, Domi." The splendid white head nodded in turn to each. The voice was a beautiful honey-and-amber baritone, sounding as unmistakably masculine as the duck did feminine. "I do hope I have the order properly."

"Uh," Kane said. "Yeah." The four and Bates entered the room. The door slid shut behind them.

"You believe you have met my colleagues, Pyrites and Rich-in-Sulfur?" It waved a furry three-fingered hand toward the duck and mouse in order.

Did it mean to say it believes we met them? Kane wondered. He shook his head slightly to clear it of thoughts that were unproductive at best.

The walls seemed to be giant monitors windowed into separate blocks. They showed a view of the undersea vent-chimney field, of a nebula glowing white and blue and purple against dead-black space, a view of an empty parking lot with what appeared to be 1970s-vintage American cars, various scenes of war and violence in the fashion of preskydark news footage and a bunch of other incongruous loops and stills Kane couldn't afford the attention to take in.

"All respect, Mr. Tower," he began.

"Old Tower," the projection said without heat.

"Mr. Old Tower, just what are you folks, exactly?"

The cat smiled. It showed more of the gleaming white fangs at its corners than Kane felt easy with.

"Colony creatures," the mouse, Rich-in-Sulfur, sang in its breathing-helium voice. It did a handstand. Inverted, it said, "We bacteria be. Live in volcano vents beneath the sea. The deep blue sea. Happy-warm life!

Energy and contentment!" It jumped back on its big splayed feet and hugged itself ecstatically.

Grant turned a single raised eyebrow to Kane, who shrugged.

"We are, I fear," Old Tower said, "nothing you can understand, my friend. Nor are you anything we can understand. Yet unlikely as it appears we share common threat in common."

Kane blinked. Is this smooth bastard going to start stuttering, too?

Domi had dug out some kind of jerked meat the Wave Children had given them in transit and was gnawing it. Kane suspected he didn't want to know what it was. Barbecued dolphin would be way too much, even if the finny creatures had been trying to kill him—was it two hours ago? Less?

"You folks aren't from around here, are you?" she asked, heedless of her mouthful of lumpy gray masticate.

The three images froze in their varied poses, Pyrites the Duck jittering as if suffering a bad case of nerves or possibly lice, Rich-in-Sulfur in the midst of doing a happy stamping dance, Old Tower with its head cocked benignly—a pose that reminded Kane of a twentieth-century politician trying his damnedest to project an image of elder statesman. Scan lines ran through their tridimensional images. The vid loops on the walls locked, and all those pictures flickered, too.

"Under the likeliness of circumstance we should never have cause to interact," Old Tower said, coming out of its fugue as if continuing what it had been saying earlier. The other cartoons and walls displays went back to normal—whatever that might be, in this damn place. "For your question, Mrs. Domi—"

"Ms.," Brigid corrected.

"Whatever," Domi said.

"—we evolved elsewhere. At the floor of a different ocean. Another planet, yes."

"You are aliens, then?" Brigid said.

"We b-belong here," the duck said, defensively, Kane thought. "Lived here long, we have, have. The bottom of the sea…our bottom."

Kane blinked again.

"This chamber," Brigid said, taking their surroundings in with a gesture of her hand. "You certainly don't need it to survive."

"We her made!" the mouse sang out.

"We bought it," Pyrites said. "Bought it from surface beings for surface beings."

"Did you buy it or make it?" Grant said.

"Let it go, big man," Kane said. "That way madness lies."

"We made this for you," Old Tower said. "We bought it from a race of surface dwellers we encountered in space. Traders. They resembled your raccoons."

"Raccoons," Grant echoed in a hollow voice.

The beautiful cat-human hybrid face frowned. It did a credible job of looking concerned. Better than Kane had ever seen an actual cat do.

"I do hope it is adjusted properly for your species," it said. "We based it upon samples."

"How did you happen to come by such samples?" Brigid asked.

Grant touched her on the arm. "Don't ask questions you don't probably want to know the answers to," he advised.

Kane nodded briskly. "I think that better be our SOP for this deal," he said. "Okay. Obviously you want something from us, Old Tower. And obviously you have something to give us, or this bastard Bates wouldn't be here."

"Ah, yes. Yes, yes," Old Tower said.

"Lev-ev-iathan," stammered Pyrites the Duck. "Leviathan threatens all, top and bottom."

"You mean above and below the surface," Brigid said encouragingly.

"What," Grant said, "is this Leviathan everybody keeps talking about?"

At once the walls all showed fuzzy, foggy shots of a great black shape, sometimes a shadow in darkness, sometimes framed by gray seabed. None showed much detail. Kane had the impression of a squat spiral shell with a mop of tentacles waving from it—and a great pair of luminous red eyes.

Of course there was nothing to show scale; the mud and pressure ridges and slabs of the seafloor could have been any size. The red-eyed black creature could have been small enough to fit in the palm of Kane's hand.

Except he knew it wasn't. He knew it was immensely huge. Immensely old. Immensely evil.

He knew it.

"Shit," he heard Domi and Grant breathe more or less in unison.

"The dreams," Brigid murmured. Her face was pale and transfigured, the face of a martyr facing the stake.

"I thought you said you didn't have the dreams," Grant said accusingly to Domi.

"I lied," she said carelessly.

Old Tower seemed to have noticed their reaction and was looking intently at each of them in turn. Kane realized that was most likely illusion, a trick or happenstance: beings as alien as these claimed to be were unlikely to be able to read human body language and facial expressions, and even their expert software was unlikely to be of use. What did alien space raccoons know about human expressions? Still, they'd had ample chances to study humanity through its electronic transmissions, as their broadcasts to Cerberus had shown.

"So you've had the nightmares, too," Bates said.

"What about you, Bates?" Kane asked. With a shock he noticed something that otherwise would have hit him in the face at once: the immensely tall man was barefoot. The features of his long, slack face looked puffed somehow. Neither his pale skin nor his one-piece one-color outfit looked any too clean, and Kane smelled stale clothing and human sweat and grease along with the indefinable alien aromas of the alien ventilation system. "You been dreaming, too?"

"The dreams are being reported by sensitives all over

the world," Bates said. "Many have been driven mad. There's rioting in some of the surviving villes in North America."

"How would you know about that?" Grant asked.

"You know I've had the ability to monitor all communications worldwide for a long time." At one time that included Cerberus redoubt, as it happened, although Lakesh swore up and down he had locked that open back door. Then again all four operatives knew how little was ever guaranteed just because the Cerberus director swore to it.

"Where you been monitoring from?" Kane asked casually.

Bates smiled as bland as pudding. "From my fortress of solitude," he said. "Or perhaps, fortress of solecism." He chuckled in appreciation of his own wit.

Kane blinked. "Fortress of Solecism" was what Team Phoenix dubbed Bates's South American stronghold before Cerberus helped them take it away from him.

"Why did you bring us into this?" he asked the three projections.

Rich-in-Sulfur shook its great-eared head. "Wants to destroy us, it. Destroy us it, wants." Its manic good humor was nowhere in evidence.

"Why bring us in?" Grant said. "Like you said, we don't exactly have a lot of interests in common. Why should we involve ourselves in a fight over the seafloor? We don't live down here."

"Some of us do," Brigid said. "Don't forget the Lemurians."

"He is threat, is, is he," said Pyrites, who seemed a lot more suited to worrying than its mouselike partner. "Threat all. Wants destroy us. Wants rule you. Or destroy. Cannot have all, destroy all."

The walls themselves seemed to take up the phrase, repeating "destroy all" in dozens of variations on Pyrites's stop-and-go voice, at different volumes and all subtly out of phase.

"Pyrites speaks well," Old Tower said through the unnerving clamor. It came as a surprise to Kane, who thought the gender-bent duck talked like Domi after seventy-two straight hours without sleep. "Silt on all rains, same."

"I don't know what that means," Kane said. "More to the point, you realize we're not exactly friends of the Lemurians, don't you? The people who live in the dome on the seafloor."

"Allies," Pyrites said, looking very convincingly distressed. The mindless replay of its earlier words faded and died. "Leviathan, surface folk under sea. Them a-allies now."

Chapter 20

"I know you understand me," the woman said to the bound creature.

The fish man sat in the darkness of the bilge. Its scaled and fin-fringed arms were pinioned behind its back. It made no response, but only continued gazing at Kiri Far-Seer with huge glabrous eyes. Ghost embers of yellow-green fire smoldered deep within.

"We have changed our minds," she said in a low voice. "Do you understand?"

Her boatswain, great Ollie with his curtain-fringe of wiry hair, guarded the hatch from the outside. She hoped he was obeying her order not to listen.

She was already arranging for the deaths of too many of her people. She could not bear more.

"I would seek terms with your masters," she said. "I know you serve the Lemurians. We would accept the terms they offered us. But there are those who prevent us. I can tell you their course, and then your masters can deal with them after their fashion."

She waited in gloom that reeked of fish and the human blood and waste that had washed down here in battle and its aftermath, scarcely daring to breathe, though not because of the smell. Does he understand? Does some flame of human intelligence flicker behind those grotesque bulging eyes? For her people had long known the truth of the fish men, that they were spawned in labs in the great dome hidden away somewhere beneath hundreds of fathoms of salt water.

She closed her ears to the groaning voices of the sea dead, past and future—for the Wave Children believed spirit was timeless—manifested in the action of waves upon the planks of the hull and the structure of *Great Sky Reef* herself.

She wasn't sure the thing spoke English. The Lemurians did, and showed no sign of speaking or understanding other tongues. But certain legends suggested they used a special artificial speech to communicate with their artificial amphibious servants.

Then slowly, almost imperceptibly, the great finned head nodded.

Relief flooded Kiri in a lava tide—and something else. The deal was done.

Tupolu's intransigence threatens all the Children of the Great Wave, she told herself. Duty requires extraordinary sacrifices of us all.

Even my honor.

Smiling, she began to recite highly specific information.

KANE LOOKED to Bates, who had an even more insufferably knowing look on his long mug than usual.

"You've been down here awhile," he said. "Do they mean what I think they mean?"

Bates nodded. "It's a surprise to everybody," he said. "One suspects, not least to the Lemurians."

"Fuck us," Kane said.

"It shall be done," said Grant.

"What was their relationship to Leviathan before?" Brigid asked.

"The same as yours," Bates said. "Obliviousness to his existence. He has preferred to operate from behind the scenes."

A pause. "Possibly for the entirety of human history. And maybe beyond."

Grant cleared his throat. "Let's all catch a grip here," he said. "We're talking about a great big squid."

"Nautilus," Brigid and Bates said at once. Brigid colored. Bates smiled and nodded her to continue.

"Whatever. It's a big mollusk. That matter, we don't even know how big it is. From these damn blurry vids it could be the size of a hamster."

The cartoon projections showed signs of animation—so to speak. Pyrites took its bewigged head in its hands and began to wag it side to side. Rich-in-Sulfur did compulsive backflips in place. Old Tower's tail bottled out to enormous size, proving that the alien AI driving the projections had incorporated some actual information on cats, as well as visualizations that the vent forms believed comforted and reassured humans.

A wall became one single image. Kane felt momentary surprise none of the projections had made a visible gesture to bring it about. Then he remembered the will or wills driving them also directly controlled the wall display.

It was a shot of Leviathan, waving blackness, with one eye burning like a red nova in the midst of triangular shadow. It looked oddly familiar somehow.

"The eye in the pyramid!" Brigid gasped. Kane realized that was true. He'd seen it before many times.

By the motion of the silty gray floor it was obvious the creature was advancing. Its tentacles quested like serpents before it. And here in the foreground came into view the towers of a vent field. It may have been the very one they were in now; Kane couldn't tell.

His memory suggested that the tallest tower he had seen on the way to the cavern was about twenty yards tall. The Old Tower? He shook it from his mind; it didn't matter.

The point was the chimney towers were fairly tall, most of them three or four times his own height. And they were in the foreground of the image, meaning they were disproportionately large in relation to the shape looming over them.

And over them…

"Holy shit," Grant said. "That's got to be hundreds of yards tall!"

"At least," Brigid said.

Suddenly a discharge like a network of purple fire enveloped the front of the monster blackness. It faded to blue, white, yellow, gone. The tentacles recoiled with surprising speed, given that the longest had to have been as long as the lost *Piccard,* which by now had joined them somewhere at the bottom of the poorly named Pacific.

Again the shadow mass moved forward. Again the net of lightnings caught and stopped it. An oceanic surge of pain and rage welled from the image, so overwhelming that Kane found himself and Domi wrapped in each other's arms.

The fear passed like a seismic sea wave. Shaken, Kane let go of Domi, who grinned impudently. From the corner of his eye he saw Baptiste and Grant disentangling themselves from each other, studiously avoiding each other's eyes.

"I was going to say 'So what? It's still a big squid,'" Grant admitted. He didn't have to say more.

"Leviathan is mighty," Old Tower said simply.

Kane found his voice. "You fought him off once, though."

"We have many times," said Rich-in-Sulfur, cheerful again. "Many-many!"

"And many times has he come b-back," said Pyrites, worried.

"Once came he close to eradicating us," Old Tower said, "as well as you surface forms. When he influenced surface dwellers to place thermonuclear devices in subduction zones seafloor."

The great white cat's head shook. "We did not know

you surface folk, in your terrible realm of heat and near vacuum, were truly intelligent, although you produced electromagnetic vibrations. These we did not know were they technological or natural emanation.

"After the terrible upheaval we—those colonies who survived—debated the wisdom of eradicating rest of the surface forms. First seemed we might not need to; our sensors detected minute change in incident radiation reaching the surface and corresponding minor, temporarily sustained drop in surface temperature. Coincided this with prolonged reduction electromagnetic activity in."

"We decided you all die soon, all-all," said Rich-in-Sulfur as cheerily as if it were passing out presents, "or harmless were."

"But didn't die out you," Pyrites said.

"We realized came to your kind were mere instruments for Leviathan's will," Old Tower said. "However, as you see can see, his physical power is vast, but limited. We successfully defend against him. Direct attack not possible, him. He must have instruments to work through."

"So why not wipe us out now?" Brigid asked. Her voice was entirely calm, level. Once again Kane realized that she was a great deal tougher than she appeared or generally acted.

"No, no," Rich-in-Sulfur said, dancing happily and waving its hands in the air. "Worse than you now."

"The overlords?" Grant asked. "They seem like a tall order even for the Leviathan."

"Leviathan made Annunaki his puppets before," said Old Tower.

Kane frowned. "But the nukecaust and skydark—that was the Archon Directorate, wasn't it?"

"That's one story," Bates said. For a full-on megalomaniac, he had kept strangely quiet, standing off to one side smiling into his wild-hedge beard and smelling like a swamper two days dead.

"They botched it, too," Domi said.

"They thought alone?" Old Tower asked. "Or thought thoughts Leviathan them gave?"

Kane looked at Baptiste. She shrugged.

"Does it matter?" Grant asked. "Big bastard's decided to make his move—that's pretty clear. He seems to be on a major global recruiting drive. Mebbe he's afraid of the overlords, mebbe he's trying to grab them, too. I don't know. I'm not a big squid. The tactical situation is you vent things are scared shitless of him, and want our help. How? And what's in it for us?"

Bates applauded softly. "An admirable appraisal of the situation, friend Grant."

"Stop that!" Grant snapped. "You sound just like Lakesh."

"You must defeat his allies, the Lemurians," Old Tower said, "and destroy Leviathan."

COMMANDER ZENO STALKED the thronged corridors of the Habitat, Lemuriaville's answer to a baronial Enclave. His casque-covered head was tipped forward, black beard flattened on his clavicle. His gray-blue eyes were clouded and scarcely spared a glance, either for the technicians of various castes or for the four men of his patrol who flanked his tall, lean form with its deep aquamarine cloak billowing from broad shoulders.

Inside his mind he walked among thoughts far more tumultuous than the purposeful bustle of the various workers scurrying by with eyes downcast to avoid meeting the fish-eagle gazes of the Deep Wardens. Why am I here? he wondered.

To be sure, keeping order within the Habitat was as much a part of his brief as extending the writ of dome law and order to the circumambient ocean. He had put in ample time on foot patrol, especially in his early years, when he had to prove himself—like any other warden who wanted to rise above a mere internal enforcer.

He had been a good and zealous dome patrolman, conscientious, courageous, filled with initiative. Had he been otherwise he never would have seen promotion to the coveted external service, first riding skimmer craft, then moving to hunter-killer crew, then on to the larger dolphin-shaped submarines. And eventually he had become the primary tactical commander for Lemuriaville's small but elite undersea fleet, a task at which he had proved himself to be abundantly qualified.

But as such it made no sense for him to be here now. It was like a twentieth-century admiral walking shore patrol on the docks. It was not—so he told himself—his pride that was wounded. It was his sense of efficiency.

But he, no less and no more than the humblest grubber in the sewage-recycling plant, served at the will of his superiors. For their will was the will of the baron himself, transmitted downward to the lesser entities who served the genetically perfected being who ruled them by right of science. So Zeno stalked the off-white corridors of the Habitat with an expression like a killer typhoon incarnate, and the techs, who had mastered the art of seeing without being seen to look, gave him plenty of room.

He was a man who had always gloried in his duty above all other things. Yet now he caught himself longing to put this duty behind him, to steal once again a few forbidden moments.

Robert, he thought, dear Robert If only I could fold you to my breast right now.

"HE CHAMPS AT THE BIT," Bennett said, raising his head from the monitor displaying surveillance video in the baron's sanctum.

The baron stared at him with his long turquoise eyes. I have no idea what the man is on about, he thought. That was another apekin weakness, to substitute metaphor for precision. It did not encourage the baron to see such weakness manifest in his very Trust. Yet unbreakable circumstance compelled him to depend upon these inferior beings.

So had his kinsmen of North America. And in time they had become gods.

And soon, he thought, so shall I.

For this was what the great wavering blackness in his head and his chest and the depths of the sea had promised him in its sibilant soft speech in his skull and in his dreams: an elevation to a being greater and more powerful even than the world's self-proclaimed overlords. He would become mightier than they—and if he was still not supreme, still he would reign as the undying and illuminated agent of the true ruler of the world.

The black words came to his mind now, as they did more and more frequently, awake as well as asleep: "Do not trust this one. He doubts."

For a moment he thought his dark master meant Bennett. But no. Bennett was sweaty and fearful and self-absorbed, but those things he had always been.

Still, the baron thought, and his perfect brow clouded with a hint of frown, I command here.

"He obeys," he said aloud. "He serves."

Bennett blinked and his pale lips became bloodless and then disappeared into a line in his florid shiny face. "He questions. I know my man."

Does the black voice speak to you, too? Baron Lemuria wondered. He knew that it had, for he had seen Bennett partake of the revelry the voice ordained. Besides, the warden commander's words coincided too perfectly with those the baron had just heard in his own mind— and he believed but little in coincidence.

Doubtless he's not even aware. They were scarcely sentient, these humans. The baron would, when he was viceroy of the world, see to creating a perfected race of servants. One more useful and obedient than the fish-man hybrids created in the dome's early days of occupancy, a botch that had cost numerous techs, high-caste scientists and even a member of Baron Lemuria's Trust their heads.

"I have further use of him," the baron pronounced with an air of finality. "Indeed, now. The intelligence you have gathered—send him to deal with it."

"Excellency, it shall be done." Bennett saluted stiffly, bowed and left.

And it is a use you have ordained, Baron Lemuria-ville told the voice, whose presence he could feel like a pressure in his sinus cavities. And when Zeno has served it, then he can be discarded. Like any tool past its use.

Chapter 21

"How the hell," Kane asked, "are we supposed to do that? Lemuriaville's got a stud undersea fleet. We've got a tubby bitch of an exploration submersible that barely made it here with air inside it. And seems to be permanently walled in that cave to boot."

"You must destroy Leviathan," Old Tower said. "It is only hope. So to do, must deal with Lemurians."

"Sure," Grant said. "No big deal, huh? We just go mano a mano with that thousand-yard-long *nautilus* and strangle him with his own tentacles. Piece of cake."

"Yes-yes!" Rich-in-Sulfur did a cartwheel. "Cake!"

"I think sarcasm may be lost on these guys," Kane said. "What my friend means, Old Tower, is how are we supposed to do anything to a creature like that that it'll even notice? Nuke it?"

"That ought to do it," Grant said with relish. "We know where to lay hands on one or two of those. Even a small one should vaporize a big bastard like our squid-faced friend. Or enough of him not to make much difference."

This caused the smaller projections to hop around. Even the pathologically giddy Rich-in-Sulfur looked disturbed, and Pyrites practically decohered. Old Tower's tail had bottled again.

"Must not!" it declared. "Such weapons cannot harm Leviathan."

"May even," Pyrites wailed, "make st-stuh-stronger!"

It wavered and blinked out.

"Is it dead?" Domi wanted to know.

"Domi, it's just a projection," Brigid said.

"How do we know what's projecting it didn't die? Do we know? Huh?"

Brigid scowled. Kane felt a thrill of guilty triumph: if he thought he hated when *she* got the better of *him*...

"The colony designated Pyrites lives," said Old Tower, unruffled once again. "Must you accept our assurance it imperative you not use nuclear nor thermonuclear, nor any large chemical explosives, Leviathan against."

"With a clear if unspoken subtext of, *if we want to leave here alive,*" Kane said.

"Kane!" Brigid said in alarm.

"Baptiste, weird as they are, you know they're thinking that. Weird as we are to them, they know we know. We know they know that. Everybody knows. Are we green?"

She definitely was. But she nodded, a trifle spasmodically.

"Okay," Kane said, turning back to the humanoid cat. "So what do we use? Harsh language?"

"A tactical implosion bomb might serve nicely,"

Bates said. His huge fingers were laced around a knee and he was rocking on the settee. "Of a destructive force roughly analogous to a kiloton-range tactical thermonuclear device."

"Yeah," Kane said, "if only such a thing existed."

"Even saying we can get hold of one of these supersized implosion bombs," Grant said, "which I've never heard of, anyway—even at that, how are we supposed to deliver the damn bomb? Clutch it to our chest and hop overboard?"

Old Tower shook its head. "Inefficient delivery means."

"I can provide your wants here, too," Bates said. "Friends, I hold the key to our joint success. You have the resourcefulness and physical prowess—I have the means."

"Why would you help us, Bates?" Grant said. "Last I heard, we chased your ass out of your secret stronghold in South America. After you made more than one or two good-faith efforts to chill us. And where'd you go to, anyway?"

"I have other resources," Bates said airily. "As to the relevant question—we are all humans together, aren't we?"

Grant glared at him like an angry bull. Then he dropped his eyes to the resilient off-white flooring. "Given a sufficiently broad definition of 'human,'" the big man mumbled.

"You know that I trade in information, gentlemen,

ladies," the freezie mogul said. "That's what I made
my modest fortune before the unfortunate events of the
war."

"Modest" was an understatement; he had been one
of the world's richest men when the balloon went up.

"I gathered a great deal of information about the
world's military and security apparatus before the nukecaust," the tall, shaggy, pale man went on. "Of course I
was an intimate part of the United States security estab-
lishment. I knew, mostly by reason of participating in
software design on a number of black projects. Such as
the drug-war fortress in the Upper Amazon to which you
just alluded, and the Gateway project, and the covert
construction of the dome, which the present self-proclaimed Baron Lemuria occupied after the civil war
among the last-stage experimental barons and the perfected products. Dr. Mohandas Lakesh Singh was well
aware of the dome's construction. Inexplicably, I gather,
he neglected to inform you of its existence."

The Cerberus four traded a single dark look. None
of them trusted the immensely tall and strangely disor-
dered-looking magnate as far as Domi could throw him.
Yet by dire experience they didn't trust Lakesh much
further. Playing his cards close to his chest—even when
it meant withholding data upon which the success of a
vital mission, not to mention the survival of his ace operatives, might depend—was as close to a defining characteristic of the ancient whitecoat as his watery blue
eyes and ingratiating manner. Had Leviathan himself

just told them Lakesh was hosing them, they'd believe it sooner than otherwise.

Bates smiled bigger. Gilgamesh Bates could not really be said to understand people, but he knew how they worked fairly well. And like any good geek, anything he found worth doing, he did with obsessive perfectionism. So he did a better than passable job of reading other humans.

"Ah, I see," he said with transparently fake concern. "In any event, I can provide you the location of a fleet of undersea combat craft—small craft, and a small fleet, but superior to anything the Lemurians possess. And I can also provide you the implosion device I spoke of before."

"Why haven't you laid hands on these supersubs?" Grant asked. "Not to mention the bomb."

Bates laughed softly. It also rang false, like a counterfeit coin in a copper cup. "I haven't had any real cause to use them heretofore. And as you know, I am not myself the hands-on type."

"One thing I don't think I'm tracking here," Kane said to Old Tower. "Why should you care if Leviathan zeroes out the human race, or even the whole surface? You thought about doing it yourselves. You said so."

Old Tower remained unruffled by the accusation in Kane's voice. "We chose not. Now Leviathan threatens us the same."

"Leviathan our enemy," Rich-in-Sulfur said. "Wants wipe us out. Will!"

"The question is," Bates said, standing up, "do we

dare disregard what they're telling us? It seems hardly likely they have any motivation to lie."

"We don't have any idea what their motivations are," Grant said. "Why should they care if Leviathan bursts all our brains?"

Kane felt his comrades' eyes on him. "We can't really commit to anything," he told Old Tower.

Suspicion dawned. He turned to Bates. "What's in this for you, anyway?"

"Abstract concern for humanity?"

"Ha," Kane said, "ha."

"After all," the erstwhile tycoon said, "disruption of all life on Earth will hardly do me much good."

"Which translates," Grant subvocalized through their implants, "what fun is it to be megalomaniac if you don't have anyone to be mega over?"

"We pay," Rich-in-Sulfur said.

"Pay what?" Domi asked. "You told us we don't have many interests in common."

"We prepared to offer technology," Old Tower said. "Specifically, interstellar teleport. Specifically."

Kane felt as if the cable on his personal elevator had snapped. "What's that?"

"How we came here," Rich-in-Sulfur said. "To world. To lovely ocean bottom. Lovely, lovely!"

"That'd—" Kane passed a hand backward over his hair "—do it. Yeah."

"Speaking of which," Grant said, "how do we get out of here? Our ride seemed pretty well cemented in place back there. Plus if the Lemurians are lurking around out there waiting for us, there's no way we get past them in that damn bathtub."

"Our friends can return you to Cerberus the same way they brought me here," Bates said cheerfully. "By their own version of mat-trans."

They stared at him. He shrugged. "If they can teleport here from the stars," he said, "jumping us in and out should be child's play for them, yes?"

Chapter 22

"I thought that in the legends," Brigid said as she and Kane waited for their eyes to adjust to the gloom inside the shop, "when the heroes went off to consult the great and mysterious sage, it was supposed to be an arduous procedure."

"Christ, Baptiste," Kane said. He wore camou trousers and a sleeveless linen shirt and was trying hard not to feel naked. "Do you have to go borrowing trouble? Anyway, didn't the volcano bugs put us through enough bullshit?"

He still felt aggrieved that the alien colony creatures had made them go through the danger and hardship of fighting their way across the Pacific and down to their vent field when they could—as Old Tower subsequently admitted—readily have sent them coordinates so that they could have jumped directly into their undersea stronghold.

"You're right, Kane," she said. She had drifted toward a shelf of books with their hard spines darkened and cracked by age. She had her finger extended, trying to read their titles. He hoped she wouldn't take one down. They looked dusty, and the musty-smelling air was making his nose twitch as it was. "Still, this seems too easy."

"No such thing," Kane said.

A tinkling noise from the rear of the gloomy shop on a little island in the Pacific that had once probably been one of San Francisco's hills drew their attention. A pudgy form an inch shorter than Brigid pushed through a curtain of beaded strands hung with dozens of little tarnished brass bells.

He had a head like a smooth polished boulder with a fringe of gray Spanish moss, a pair of round glasses with impermeable sapphire lenses, a wide nose, cheeks appled in a smile of questionable antecedents, and a beard also of moss-gray, which was entirely dominated by an astonishing mustache like a pair of downward-angled foxtails.

He folded left hand over right fist before his breastbone and bowed. "Lady, gentleman. May I serve you?"

"Silas Wu?" Kane asked. "Dr. Silas Wu?"

The man stole forward. He wore faded jeans with blue suspenders over a gray-and-black check flannel shirt. He had a belly like a small Galapagos tortoise strapped to the front of him.

An eyebrow arched. "Do I face Magistrate's justice? The hour seems late for the service of a termination warrant."

"I don't know what you're talking about," Kane said levelly.

"You don't?" Crooked teeth showed in a little smile. "Once a Mag, always a Mag, my friend—the clues are plain for anyone with eyes. But I see that I mistake myself. You can only be the renegade Magistrate Kane."

He turned and bowed again to Kane's companion. "Which can only make you Brigid Baptiste. A pleasure to meet you."

"How do you know all this?" Kane demanded. He saw no mileage in denying anything.

"Information is my life, Mr. Kane," the man said, "as well as my business. My passion, one might even say. Strange to think that once it was thought that information was considered the new wealth, the new Comstock Lode. Now, I find that I have little competition, at least in my own little niche."

"I have no idea what you're talking about," Kane said. "But if you want payment, you'll have to let us know what."

Walking as if his feet—nails cracked and somewhat dirty in tire-rubber sandals—were sore, the proprietor tottered past the two and clambered up to perch on a stool behind the counter. He waved a hand around a room crowded with shelves of all kinds of indistinguishable trash, and a stuffed alligator hanging from the ceiling at such a height that its toothy fixed smile endangered Kane's head.

"I deal in many things as well as information," he said. "Herbs. Medicines. Ritual items of all sorts."

He crossed hands on the counter and leaned forward.

"As to what you can pay me, first tell me what I can do you for."

The expression made Kane blink. "We're looking for information on Leviathan," Brigid said.

"Of course you are," Wu said. He gestured toward a few other stools with cracked leather seats and stained wood and canvas director's chairs. "Sit."

They did. Kane moved gingerly in a not altogether successful attempt to keep the muzzles of the hand-blasters he wore in shoulder holsters in either armpit from clunking on the arms of the chair he chose. They were blocky black Glocks, with polymer grips and frames and ceramicized steel slides. He had chosen to wear them because, on the mainland, Sin Eaters worn openly were too distinctive, brought too much static. Basically only two classes of people on Earth packed them: Mags and baron blasters. It could be dangerous to have people assume you were either one.

Brigid carried her usual Heckler & Koch 9 mm Universal Service Pistol in a hip holster.

"So," Kane said, gesturing at the dusty clutter surrounding them, "all this is really, like, lost and found? I mean, the sign over the door reads Wu's Lost and Found Emporium."

"It is to the extent," Wu said with a smile, "that everything I stock is lost to its former owners and has found its way to me."

He picked up a skull of clear amberish crystal a little smaller than Kane's fist from the counter and began to polish it with a grimy-looking rag. Remarkably the rag did not succeed in smearing the object worse than it was.

"What specifically about Leviathan do you wish to know?" he asked, looking at what he was doing, not his guests. That they carried openly didn't seem to phase him. It wouldn't. Pretty much the only types of people in the Outlands you didn't see carrying weps were those too wretched to have them—or those hiding them.

Kane shrugged. He winced as one holstered hand-blaster made small scraping sounds on wood. "Everything."

Wu smiled. "There's half a billion years to talk about, son. I'm afraid you'd better be a little more specific."

"To start then, Doctor," Brigid said, "what do you mean, 'half a billion years'? Do you man the evolution of life-forms that produced Leviathan?"

"I refer to the creature's life span."

"You are not seriously suggesting the fucker's five hundred million years old," Kane rasped.

Wu had fastened on his head a band with a magnifying glass clamped to it, so he could swivel it before his right eye or away as he desired. He grinned beneath it at Kane. "No, Mr. Kane. I am *telling* you that according to our best intelligence, Leviathan is a spiral nautiloid who, as an individual, has survived for five hundred million years. You don't get that big overnight, son."

Kane blew out a long breath. Half disgusted, half… something. Awed? Disbelieving? All of the above?

"Can a single organism subsist for half a billion years?" Brigid asked.

"One has," Wu said. He was polishing the skull again.

"How is that possible?"

The round man shrugged a round shoulder. "Some creatures appear to continue living and growing until something kills them. Many dinosaur species are believed to have been that way. So are some modern carp. The point is that not everything dies of old age."

Wu held the skull up to the milky morning light dribbling in through water-stained windows. "Or maybe our Leviathan was an extraordinary individual, a freak—a mutant. Although I personally favor the hypothesis that he survived all these millennia on the basis of unbendable willpower alone."

"So he just kept eating," Kane said, "and getting bigger. And meaner. And smarter."

Wu nodded. "Precisely."

"What does he eat?" Kane asked. "Seems pretty damn desolate down there, except for the black smoker farms."

"Everything," Wu said, studying his artifact. "Everything that dies in the sea eventually falls. If you think about it, most things on land find their way to the sea, in time. The rains wash their remnants to the rivers, the rivers to the sea. Leviathan receives the tribute of the rivers. Desiring to be above all, he places himself beneath all. And so he thrives, and grows."

"Forgive me, Doctor," Brigid said, perching on her

stool as if she were too worked up to commit to just sitting on it, "but your biography seems to leave a very great deal unaccounted for."

"Very perceptive, Ms. Baptiste."

"How did he get to be—" she waved a hand in the air, seeming as much befuddled by the fact that words for once failed her as by the conundrum that had caused the meltdown "—the way he is?"

"Postulate that at some point our specimen developed a form of psi," Wu said, head back down and burningglass before his eye. "Perhaps it was the challenge of confronting a changing but ever hazardous environment, perhaps it was a natural development once his cortex reached some critical mass and threshold of neural connections. Or perhaps it was part and parcel of the mutation that led to his unimaginable longevity and size—there's no knowing. For all his inconceivable intellect and lore, the odds are very good that he himself does not know the truth.

"However it came about, he discovered within himself the power to influence other entities. To cause them to take action. Primarily, it would appear, through the induction and manipulation of fear. Again, whether this is the sole or the naturally strongest manifestation of his ability, or simply the one he has come to prefer, there is no way to tell."

He sighed and set down the skull. "My personal hypothesis is that fear is the very key to understanding him. He developed his gift out of fear. He ate until he grew to vast, and finally unchallengeable size, out of fear. He may have literally forced himself to become intelligent, so great was his fear. And he seeks, over time, to seize and exert power over all things of this Earth. Out of fear."

Kane looked at Brigid. Her eyes burned like emerald coals. His lips and throat were dry, his stomach a knot.

"I think," he said slowly and raspily, "that we both have an idea why you think that way."

"The dreams," Wu said, nodding. "For long and long has he worked through dreams."

"You're familiar with the dreams, then?" Brigid asked. Kane knew that, while tact wasn't normally a much greater part of her arsenal than his, she felt reluctance to ask the doctor to bare his soul to the extent of outright asking if he'd experienced the brutal nocturnal combinations of seduction and horror himself.

Wu nodded. "People are having them throughout the world," he said. "I listen, via shortwave and other means it is not necessary for you to know the particulars of." He had a very precise mode of speaking, almost exaggeratedly so, rather than any identifiable accent.

"There have been similar outbursts in the past," Wu said. "The recent wave of dreams is the most powerful I have discovered evidence of. And I must tell you, my young friends, I believe it is growing in strength and intensity. Which, indeed, I infer is why you have sought me out at this juncture, to ask me about Leviathan."

" 'The Call of Cthulhu'!" Brigid said. "That's what this worldwide epidemic of dreaming reminds me of.

I've been trying to put my finger on why it seemed familiar, the dream phenomenon."

"I thought you had an eidetic memory, Baptiste," Kane said.

"It's all there," Brigid said testily. "But I can't necessarily retrieve any given datum until I have sufficient referents to locate it."

"'The Call of Cthulhu' indeed." Wu nodded.

"But that's just a story," she said.

A smile. "So far as Mr. Howard Phillips Lovecraft believed," Wu said, "it was."

"But Lovecraft created the Cthulhu Mythos out of whole cloth."

"What makes you think Lovecraft invented the Cthulhu Mythos?" Wu asked.

"Well, we have certainly encountered elements that seem likely to have inspired bits and pieces of it," Brigid said.

"Indeed, indeed. I'm aware of them as well as you, of course. Better I daresay. But what I suggest is that Lovecraft had the mythos from the source itself—the mind of Leviathan."

Brigid frowned. "But didn't Lovecraft profess himself an extreme rationalist who didn't believe there was any truth whatsoever underlying his fantasies?"

"You give yourself too little credit. You know that for a fact, having perused Lovecraft's fictions and letters during your tenure in the Archives Division of Cobaltville. I've seen your dossier, Ms. Baptiste."

Brigid flushed. Kane scowled and crossed his arms. They already knew Wu had been a big crank in the baronies—like Lakesh, an architect of the new world order itself. And they knew that both Lakesh and Gil Bates had penetrated the nine baronies' databases pretty thoroughly. Still, he didn't like thinking of their backstories as common knowledge.

"Consider the possibility that Leviathan infected Lovecraft with the concepts and conceits he developed into the mythos," Wu said, "through the medium of dreams. Lovecraft was much concerned with dreams and their power—his writings make that abundantly clear. Who is to say that Leviathan sent him nightmares, and that Lovecraft recast them as his fictions?"

"You're saying Leviathan dictated his stories?"

"Not at all, Mr. Kane," Wu said with a smile. "Indeed, as far as I am able to ascertain, Lovecraft's details almost all miss the mark of reality. It's in their broad outlines—the conception of an ancient, Cyclopean horror—"

"With a squid face," Brigid said.

"Just so. It is in the outlines of the mythos that we glimpse the outlines of the truth of Leviathan. Nor there alone. A rather closer portrait of him appears under the very name Leviathan, in the 1970s science-fantasy Illuminatus! Trilogy, by Robert Shea and Robert Anton Wilson—"

"Yeah, that's great," Kane said. "But what does the bastard want?"

"He has maintained his cults for millennia," the mustached man said, setting aside the crystal skull he had been polishing with seeming regret. The empty eye sockets stared at Kane with prismatic ambiguity.

"He must work subtly and exercise patience. Long has he been patient. But he craves the hot blood, the wild passions of torture and fear. They nourish his soul, if you will, as the falling organic silt nourishes his body. So the wild cults he has fostered over the millennia have been his vice and his balm. And, of course, his tools."

"What about these fish guys?" Kane asked. "Do they belong to this Leviathan creature?"

"Yes and no," Wu said, boosting his saggy butt onto an old-fashioned bar stool covered in what Kane suspected was old, grease-darkened human skin. "All things are his, or so he believes, and when he puts the force of his will behind a command, so do I."

He took a pipe from somewhere inside his coat of many pockets, began tamping tobacco into a bowl carved in white clay or ivory to resemble a skull with ram's horns curling back along either side.

"But they are creations of Baron Lemuria," Wu said, putting the pipe in his mouth. "Of his pantropic science. As our scientists experimented with various land forms to produce organisms that might survive in the postnuke environment. Men as well as beasts."

"They're human, then?" Brigid said. It was actually inflected like a question.

Wu struck a match with a long cracked thumbnail,

sucked flame into the horned skull and puffed the pipe alight. "They are descended from men," he said through greenish smoke. Its sweet aroma made Kane's skin crawl. "There are fish genes grafted in, and whatnot. As the refugees were not barons of the first water, the scientists they took into exile with them weren't first-class, either."

He set the spent match down carefully in a tarnished brass ashtray. "And then again, Leviathan got the better of Baron Lemuria in that, as well. For the nets he cast in dreams caught him cult converts within the dome of Lemuria itself. Among these were the fish men. Indeed, I do believe all the fish men serve him, knowingly and gladly, for they hate their human masters, who treat them as animals and relegate to them the most unpleasant and dangerous tasks."

"How do you know all this stuff about Lemuriaville?"

Wu smiled beneath his extravagant down-sweeping mustache. "Like Leviathan—albeit in a far more modest way—I cast my nets wide."

He stood up. "And now I fear I must take leave of you. I've business to attend to."

"But, Dr. Wu there are questions we still need to ask you," Brigid said.

"We haven't yet discussed payment."

At the bell-beaded curtain Wu stopped, turned back, waved a pudgy hand. "Return tomorrow, my friends, and we will talk some more. And now I must ask that you excuse me. But because I like to leave my audiences wanting more, I leave you this tantalizing hint—you may be sure what schemes Leviathan has in train involve *energization*."

Chapter 23

"I can't believe," Grant said over the sounds of their passage, "they made us go through all that crap when they could've just jumped us straight in."

The noise of the wake churned up by their passage, almost luminous white in the diamond light of the stars, was louder than the purr of the motor driving the inflatable black Zodiac boat. "I thought you hated jumping," Domi said.

Ahead loomed a dark monolith with a jagged, angled top. Domi turned the tiller to steer well clear of the ruined skyscraper jutting from what had once been a part of downtown San Diego. Because he didn't much care for boats, Grant for once had given in to the albino woman's ceaseless importunings to be allowed to drive. She was doing a credible job, he had to admit. Still, it was all he could do to keep from tensing in the bow like a tomcat on a fence looking down at a Rottweiler for fear she'd do something wild-crazy. The Pacific wind was unseasonably cold in his face.

"I do," he admitted. "But this one didn't feel like most others. Smoother."

"Was," the girl agreed. She wore a black wet suit. The big man wore shadow armor, which served even better; it was watertight and insulated against environmental temperature, as well as more extreme phenomena.

The ocean opened beyond them. A strange cry issued from the shadow depths of the gutted skyscraper stub. Reflexively Grant aimed his suppressed MP-5 at it.

Domi glanced down to check the backlit screen of the little satellite-fed map display. Their objective lay about eight miles dead ahead. She opened the throttle and the Zodiac accelerated, lifted its prow out of the water and began to bang across the long slow ocean swells. Grant let the blaster hang by its sling and grabbed a handhold. He said nothing, not wanting to give her the satisfaction.

"Be a piece of cake," she said. "You're just a big worry-butt. You'll see."

"WE SHOULD BE WARY," Lakesh said, "of taking what the good Dr. Wu says too seriously."

"You mean about how Leviathan mebbe influenced the Archon Directorate over the years?" Kane said, sipping coffee. "You're the one sent us to talk to him."

He and Brigid sat side by side at a table in the commissary. It was deserted on this late-night shift—not that sidereal time meant anything in the eternal false sunshine within Cerberus Redoubt—but for them, Sally Wright, who perched like a bespectacled gray ghost on a counter, and Lakesh himself, who paced as he often did when he spoke. It seemed to enhance his pleasure in listening to the sound of his own voice.

"He is the greatest authority on the curious phenomenon known to legend as Leviathan," Lakesh said, his hands clasped behind his white-coated back. "However, over decades of study interest turned to obsession. It affected his judgment, I very much fear. His sense of balance, of perspective, you know."

"You never told us anything about this Leviathan before," Kane said.

"I encountered no mention of such a creature in my researches," Brigid said. She was drinking green tea from a beige mug with a hairline crack down the side.

Lakesh stopped and looked at her with his head tipped to one side. When he struck that pose he looked like nothing so much as a curious baby bird.

"Why, dear Brigid, you fail for a rare occasion to speak with your customary precision! You yourself reported mentioning having read of Leviathan in the Shea and Wilson trilogy of novels."

"Forgive me, Dr. Lakesh," she said, speaking with more than her customary precision. "I should have said, I encountered no mention of such a creature as anything but a legend or a fictional device. I encountered nothing, in other words, to indicate that Leviathan was real. No hint indeed that any such being existed."

"For all the infinite capacity of that perfect memory of yours," Lakesh said, "stored beneath those radiant red-gold locks, for all the zeal with which you pursued your research duties in Cobaltville and afterward, there are many areas to which your attention has never been directed. Even you have but twenty-four hours in a day, dear child, so that there remains and always shall, far more data stored outside your lovely head than in it."

"Also," she said, still crisply, "the Directorate and then the Trust presumably didn't want to encourage unauthorized persons to speculate about the existence of such a formidable rival to their own power."

"If you knew about this Leviathan," Kane said, "why didn't you try to take it out? Him out? Whatever." He was referring to Lakesh in the days when he was a trusted operative of the Archon Directorate.

Lakesh smiled thinly. "There was much debate as to whether he really did exist," he said. "There was also, although never voiced openly, some doubt as to whether we could do anything to him. So my colleagues overall preferred to deal with him as with the proverbial tiger in the drawing room—pretend he didn't exist. If it should even eventuate that he does."

"Oh, he does," Kane said. "Unless those hoodoos were showing us some top-quality computer-graphics imagery."

"They certainly possess the ability to generate false imaging of any desired quality or subject," Brigid said.

"Indeed they do," Lakesh said, "but, without attempting to speculate as to their possible motivations for doing so, I think we can take it as given that the video they showed you of Leviathan attempting to attack their colonies was real."

"I reckon it was, myself," Kane said.

"I am inclined to believe so, as well," Brigid said.

"I provisionally regard his existence as proved. The dreams you and others have reported over the past few weeks tend to substantiate the accounts given you by both Wu and the vent organisms."

Kane took another hit of his coffee and sprawled back in his chair. "What's the story with this Wu character, anyway?"

"He grew frankly cracked on the subject of Leviathan," Lakesh said. "He began to evolve increasingly crackpot theories—such as that Leviathan was the secret controller of all events on Earth, manipulating the Archons and even the Tuatha de Danaan and the Annunaki by playing upon their emotions—all with the goal of strengthening himself through a form of psychic vampirism that feeds upon fear and pain. Indeed, that Leviathan was continuing to manipulate us."

Lakesh smiled thinly. "Needless to say, such speculation was unwelcome. At last he was allowed—encouraged, in fact, albeit indirectly—to flee into exile."

"It isn't easy," Brigid said through the steam rising off her mug, "to concoct conspiracy theories wilder than reality."

"You got that right, Baptiste." Kane laughed. "Why didn't you just hang a termination warrant on his neck and have done with it?"

"It was argued by many, myself included, that he remained a potentially useful tool, of a kind far too rare to waste," Lakesh said with a sigh. "Alive in exile, he was still available to us at need. Provided, of course, that he succeeded in staying alive.

"It may be that sentiment did not fail to play a role in that decision."

Normally, for all the florid and precious affectations of his speech, Lakesh harbored as much sentiment as a cinder block. Although he had to have possessed some actual sentimentality, or else he would never have been sufficiently appalled by the Archon Directorate's actions to begin planning to betray them, not long after being awakened from his frozen sleep. Unless, of course, it was merely incipient megalomania that caused Lakesh to strike out on his own, first morally and eventually in physical fact. As Kane sometimes suspected.

"But if he's so unreliable," Brigid said, "why is it necessary that we interview him?"

"Because we need to know whatever we can to deal with a half-billion-year-old lobster the size of a battleship," Kane said.

"Nautilus," Brigid corrected. "Spiral nautilus."

"Whatever. He's still militant seafood that can give people nightmares on the other side of the world. He's reaching into *our* heads, Baptiste. He's screwing with *our* souls. And we basically, of this moment, know dick."

"Inelegantly put, friend Kane," Lakesh said, "but cogent withal."

He stood up and stretched, enjoying the way Lakesh cringed lest his slop coffee from his cup. It was empty anyway.

"Okay," he said, "we go back tomorrow and see what more we can get out of this mad scientist of yours."

"Researcher," Lakesh corrected. "He was never, strictly speaking, scientifically trained."

"He's a crazed whitecoat," Kane said. "That's the story of this suffering old world of ours right there, isn't it? It all comes down to another fused-out whitecoat."

"One thing," Sally Wright said timidly, as she always did. "Since he didn't yet name a price for cooperation, you might consider taking him a bottle of some sort of liquor from our stores."

Kane flicked a glance at Brigid, who had likewise stood. "Don't tell me he's a soak, too," he said.

"He was partial to strong drink," Lakesh said, "which was unusual at his level. Nonetheless, if he's become alcoholic, that's a new development."

He took off his glasses, cleaned them with a handkerchief, peering over top of them at Brigid's assistant, and stand-in when Brigid was in the field. "Have you come into possession of information regarding Dr. Wu's current status of which I'm unaware, Sally dear?"

Sally's gray cheeks went pink and she looked down at the floor. "No, sir. I just thought it would make a good gift. And even if he doesn't drink it himself, he can always trade it on advantageous terms. I'm sorry, Dr. Lakesh, if I've said something wrong...."

"Not at all," Lakesh beamed. "What do you think, Kane?"

The tall lupine man shrugged. "Sounds like a plan to me," he said. "Besides, I always trust info more when I've paid for it."

They started toward the door. Sleep had not been in abundant supply recently. Kane was just as glad Wu had fobbed them off till the following day, given them a chance to jump back to Cerberus, get a shower and a hot meal, sleep in a real bed.

He wondered briefly how Grant and Domi were doing. About the same as usual, no doubt.

At the door to the corridor he stopped and turned back. "How're you doing with the simulator software Bates blipped us?" he asked Lakesh.

"I have personally insured that it contains no back doors or other unpleasant surprises," the whitecoat said. "We have some of our techs trying it out. Initial reports are positive. Will you try it tonight?"

"No," Kane said. "I'm going to bed."

THE SENTRY WALKED along the barren ridge with his musket slung over his shoulder by a length of grimy hemp rope. It was a bare heave of sandstone, highest point on what the legends said had once been no island at all, but part of the mainland.

The sentry spared little thought for such things. All that mattered was preserving the holy secrets. Why or what for—such questions were not encouraged among the faithful. Those who doubted the sacred mission were weeded out ruthlessly in childhood.

That none knew the blessed secrets, not even the shamans, did not trouble the sentry. What else, after all, were secrets?

He trudged on, peering out into the blankness of the Cific with his small, weak, blue eyes.

WHEN HE HAD GONE, down the gradually declining knee toward the end of the island, two forms slipped over the crest of the hill in his wake. First a small, slight figure. Then one taller and bulkier, especially above the waist.

"Where's that entry Bates told us about?" Domi asked quietly as they both dropped into the lee of a weathered granite boulder. Like Grant she had a balaclava on her head, the bottom rolled like a stocking cap. If they had to get close to any bad guys out here in the dark, they'd roll them down and bless the fact the sea breeze was cool, more than they were already. Until and unless it became necessary to reduce the reflectivity of their faces, they'd leave them rolled up. The things made it hard to breathe and quickly got spit-logged, making them even harder to suck wind through and smell bad into the bargain.

Grant jerked his head. "'Bout twenty, twenty-five yards that way."

"What if some of the cultists are waiting down there?"

"We take our chances." Grant held his MP-5 muzzle

up toward the mostly cloudless sky. "And they take theirs."

He grimaced. "Just what we need, more cultists. We're ass-deep in cultists on this mission."

"Least these're different cultists."

The people they'd talked to on the mainland, at a little fishing and trading community called San Juan De-Marco, said the island was inhabited by a sect that guarded it with fanatical zeal and neither came to the mainland to trade nor permitted traders to visit the island. Well, that wasn't quite right: what they said was that they never permitted anyone who landed there to leave. Alive, anyway. Legend had it that the cultists descended from the security garrison that protected the facility at the time the balloon went up for the nukecaust. It was a common enough story, enacted in a number of places, and not just in and around North America.

It seemed likely enough. The male sentry who'd walked by had worn what looked in the starlight like an oft-patched olive drab blouse, oversized and hanging far down pale bare legs above bare feet. What, if anything, he wore beneath neither had a clue. Not even the usually prurient Domi felt much interest in knowing: he hadn't smelled so good walking by—and had never gotten within five yards of where they crouched behind some scrub.

With Grant overwatching, suppressed Heckler & Koch machine pistol ready at his shoulder, Domi slipped toward the opening he indicated. A small hump of sandy soil and a clump of brush masked it from where he sat.

She darted noiselessly toward it and vanished. A quick scowl of annoyance washed across his face. Bad field-craft to get out of his field of view. But that was Domi.

A moment later her head popped up, face glowing white between black cap and black pullover. She held up a thumb and then gestured for him to hurry up. He glanced quickly around to make sure he was alone, then complied.

He went over the top of the hump and dropped a yard to a soft three-point landing on a pool of soft sand collected in a small bowl-shaped depression. From the midst of it a concrete cylinder jutted like a decapitated giant mushroom, three feet high and about four broad. A round metal hatch, white paint peeling from long exposure to the sun, was set in the center of it. It had a handwheel on top about two feet in diameter.

"Subtle," he said.

"Mebbe they used to have a shack here or something to cover it up. Lotta things coulda happened to it."

"What, aside from a world war, killer earthquakes, killer waves and a couple centuries? No big thing, girl."

She grinned and fisted him gently in the ribs. Not all that gently, really—her sense of play was that of the wild young predator she still was at base. But he showed no reaction. Just grinned back and bent to see if by working the wheel nice and slowly he could open the hatch noiselessly. Domi crouched, watching him with her own MP-5 across her thighs.

Behind them, a dozen forms rose from the brush and slipped over the ridge, as silent as shadows.

Chapter 24

Grant had just felt the lock disengage beneath the hatch when he heard a pebble roll down a short slope and land in the sand with a soft plop. A heartbeat earlier he wouldn't have heard it for the muted squeal-rumble of the mechanism.

"Damn," he said aloud. He already knew there was no more point in keeping quiet.

Quicker or maybe just keener eared, Domi had already swiveled to bring up her MP-5 and swept their attackers with an extended burst.

Pale shapes leaped over the bush at the back rim of their little hole in the hilltop. They wore rags and shreds of what looked like military kit. She raked them with a single long burst. Several fell howling and thrashing. One or two others fell and didn't do much more to speak of.

A man with a dark rag tied around a brush cut head clubbed the MP-5 from Domi's hands, paler even than his own, with the barrel of his musket. It rang like a bell. Grant hoped the MP-5's integral suppresser hadn't bent. Those blasters could produce some pretty spectacular failure events when fired after something like that happened to them.

He had the butt-piece of his own extended stock to his shoulder and fired a triburst. The man's head came apart, and he slumped motionless.

Hands clutched at Domi. She squalled like an angry cat. One attacker reeled away, clutching at a slashed throat that squirted blood like a ruptured fire hose. A second went down screaming louder than the outraged albino girl, kicking as if to free his skinny white legs from the greasy, starlight-shiny loops of his own guts entangling them.

By this time Grant had dropped two more cultists with controlled tribursts to the head as they jumped over the bush, conveniently silhouetting themselves against the starry sky. Domi went down kicking and thrashing under a rush of assailants.

Grant raked his blaster in a long right-to-left burst at a level higher than Domi's close-cropped head would be if she were standing.

As cultists dropped away, Domi jumped up and tried to run, her face a mask of what Grant hoped was other people's blood. She darted to the side.

A hand grasped the thick barrel of Grant's MP-5. He heard a small sizzle of sound, smelled cooking meat cutting through the sour reek of the bodies surging around him. The cultist screamed falsetto and tried to yank his hand away. Unfortunately his palm and fingers had gotten stuck to the hot shroud of the integral suppresser.

Those bastards got hot when you fired them a lot. The H&K machine pistol fired from a closed bolt, making it far more accurate than the more usual open-bolt blowback submachine gun. But the H&K also didn't bleed heat nearly as well, and with the suppressor shroud building up heat from retarding the flow of all those hot propellant gases, the blaster could overheat and shut down fast in a real firefight.

Grant ducked his head, letting the sling slip over it. He let the cultist have the piece. Little as he seemed to want it—shrieking and prancing and swinging his arm around as if the sleeve of his blouse was on fire and he was trying to put it out. Grant felt a flash of surprise; the metal shouldn't be sticking to him that hard, and the seared skin should tear away fairly readily. Mebbe the pain and nerve damage had sent his hand into some kind of cramp reflex and he couldn't open it.

Grant put out his arm and made a fist. The Sin Eater strapped to his forearm slipped into his hand and instantly made much most satisfying sound and noise and big dancing fire. It wasn't even close to being quiet, but you didn't have to worry about it going all temperamental on you if you had to chill a bunch of fused-out attackers in a hurry.

The depression was full of smell and jostling bodies. Grant saw Domi's legs caught from behind in a tackle that planted her face just shy of the top of the bowl. Grant slashed the blazing handblaster as if it were a sword in front of him, drawing a figure eight of yellow flame before him in the night.

Sudden impact jarred the left side of his head. Supernovae exploded into galaxies of whirling white-and-crimson sparks behind his eyes. A club of some kind, a musket butt, maybe. He had no way of telling.

Trying to ignore the slow barrel rolls in his stomach, he pivoted toward the attack, bringing up his left arm both to fend off a second strike and clear the muzzle of the Sin Eater, which he triggered in a triburst from hip level with his elbow locked against the tip of his pelvis for stability.

The muzzle-flare illuminated a very surprised face painted in red stripes, possibly blood, and a pair of arms raised to strike again with a silvery chunk of driftwood. The local hollered and sprayed and died.

But it seemed there were plenty where he came from. A pair of arms draped Grant from behind, tangling his burly upper arms. A nose streaming blood or snot was pressed against the back of his neck, and thunder breath like a fumarole enfolded the left side of his face and stung like a caustic.

He brought his left hand up in a back fist to the face. A crunch, the head snapped back. The chill trickle down Grant's neck was replaced by a warm gush of blood.

Before he could turn to deal with the disoriented attacker behind him, another darted in to make a grab for the Sin Eater. Either lucky or learning a quick lesson from the guy with the H&K stuck to him, this attacker stayed away from the perforated muzzle shroud. Instead his black-nailed, almost taloned hand snatched the box magazine right out of the front well.

The Sin Eater did *not* fire from a closed bolt. That meant no chambered round. When the trigger was pulled the heavy bolt slammed forward and sucked the top cartridge off the magazine stack. That meant all the bullets had gone away with their happy little house, and Grant was holding a hot, unwieldy club.

Snarling a curse, Grant spun and slashed the blaster transversely across the blood-spurting face of the cultist who'd grabbed him from the rear. The steel lip of the violated magazine well cut his right eyebrow adrift from its mooring. It dropped like a sort of forlorn broken wing in front of the eye, with attendant sprays of blood. The cultist staggered away shrieking like an air-raid siren and trying to stick various components of his face back together.

More arms grabbed Grant from behind, this time in a tight bear hug. "Jesus," he roared, "don't you guys know when you're beat?"

He slammed his head back into the face of the man holding him from behind. But the man had lowered his head, and the back of Grant's head cracked against his forehead. He saw more stars. Pretty much a tie.

Then others swarmed him and bore him down, then trussed him firmly in hairy, fish-smelling rope. The steel hatch was opened. He and Domi were borne down into darkness.

"KANE," HE RESPONDED, sitting up in bed rubbing his face.

"Urgent message for you, sir," the wall said. The

voice on the intercom was young, oddly deferential, unknown to Kane's conscious mind. A Manitius tech he didn't know? One of the outlanders brought in for training and force augmentation? Place is getting too big, he thought.

"It's Grant and Domi—their biolink transponders indicate they're in trouble."

GRANT ROLLED HIS EYES. The chamber beneath the hill extended in a hemisphere well beyond the dubious reach of the light cast by smoky torches. It had to have occupied a sizable percentage of the whole island. But not the whole thing by any means—as Grant knew well.

A concrete waterway bisected the cavern, running out through a thirty-foot tunnel to a semicircle of dark that was just lighter than the dark of the dripping stone walls at that point. Apparently it just opened right out onto the broad Pacific. Presumably at one point the outer entrance had been sealed or at least masked for security.

These days, Grant guessed, any explorers or pirates, to the extent the two professions differed in this brave new world and this little happy corner of it, who let their curiosity drive them inside the sea cave ended up right about where he and his slim albino companion were.

And where they were going, unless events took a drastically different turn in a hell of a hurry.

Thirty yards away from the captives, in front of concrete doors as tall as a four-story building, the native islanders held a ritual by the light of a couple of great big bonfires. They had to have raided or traded big time for all the fuel, as there wasn't enough brushwood on the little island to have accounted for all the torches, much less the fires.

Grant's fingers continued to pluck relentlessly at the wet ropes securing his wrists behind his back. The reduced circulation made them numb and responsive as so many sausages. But that was probably a blessing, because he guessed he'd long since ripped the skin off the tips of them.

What looked like random slabs of busted concrete had been piled into a sort of dais on the platform to the left of the huge doors. A matching platform ran about forty yards down the far side. Apparently it had constituted some kind of dock for the hidden facility at one time.

"Hooah!" the apparent high priest screeched, flinging skinny arms into the air. He wore a loincloth, apparently random smears of body paint whose color Grant couldn't make out in the torchlight but looked way too suggestive of semifresh blood, and a headdress in what he took to be the semblance of a bald eagle.

"Hooah!" the faithful howled in ecstatic response. Their collective shout echoed from the unseen walls.

"Hail to'uh chief!" the priest screamed.

"Hail!" Grimy pallid right arms shot forward with hands extended, palm down.

Grant grimaced and turned his head to Domi, who lay on her side facing him, her face fisted in concentration.

"How long you figure this nutcake ritual will go on?" he asked her.

She opened her eyes to glare at him. She looked feral and intimidating in the torchlight, like an angry albino weasel. "What you think I am?" she snapped. "You think my people like this? Huh?"

She was reverting to her clipped Outlander speech as she did under times of stress.

"Don't bust my balls, girl. If either of us knows anything here it's you. Talk to me."

She scowled and her shoulders continued to work inside her black pullover. They had not been searched; only the visible blasters had been removed. Which meant that their trans-comms in their special sealed pouches were still in place, as were the bone-conduction microphones and speakers fastened to their throats and behind their ears by special adhesives.

"Dunno 'bout savages like this," she spit. "But looks like they havin' fun. This big social occasion them, like fiesta. Gotta draw it out, long's they can. No TV here, long time."

It wasn't good news, but it was the closest facsimile they were likely to get.

SITTING BOLT UPRIGHT in his bed, Kane stared without seeing at the wall of his small compartment. A low amber night-light glowed along one baseboard so the occupant would be able to see in an emergency without having to turn the lamp on; otherwise it would've been dark as the inside of a black hole in this sealed room in the middle of a mountain peak.

The nearest jump spot accessible to interphaser was eighteen miles from Grant and Domi's current location, with a good sixty miles of open water intervening.

"Manta," Kane said aloud, referring to the transatmospheric craft they'd gotten from Manitius Base. "Baptiste and I can dump her in the water right outside the cave there and either swim in or use an inflatable."

Chapter 25

"Hooah!" screamed the multitudes.

"Your ass," Grant grunted sotto voce.

He and Domi lay facing each other on their sides on a slab of concrete about two yards by three, maybe a foot thick and relatively level, right in front of a small door set into the sheer concrete wall that flanked the huge doors. Grant was trying real hard not to think about the implications of the brown crusty stains like lichen growths beneath them, or the lingering aroma of old death that swam in his head and kept his stomach churning.

At least they hadn't been knocked out. That usually meant subdural hematoma, which under these circumstances meant death as surely as decapitation, and only a touch more slow. If that was a blessing and not a curse... Grant tried real hard not to think about human-sacrifice techniques they'd had the happy privilege of viewing worldwide, in the Valley of Mexico and elsewhere....

"There!" Domi said, a soft explosion of satisfaction.

"What?" Grant asked. He didn't bother whispering. The high priest stood barely five yards away with his back to them and his unlovely face to the less-lovely crowd. The ceremony was clearly working its way to a crescendo. Which approached rapidly; the faithful were starting to get mighty hoarse and would be all out of voices any time now.

"Roll over," the albino girl said.

"What?"

"Just do it," she hissed fiercely.

The locals seemed to pay them no attention. The high priest was capering around waving what appeared to be an ancient baby doll, cracked and naked, on the end of a stick with a bunch of feathers. The mob responded to his screeching with howls that were almost intelligible as some degraded kind of English.

Seeing no risk, Grant obeyed. That gave him his first really good look at their captors of the evening.

The priest, Grant now saw, had six fingers on one hand and seven on the left. A lot of the faces turned adoringly toward him had receding chins and bulbous foreheads. A sizable proportion had noticeable hare lips. The arms they were waving ecstatically at the air were tipped often as not with hands sprouting extra fingers, and sometimes two or three fingers that seemed grown together like partial mittens. "Are these fuse-jobs taints, too?"

"No," Domi said. "Not rad damage. Inbreeding. Been fucking each other, ten generations. Cousin-cousin, brother-sister. Mebbe mom-son daddy-daughter. Stop squirming."

"Huh," said Grant, who was unaware he had been squirming. "What're you doing back there?"

As if in answer he felt the rope that bound his wrists relax.

"Roll on back!" Domi ordered. "Right now!"

He did. She already lay supine, looking as trussed and helpless as an old-time melodrama heroine on a railroad track. Grant had never seen any of those old-time melodramas, way in the past by skydark; Brigid had shown him cartoons parodying them, for reasons he'd long since mislaid.

"How'd—?" he began.

"Shut it," Domi whispered.

The high priest came prancing up to them, shaking his doll and chanting. His overpowering sour-foul body preceded his coming into view. He leaned over the captives, still to all appearances safely tied up, giving Grant a good look at his face. Up close his painted bald-eagle headpiece looked even cruder. It might have been made of mud smeared badly on a rude frame and painted by somebody with the aesthetic sense of a drunken sow and the hand-eye coordination of a long-term jolt-walker.

Then the priest danced away, toward the human-sized door set next to the ones that shut off the waterway. They were so awesomely proportioned that the ordinary door looked like an afterthought or an accident beside them. He began to make passes in front of the keypad beside the door with his six-fingered free hand.

"How did you do that, girl?" Grant said. "I know they

got that saw-back knife of yours. You gutted some of 'em with it, and not even these pukes are that damn dumb." Although he spoke the last without particular conviction.

She grinned at him. "Swiss Army knife," she said. "Found it one time, few gigs back. Pretty toy. Useful, too."

Suddenly they were surrounded by pale misshapen bodies, each elbowing the others to get close to the makeshift altar. Their weird hands clutched an assortment of knives, some rusty-bladed Ka-bars and hunting knives, some machetes, others seeming flaked from stone.

The priest jumped up on the altar between the two captives. His six-fingered hand now clutched a knife with a strange curved blade. It might have been an Arab kindjal or a linoleum knife; Grant couldn't tell in the uncertain light.

"Kiwemaw!" the priest screeched, throwing his head back so far the eagle-head hat wobbled dangerously and holding blade and fetish up so hard his skinny arms trembled with effort. "Le'gawsordem oud!"

"Le'gawsordem oud!" the faithful responded ecstatically.

Grant kicked out straight-legged. His foot struck the priest between the shoulder blades. He seemed unnaturally light, or maybe Grant's system was just that far into adrenaline overdrive. The priest went flying with a shriek even less articulate than his usual, flailing arms and legs until he hit the wall face-first with a smack clearly audible over the sudden hush of the crowd.

Grant arched his back, thrusting his pelvis toward the distant shadow-hidden ceiling. Then he jackknifed powerfully, snapping himself up onto his feet on the slab.

The mob had recoiled at the utterly unexpected attack on their high priest. Now growling like animals, they closed in.

Letting the ropes Domi had severed with her pocketknife uncoil down around him like a dying constrictor, Grant raised his big muscled arms above his head.

An especially large adversary jumped up to confront Grant toe-to-toe. He was almost as tall as the former Magistrate. For all his bulk his head was still disproportionately large beneath its blond crew cut, with a bulging forehead overhanging a button nose, almost-MIA chin and goggling blue eyes one of which looked fully twice the size of the other. For all the mushroom pallor of his skin, so unlike the bleached and polished bone perfection of Domi's, he was as wide in shoulder and chest as Grant, as well.

Having seen him as he started his leap, Grant met him with an overhand right. Lined up with his radius to transmit maximum kinetic energy, the latter three knuckles of his fist drove into the outsized forehead with an audible crunch. The mismatched eyes rolled up, showing half-yellowed whites, as if looking at the unmistakable dent above them. The cultist toppled over backward.

"Hold 'em," Grant said to Domi.

"Easy you to say!" she snarled as he leaped off the slab—right toward the smaller doorway.

He began to stab a forefinger at the buttons, from which any kind of identifying numbers or legends had long been rubbed or otherwise eroded, as Domi shucked her own severed bonds and grabbed the wrist behind a knife poked tentatively at her. She rolled away from her attacker, into the slab's center, locking out the attacker's elbow over her own right upper arm. Her momentum easily supplied the necessary pressure to snap the joint like a celery stalk.

The cultist understandably shrieked and even more understandably released the knife. Domi grabbed it up and rolled back, slashing at the man. He jumped back hollering, clutching and spurting.

She leaped onto her feet and ran to stand behind Grant's back, where she crouched, slashing like a cornered panther at any who came near.

Somewhere deep down in the earth beneath them, a rumble as long-dormant machinery groaned and ground to life. A thunk as of God's own front door closing vibrated through the soles of Domi's black low-top athletic shoes.

With a suppressed squeal, the gigantic concrete doors slowly parted.

"I HOPE WE'RE NOT TOO LATE," Brigid said as Kane finished fitting the small electric motor to the stern of the little self-inflating boat riding on the swell a hundred yards from the cave mouth in the gray dawn light. Whether by accident or design, it was hard to see from open water, by reason of a frowning overhang and a couple of tide-rounded rocks jutting from the water in front of it.

The blazing yellow boat wasn't hard to see, since it had originally been designed to make ditched aircrew easy for rescue aircraft to spot. But they hadn't exactly been in a position to be choosy mounting this slam-dunk rescue mission. Kane settled himself in the stern, gingerly, to keep from upsetting the inflatable. He didn't want to risk dumping the gear in the heavy packs that were driving the little boat dangerously low in the water, even though they were tethered to the boat. They were coming loaded for bear.

Their Manta TAV bobbed on the waves behind them. Kane had put it down in a vertical landing as near the cave mouth as he dared for fear of bending the airframe and busting their necks, which would do their imperiled comrades no good at all. They might have swum the intervening distance, though neither was a distance swimmer. But the little boat would get them more quickly to the cavern mouth. And what with all the sharks and killer dolphins they'd encountered the past week or so, Kane was not all that eager to spend more time in the Pacific's greasy green embrace than absolutely necessary.

"We're about to find out," Kane said grimly, steering them to the near side of the half-hidden cave mouth.

WITH A COLLECTIVE GASP and gushing of drool from awe-slackened jaws the holy guardians of the underground base fell back.

"Just what I thought," Grant muttered to himself in satisfaction. "Inbred idiots had no more idea how to open their holy of holies than they have how to read."

He strode past Domi, who was suddenly menacing a slowly widening semicircle of empty air with her blade. He held his big arms up and out.

"Listen to me!" he declaimed in a voice that boomed like thunder from the distant stone walls. "The ancient prophecy is come to pass! Long has it been foretold," he said in a voice that rang like a trumpet, "that a mighty black warrior and a beautiful white goddess would arrive to open the holy place and lead the people into the cleansing light of day!

"Well, that day has come."

"WHAT THE FUCK," Kane said, "over?"

More because he thought his greater mass would stabilize the little balloon boat better than out of any sense of gallantry, Kane sat still while Brigid daintily clambered onto the concrete apron next to Grant and Domi. Then he let Brigid reach a hand back and help him ashore.

"Good heavens," the flame-haired former archivist said, waving a hand in front of her face. "Personal hygiene does not appear to be included in the ancient lore of these people, does it?"

"You and Domi were supposed to be lying on an altar having your chests carved open," Kane said aggrievedly. He covered the groveling multitude with an

M-60 E3, a .308 machine-gun variant of the warhorse M-60 designed for the U.S. Marine's Force RECON, with a chopped-down barrel and gas tube and a pistol-style foregrip. The 105-round belt of linked cartridges was looped over one shadow-suited shoulder. Brigid carried a Street Sweeper shotgun, pump action with a fat drum magazine. They had prepared rapidly for this mission, but they had come seriously prepared.

"Change of plans," Domi said brightly.

"Disappointed, Kane?" Grant said with an uncharacteristically huge grin splitting his face.

"How did you accomplish—" Brigid waved her free hand again, this time indicating the worshippers, who moaned sacramental gibberish as they prostrated themselves "—this?"

"Told 'em all about how the ancient prophecy was fulfilled."

"About the great black warrior and beautiful white goddess," Domi said.

Kane turned to his partner. "What prophecy? How did you know what prophecy these slaggers had?"

"Didn't. I made it up on the spot, Kane." He waved at the portal into the inner island, now yawning open for what had to be presumed the first time since the nuke-caust. "I opened up their inner sanctum for 'em. Major miracle. After that they were in a frame of mind to believe whatever I told 'em."

"Even an ancient prophecy none of them had even *heard* before?"

"Look at them, Kane. They're inbreds. Among them I figure they about got the sense to pour piss out of a boot with the instructions printed on the heel. Which makes me and Domi look triple stupe, getting caught out by them. But they're sneaky bastards—give 'em that."

He gestured grandly at the great opening. "But take a look at the prize that was waiting for us behind door number one."

Perhaps it was because the dimensions of this outer cavern were concealed in shadows that firelight could only feebly shove back, but the chamber beyond the gates seemed to have a lower ceiling. From it blazed white lights powered from an ancient generator that had awakened in obedience to the code—provided by Gil Bates—Grant had punched into the outer keypad.

The waterway ran on into it. A craft rested on a framework of massive vanadium steel struts above it. Not a craft such as they were expecting to see—a small, agile submersible—but a long gleaming spun-titanium torpedo studded with strange pods like longitudinal blisters.

"It's an undersea carrier," Kane said.

"So it is," Grant said. "I reckon that when we check it out the little undersea fighter craft we were promised will be tucked away all safe and neat inside those bubble things."

"Bates actually told the truth," Brigid said in tones of wonder.

"And somehow," Kane said, "that makes me trust him less."

The others looked at him. "I don't know why," he admitted. "I just feel in my gut that he's got some kind of sting waiting for us at the end of this."

Grant's face started to reassume its more typical scowl. "Point man's instinct?"

"Just about."

Grant shrugged. "Well, let's go check out our shiny new toy. Who knows, mebbe the faithful here might actually turn out to be of some use."

"I doubt," said Domi.

Chapter 26

The sea surface boiled outward in a ring away from the thrust of the Manta's maneuvering jets, tilted downward for vertical descent. A close approach by air followed by a water landing had worked for their first island appointment of the day. So Kane figured it would serve him and Baptiste for a return visit to Dr. Silas.

Kane set the craft down with considerable more gentleness than he had the first time today. Then with the craft rocking gently they reinflated their gaudy yellow boat and used it to putt to a landing on the white sand of the spit.

IT SEEMED EVEN GLOOMIER in the shop today than it had yesterday. Brigid's nose wrinkled. "Did it smell this much like fish yesterday?"

"Dunno. My nose is still overloaded by the assault it underwent earlier, down south." For a fact, though, Kane did notice a strong smell of fish. Along with something else the fish reek seemed to be doing a good job of masking.

They had left Grant cooing and clucking like a

mother hen over the wondrous undersea fighter craft. His odoriferous flock, now listless and docile, had been content to hang in the background and gaze adoringly at him and Domi.

"Anybody home?" Kane asked as he and Brigid moved cautiously through the cluttered aisles toward the rear.

Although he and Brigid had left their heavyweight crowd-control longblasters in their ride, Kane was well-heeled, just the way he had been yesterday: his pair of boxy Glock handblasters with extralong mags, riding in open-carry holsters under each arm. Brigid had her USP in its Kydex combat rig at her waist.

"Here we go," Kane said. He had caught sight of the whitecoat's dumpy form, indistinct through the bead-and-bell-hung strands that formed a curtain between the front and back rooms. He walked more assertively toward the divider with Brigid trailing dubiously behind.

Something tickled his subconscious before he stretched a hand to the beaded curtain. Before he heard the buzz of busy flies. Before he smelled a tang unmistakable even through the thickening odor of fish.

He stretched a bladed hand and parted the strands with a tinkle.

"Oh," Brigid said.

It wasn't the dumpy doctor who stood there, but what Kane guessed was a tailor's dummy. But it was wearing the doctor's tie-dyed lab coat.

Also his skin.

His face had been stretched over a brass globe, his heavy-rimmed eyeglasses perched askew on his nose, itself askew.

Across a heavy butcher-block table to the right was sprawled a shocking-red parody of a human body. Its lidless eyes gaped, its lipless mouth opened in a frozen scream, its arms and legs were outstretched and its back was arched.

Kane looked down. "Shoulda looked before," he said. The tip of his right boot was encroaching on a puddle of blood that had turned blackish and congealed to the consistency of custard. An encrustation of green-bottle flies like animated mold fed on it as avidly as if it were custard.

Brigid stood by his right shoulder, staring at the body arched over the table. Her breath came thready and shallow. Her eyes were large. Her cheeks were very pale.

"Hard way to die," Kane said. His throat felt raw. Raw as the gaping wound Dr. Silas Wu's entire body had become. While he was still alive, by the looks of things.

From somewhere there reached Kane's ears a faint squeak, as of gravel crunched beneath substantial weight.

"Shit!" Kane said. "We've been set up!"

Turning, with his left hand he thrust Brigid stumbling into the small backroom, which looked more like a retreat for the erstwhile scientist than a bedroom; evidently he slept somewhere else. At the same time he drew one of his Glocks with his right.

One of the fish men from the Lemurian labs was shambling in, its already hunched form bent lower to clear the top of the front doorway. Other shadows moved across the salt-blurred and fly-specked windows. The creature wasn't alone.

It advanced through the shop, shouldering aside a bookshelf with curious figurines on it, and various polished rocks, oddly shaped and colored. Some of these tinkled into pastel dust as they fell. More did so as they were crushed beneath the being's enormous weight.

Kane fired. The handblaster was a Glock 18, a selective-fire machine pistol with a high cyclic rate. It shot 9 mm Parabellum rounds like the Model 17 it closely resembled. It would also overheat quicker than the Heckler & Koch subguns Grant and Domi had taken to the hidden seabase, which was why he brought two.

He already knew 9 mm ammo would not have a terrific effect on the oversized hybrids. He was prepped for that, too. He aimed right for the creature's crotch and ripped off a 5-round burst.

The monsters could take enormous punishment. The Cerberus crew had long since learned that to their pain. But they couldn't violate the laws of mechanics, no matter how hardy they were. The copper-jacketed 147-grain slugs lanced through soft-scaled and pale belly skin. Three struck the creature's pelvic girdle, in the center and two strikes on the right wing. The center hit did it: the pelvis buckled.

In horrid silence the creature folded to the floor.

Without a structural brace its legs would not work, period. A well-adrenalized human could run even with both femurs broken, but nothing bipedal could stand, much less run, with the pelvis gone.

Another creature lumbered in the door. Nice and slow, guys, Kane thought. It was like old black-and-white horror vids he watched with mummies as the bad guys: how big a threat, really, was something that could easily be outrun by a reasonably fit granny in a wheelchair? He gave the newcomer a triburst, deliberately aimed, in the same location. With the same result—and the added bonus that this immobilized monster now blocked the doorway to its fellows.

"Kane!" he heard Brigid scream.

He snapped his head around. One of Leviathan's cannibal cultists had her around the throat with a forearm twined in jagged dark green tattoos. The eyes staring from a tattoo-covered face above the former archivist's right shoulder were bright blue.

"Drop," Kane commanded.

Brigid obeyed. Keeping her presence of mind in a crisis had always come naturally to her—which was why she was still alive. She went limp. Her not inconsiderable weight dragged her captor's arm inexorably down. Taken by surprise, he didn't even try to bend with her.

Kane drew his other Glock 18 with his left hand, snapped his arm out straight, squeezed the heavy trigger. The burst ripped out in a parabola up and to Kane's right. Wiry-strong as his wrists and forearms were, there was no way to keep the lightweight blaster from rising to the force of recoil. There was also no way to keep the rifling bite of the lands and grooves imparting spin to each successive projectile from torquing the weapon clockwise in his hand.

The first shot hit the cultist's skinny illustrated chest just inboard of the right nipple. Succeeding shots walked up the side of his throat, shattered his chin, smashed his right cheek and punched just between his nose and the inside of his left eye. Blood and brains puffed out behind him, decorating the half-open blue-painted doorway to the bathroom where he'd been lurking before he jumped Baptiste.

He went down. Kane stood with his Glock turned sideways as another cultist came out of the tiny unlit bathroom in a low dive and tackled Brigid before even Kane's rattlesnake reflexes could get a shot in him.

There was a crash of glass from the main shop. Frustrated trying to clamber over all the corpses blocking the doorway, somebody had decided to try an alternate route. Kane spun in time to see a cultist tuck and roll in a shower of glass shards, then hop up to his bare feet, seemingly oblivious to the blood that streamed from a dozen cuts.

Kane gave him a triburst in the chest. The fish man flew backward, arms eagled, into a rack of candles and brass bowls and lanterns. They all went down in a noisy heap.

Kane heard five muffled gunshots from behind. He turned. Brigid was just rolling off her erstwhile attacker.

He had five cup-sized exit wounds in his back and didn't seem to be resisting.

Kane's head snapped around again as something twanged loudly in his right ear. The barbed black iron head of a spear was embedded in the door frame right by his ear. The human cultists had figured out that they could get through the door by scrambling over the crippled fish men on all fours like animals. Others were crowding in through the busted window.

He held out both handblasters and blasted. Bric-a-brac tumbled. Glass crashed.

The main shop wall bowed to an impact that reverberated through Kane's feet like one of the frequent earthquakes that rocked this region. For a flash he thought that was what it was. Then came a second heavy thud, and the lath-and-plaster wall began to split open. A little cupboard toppled noisily, sending a globe of Venus rolling across the floor.

A fish man was coming in the hard way. More cultists tumbled through the windows and scuttled through the door like spiders. Kane shot them until both slides locked back.

Brigid stood behind him. There was no room for both to shoot through the beaded doorway. But she had her USP muzzle up and ready to rock.

"Forget it," he told her, jamming one blaster back in its holster while thumbing the magazine release on the other. Good thing about these 30-round double-stack boxes: they dropped free a lot easier than did the standard mags. "Too many. We gotta get out of this place."

Her green eyes widened. "How? No door."

He grinned. "Not yet."

MORE THAN TWENTY human cultists, painted and tattooed and armed with spears, clubs studded with shark teeth, and machetes thronged with half a dozen fish men around the front part of the former Wu's former Lost and Found Emporium, all jostling to get in and get killing.

The back wall of the small structure exploded in dust and splitting rotted planks, beneath the coordinated weight of two strong and sizable adult humans.

Kane sprayed both his handblasters as he flew to a somewhat rough and unsatisfactory landing, fetched up against the sand mounded around the base of a clump of tough long grass.

Firing her own USP left-handed into the chest and face of a cultist who ran at them with a sort of wooden sword edged with shark teeth, Brigid reached down with her other hand, caught Kane by the back of his shirt and hauled him onto his feet.

"Let's move," Kane said.

They raced down the head of the spit to their boat. Apparently the cultists and their fishy friends had already been in place, lurking out of sight. Or if they'd emerged from the sea had been so fixated upon their prey they'd left the boat alone.

Brigid jumped in and fired up the motor as Kane pushed the yellow inflatable into the surf. As the screws bit water and began to push he flopped backward into the boat, causing it to wallow alarmingly but not tip.

A spear splashed into the water to one side of the boat. Another nicked the other gunwale. Air immediately began to hiss out.

"Kane!" Brigid cried.

"All right," he said, rolling over. "We're all right—short trip."

He stuck out his right arm over the balloonlike side of the boat and fired a burst at the cultists standing knee-deep in the gray-brown froth, cocking their arms to chuck more missiles at them.

He missed, but the cultists ducked. Two went through with the casts they had in progress, but their spears flew wide.

Overheated, the Glock's slide locked tight—fortunately, in the act of returning to battery from ejecting an empty case. Had it seized up under the forces of a round going off, the sudden overpressure might have done some very nasty things. The Glock had a mighty strong action, but Kane wasn't eager to put it to that kind of test. He cursed and dropped the handblaster into the water, then reached for his second Glock.

They were already out of spear range and almost at the bobbing Manta. The cultists stood on the beach dancing and waving their arms and shrieking.

Kane rolled onto his back. "Whew," he said. "So

much for Wu." He boosted her up to the Manta and prepared to follow her when something locked around his right ankle. He looked down. A fish man had half emerged from the water and grabbed his leg. It started to pull him back down.

Kane grabbed at the Manta's cockpit rim with both arms. The fish man was twice as strong as him and no doubt weighed half again as much. It was a question of how few heartbeats before his grip failed and he went into the water.

What would happen there he refused to think about.

Grabbing the back of his shirt with one hand, Brigid leaned way out of the cockpit to empty her USP into the fish man's face. The big goggling eyes exploded like bags of ink. The death grip let go of Kane's ankle.

With added impetus from Brigid, Kane flung himself into the cockpit and dropped into the pilot's seat. Brigid hurriedly strapped herself in. With a whine of impellers the craft lifted off the water before the canopy had even sealed itself.

Chapter 27

The armaglass walls of the Cerberus mat-trans gateway lent a strange dead sepia cast to objects that materialized within them. Such as the four-foot stainless steel cylinder with flared end caps of a black synthetic.

"Hoo," Grant exhaled. "That's what a tactical implosion bomb looks like."

"Not much," Domi commented.

Thankfully it wasn't leaking radiation. At least, not in any slice of the spectrum nor any family of particles recognized by the instruments Philboyd waved at it.

"The rough equivalent in destructive capacity of a five-kiloton thermonuclear device," Lakesh intoned.

"That oughta take a big bite out of Leviathan," Kane commented. "Wonder why a plain old tactical nuke wouldn't do the trick?"

"Poor Silas believed that Leviathan might possess the ability attributed to the imaginary Cthulhu in a certain Howard Phillips Lovecraft story," Lakesh said, "to re-form his corporeal being after physically knocked to pieces—in this case, after having been rammed by a ship, I believe."

Grant rubbed his chin. "I reckon the vent-forms know what they're talking about where Leviathan is concerned," he said. "After all, this whole thing is about us getting him out of their hair, or whatever they have. Doesn't seem likely to me they'd give us false dope on something like what's needed to take him out."

Again Lakesh nodded sagaciously. "Astute, friend Grant. We find ourselves in a position of being compelled to trust our alien allies. Certainly they have delivered upon their promises so far."

"So has Bates," Kane said, as two techs, grunting, laid the device on the black rubber mat spread atop a trolley. "That doesn't mean I trust him."

"I do," Grant said. "To screw us royally, first chance he gets."

"Big time," Domi concurred with a nod.

"We didn't exactly trust him for this," Brigid said.

Bates, per his promise, forwarded the device to them via a mat-trans gateway.

"Trust Bates to materialize a bomb in the middle of Cerberus?" Kane asked with a harsh laugh. "That'd be way too much of a temptation. And Bates seems to be a boy who can resist anything but that."

"And indeed poor Gilgamesh took on most lamentably about our lack of trust," Lakesh said. The four companions glanced at him, then at one another; they hadn't known, for sure, that Lakesh had been in communication with his erstwhile associate.

Kane slapped Grant on a rock-jut shoulder. "You

ready for this, big man? Going up against a critter who makes the last of the redwoods look young and small?"

"Will be," Grant said stolidly, "after I pull some more time in the DeepFighter simulator."

"If those underwater attackers act like their simulators do," said Domi, rubbing bone-white hands together, "this is gonna rock."

"KIRI," THE RADIO RECEIVER said, crackling with sunspot static. There was a major solar storm in progress, unprecedented for a century; the Wave Children kept close track of such things. "There is bad news."

Her body turned cold within her skin, still warm from the sun outside the cabin.

"What is it?" she asked, although she knew what it had to be.

It was Meherio, the golden-haired captain of *Waverunner,* into whose care Kiri had entrusted her son, Reva....

"Our engine broke down," Meherio said, "and the wind blew foul for home. By good luck Tupolu came upon us, homeward bound, and took us under tow."

Kiri gagged on the breath she was drawing in.

"In the night a squall overtook us. Under its cover we were attacked by the undersea marauders. It must have been a torpedo—my ship was shattered in a white flash and thunderclap of noise."

"Reva—" Kiri said. She fell to her knees.

"I was stunned, Fleet Mistress." The voice was flat, empty of inflection. Only the crisp crackling that betokened the distant anger of the sun gave it color. "I came to my full senses floating, clinging to a piece of decking. The rain fell fiercely—it made it hard even to see the wreckage of my ship, burning fiercely before the sea finally put her out of her pain.

"But I was close enough to see Reva. That was how I know the undersea folk attacked us, for the dolphins... took him. They tossed him for twenty minutes. He screamed and struggled for a time, but you know there's no escaping those devils.

"I tried to paddle toward him, to help him, Fleet Mistress. I tried with all my strength. But the waves and wind were against me. They kept throwing me back, though I came so close twice I could almost touch his fingertips. It was as if the sea herself helped those smooth-skinned devils.

"Some time after the dolphins tired of their play and dived a light fell upon me. It was the war leader in his vessel, braving storm and the unseen enemy to look for survivors. Only two of my crew and three of the wounded did he ever find. Fifty-one were lost. Including Reva."

After a moment, popping with radiation, Meherio continued, "I have made my report. My ship and my people are gone. As is your son, whom I loved as my own. I have failed them as I failed you, Fleet Mistress. Now I have made my report, and fulfilled my final duty to my fleet mistress and my tribe. I shall now go and cast myself over the rail and join those whom I have let down. Goodbye."

"No!" Kiri screamed. "I forbid it!"

But Meherio had gone. Only the sun's fury answered Kiri. She thought to hear mocking laughter in its fire sounds.

She vomited onto the woven-palm matting that covered the deck. Then she fell forward to lie with arms wrapped around her knees, shaking and weeping with the agony of unendurable loss.

After a time, during which her crew feared to enter the cabin to aid their beloved captain, she regained control of herself. She rose to her feet. She swayed, then firmed her balance by exertion of sheer will.

In serving my folk I have sent my son to his death, she told herself. It is done. If this is the sacrifice I must make to save my people...

Doing no more than wiping the stinking clots from her mouth and eyes, she turned back to the radio. There she established communications with the island that currently served the Wave Children as home base.

"Tupolu should raise the island later today," she said. "He has betrayed the people. He must be arrested and held for trial upon my arrival. This upon my authority as fleet mistress."

This command quite exceeded her authority as fleet mistress. But such was the titanium authority in her voice, even attenuated by distance and noise, that the voice at the other end said, "It shall be as you command."

She broke the connection and turned away. "You

have cost me my son, Tupolu," she said hoarsely, aloud. "But you shall pay with your own life."

She went then to cleanse herself. Her son's sacrifice could not be in vain. She had to seize power now, the power to make the Wave Children safe.

She would not fail in her sacred task.

"COMMANDER."

Zeno turned from the locker in which he had just stowed his undersea gear. His heart was already clouded as the sky above the sea had been. Something set poorly with him, about his nocturnal shadowing and sinking of the surface-dweller ship. Even though it was far from his first time.

He turned to see a pair of sea wardens in their full Bilge patrol regalia: figured ceramic-steel breast and back, greaves and vambraces, bullet helmets with dark blue-green visors. He himself had scorned to wear armor on foot patrol, even in the worst-smelling, darkest, most dangerous sections of the Bilge, since he had been promoted to lieutenant.

From their attitude he divined their mission at once. He cocked a dark arched eyebrow. "You come for me?"

"Affirmative, Commander," said the one to his left. It was Warden Sergeant Wales, a veteran of thirty years. Though the dark polycarbonate of the visor hid his features from bearded chin upward, his voice and the tendency to shift his weight all but imperceptibly from foot to foot betrayed his mortification. "Sea Marshal Bennett has ordered this."

For a long moment Zeno stared at him from dark intense eyes that seemed naturally lined with black. Then his shoulders rose beneath their epaulets in a deep breath, and he let the air out of him in a long sigh.

He held out his hands before him. "Then, Wardens, do your duty," he said firmly.

Chapter 28

"Remember," Kane said to the mike molded into his skull-hugging polycarbonate helmet, "our job is to make lots of noise and draw lots of attention to ourselves. Not get chilled."

"Are we really sure the Lemurians can't hear us, Kane?" a female voice asked. A tag on the plasma display built into his visor IDed the speaker as Cairns, Keiko, a volunteer pilot originally from the Moonbase. The Cerberus team had been three days at sea on the DeepFighter-carrier, running submerged to within the remarkable subsea fighters' short striking range of the submarine dome of Lemuriaville.

"Negative, Black Snake Four," he replied. "They might be able to detect our comms, but it's all encrypted in real time. So they sure can't understand what we're saying."

"Can we really rely on Bates that far?" Brigid asked over a restricted sideband that permitted her to talk privately to Kane. Cairns's question and his answer had been exchanged on Black Snake's general frequency.

"I rely on Gil Bates for two things, Baptiste—looking out for his long skinny ass and ace crypto. He seems to see profit in us doing this deed. So if he says the Lemurians can't crack our comms in any tactically useful time span, I think that's about as sure as that he'll jack us in the back first opportunity he sees. Which I guess makes it three things I trust him for."

"TODAY IS A GREAT DAY," Kiri told the fleet.

She stood on the foredeck of her big powered trimaran with the salt-laden wind whipping her curls like purple-black flames. She stood naked before her assembled people in the mother-of-pearl predawn light, in a traditional sign of her sincerity.

She spread her arms to the fleet bobbing on the rising chop to port of the flagship. "Long have we been oppressed by the people from beneath the sea, and the fish demons they have sent to harry us. They have cut our nets and sunk our boats and enslaved our people. They have taken away our children—as they took mine from me!"

Although she possessed a strong set of lungs and a ringing voice, she made use of a microphone and hidden amplifier powered by high-efficiency solar panels to increase the force and range of her words. Appropriate technology, the ancestors would have called it.

"This day it ends!" she cried.

"But why?" Aiata asked from the nearest ship, the catamaran *Angelfish*. Kiri scowled fiercely down. Aiata was *Angelfish*'s navigator, an older woman with silver in her long hair. "Haven't we sacrificed enough? What can we do against the undersea folk, with their death beams and torpedoes?"

"Have we not met them and triumphed?" Kiri demanded. She marked Aiata down mentally for future… disposition. There would be a great purge when this fight was done, and not among the Shark Tribe alone. For too long had they allowed timorousness to hinder their pursuit of their destiny. And now it's cost me my beloved son!

"Yet you are right." Thought of her lost darling brought huskiness to her voice, which sounded to her audience like passionate conviction. "We cannot hope to withstand the undersea folk forever. That is why today we must once more aid the mainlanders as we have promised, to deal with the threat once and all! Once they have defeated Lemuria, we will roam the ocean in peace and freedom yet again. The Wave Children will once again rule the waves!"

She threw up her arms. As coached beforehand her boatswain, Ollie, likewise raised his big meaty arms and roared approval, followed a beat later by the rest of her crew.

The answering roar from her assembled fleet beat at her like surf, and warmed her like a mighty bonfire. She had them, now. And when the battle was won and the haughty Lemurians humbled, she would have all the Wave Children and could begin to rebuild her world in such a way that she and they need never fear again. For then she would have the power.

And if certain others tried to stand in her way, such as Aiata or the elders…nothing great was ever bought without cost.

THE SOUND WAS like the knuckles of a huge fist rapping on a great oak door.

"Easy," Kane said, flicking his eyes across his display. He felt a pang of missing Grant; Grant was the master combat pilot, although Kane was fully rated and highly skilled. But Grant had his own job today.

In fact, the real job. This attack was all a feint.

"We're coming up on our tribal pals," he radioed his own flotilla—or squadron, he guessed, since the Deep-Fighters were closer to aircraft than ships, at least to his mind. Their streamlined small craft still rode in pods arrayed around the mother ship's hull. "Dropping timed explosives to draw out the bastards."

Kane could see in a window of his display that their adversaries had started to swarm out of the distant dome in hornet fury. It lay four hundred fathoms down and a bit under a half mile away—a long way from being visible, either to Kane's eyes or visual sensors. As he knew from the simulator, he was seeing now via terawave radar, which pulsed out signals of extraordinarily high frequency. They could be selectively tuned to "see through" virtually any substance, including metal and, of course, seawater, and return imaging of any other material with far greater resolution than sonar, radar or lidar. Best of all, Bates and the vent-forms both assured him, the Lemurians didn't use terawave radar, and thus couldn't detect it.

His own detectors showed no sign of any terawave transmission from either the dome or its reacting undersea warfleet. Kane trusted that.

Bates had also promised that the stealth features of the carrier sub, which according to its computers was called USS *Cheney*, but which its crew had apparently called *Sneaky Bastard*, would render its approach invisible to the Lemurians until it got within a thousand yards. The plan had been to launch at two thousand yards, just for a margin of safety. Evidently it worked, because they hadn't been attacked, even though egg craft had twice patrolled well inside the two-thousand-yard safety margin without responding to *Bastard*'s presence.

And now the Lemuriaville submarines, three of the big mother ships and more than a score of egg craft were all streaming furiously toward the impudent surface runners—and away from the carrier and its cargo of Kane's three four-ship DeepFighter elements, Black Snake, Yellow Snake and Green Snake.

"All right," Kane radioed. "Let's go. Mother?"

"This is *Sneaky Bastard*," came the response from the carrier. "Letting go...now."

The pods concealing the craft clinging baby-opossum style to the mother ship had already opened. Kane felt a jar as the clamps let go. A breath of compressed air pushed the smaller craft gently but firmly away from the larger.

He fired up the electric impellers. The little craft seemed to shake herself, then settle as her control planes bit the water that flowed past her as she got under way.

"Snake Squadron," he radioed to his twelve-ship squadron, "Snake Lead. All elements execute attack plan. Green Snake, you stay high to jump intercepting bandits. Yellow and Black Snake, fly straight for the dome. Remember, we want 'em to think we're making a firing pass on their house itself."

"Good hunting, Kane!" *Sneaky Bastard* called.

"SOMETHING HAPPENS," the white cartoon cat said from the screen.

"What do you mean, Old Tower, my friend?" Lakesh asked. The rest of the duty shift in the Cerberus operations center all gaped at the screen. Nobody had really gotten used to being addressed with great earnestness by an anthropomorphic cartoon animal. Especially one dressed as a cavalier. "Are our friends in greater danger than we anticipated?"

"All is in danger, my friend." Old Tower's voice was a masculine baritone, although as far as Lakesh or anyone could tell the vent-dwelling aliens lacked sex, either as individual microorganisms or collectively. "As we have discussed, a solar storm of ferocity unprecedented for millennia is occurring upon this system's primary. We now track a coronal mass ejection from the primary that will strike this world's outer gas envelope in…fifty-eight of your minutes."

"Our communications are proof against disruption," Lakesh said, "even from such a powerful solar discharge."

"That the concern is not. We monitor…Leviathan's energies," the bipedal white cat said. "He must have calculated such a solar storm was in the offing. He…prepares."

"Prepares what?" Lakesh said. He kept his exasperation from showing on his face or in his voice. Then realized the being he addressed was almost certainly capable of reading neither. The third-party alien AI they used to communicate with the humans seemed able to process some degree of human nonverbal communication—but only to a degree, say, that it might have registered had he chosen to turn handsprings the way that annoyingly manic cartoon-rat personal visualization did.

"Sacrifice," the impassive white-furred face said from the big screen.

"HERE THEY COME," reported Black Snake Three, a former outlander named McDougall.

Kane already saw the news on the visor display. The whole Lemuriaville undersea flotilla had turned back from the surface decoys and were streaming out to intercept Snake Squadron.

He grunted. Amazingly, the plan was working so far. Just as planned, the submarine dome's defenders had gotten themselves strung out, both the eggs and the beefier attack subs, so that they couldn't support each other effectively.

He heard a harsh buzz. A cyan lance stabbed from

one of the larger, trailing craft. A cry sounded in Kane's ears, then abruptly cut off. A second voice said, "Snake Lead, Yellow Snake Three. Yellow Snake Four is down. I say again, Yellow Snake Four down!"

Kane's eyes flicked to the right-hand side of his display. The four-ship element to the right of his own Black Snake was now three, represented as little yellow arrowheads. Reflexively he turned his head aside. Although the craft had a clear front port and smaller side ports, they were for emergencies only. What he saw was a seamless image as if he looked out into the water with nothing intervening, gathered by an array of minute pickups in the undersea craft's outer skin, assembled by the craft's artificial intelligence and reproduced in the visor plasma display. He could change his point of view by turning his head, or he could direct the viewpoint to scroll across his field of view.

Brigid's DeepFighter, Black Snake Two, hung green-and-gray off his starboard quarter. Despite her inexperience, Kane felt good to have her at his shoulder. She'd always come through before....

"All Snakes, Snake Lead," he called. "Yellow and Black, close in tight with me. And keep aware—your systems will alert you when a big laser's getting ready to fire." The Lemurians' electrochemical lasers were imperfectly shielded; the DeepFighters' sensor arrays could pick up the characteristic emissions indicating one was charged up.

"Green Snake, stay frosty and look for targets of opportunity."

As he spoke, his enhanced underwater vision saw a line of turbulence to his right, drawing itself behind a barely glimpsed torpedo shape toward the enemy mother ship that had fired. A tiny blue-white star of exhaust flame shone from the rear of the object. It was a torpedo, in fact, an underwater ship-killing rocket that was guided by the operator by maser beam or depended on its own sensors in its head.

He heard a buzz and saw an egg craft line up on him. He rolled his fighter left. It moved slowly, but so did everything down here—except the light-speed blue-green laser lance that boiled water where he had been a moment before.

The ship shook. He heard a clap like thunder as water that had flash-boiled away from the superhot beam collapsed back on its track. The Lemuriaville lasers didn't have too much range down here, although more than they'd anticipated, as Yellow Snake Four had found out.

The DeepFighter weps had even less range, except for the big guided missiles each carried concealed in its belly—like the one he'd just seen launched to starboard. But they were big-game munitions, not maneuverable enough to take down an egg craft. Kane triggered off a smaller "dogfight" missile from its recess beneath one stub wing at the egg craft that had shot at him, just to keep the two-man crew busy.

Another explosion, deep and low and far away. The noise went on and on, like Neptune crumpling the cardboard box a full-sized city bus came in: the Lemurian submarine apparently had sucked in Yellow Snake Three's torpedo.

It was the sound of a ship dying. And incidentally the fragile little protoplasm blobs trapped inside...

Kane's lips compressed. Doesn't take much to chill a body down here, with all that water pressure trying all the time to get in, he thought. Just the slightest little crack. Even a pinhole.

What else is new? he asked himself. It's not like it takes a lot to make even a Deathbird into a smoking hole in the planet.

The egg craft was close now, just fifty yards. He lined up a spidery yellow pipper until it flashed white with gleeful urgency and pressed a trigger on his right-hand joystick.

A milliwatt laser stabbed from either side of the snout of Kane's ship. It flash-boiled clear a narrow linear path through the water. Before even the colossal pressure could recollapse the skinny tubes, quick twin pulses of antimatter blobs streaked down them. To the eyes of Kane's sensor array they looked like orange-red golf balls with searing white cores. He had no idea how they were stored or generated in his little craft; he vaguely knew that they seemed to employ a similar principle to the antimatter beams that formed part of Cerberus redoubt's external defensive array.

At least three antimatter blobs struck the egg ship, where they catastrophically combined with normal matter in violet-white minisupernovae of mutual instantaneous destruction. Kane's visor showed him the bearded face of the enemy pilot, eyes wide open in shocked dismay. Then a sheet of water burst in between two of the holes the antimatter pulses had blown in the craft's front screen. It cut the man's head in two like a buzz saw.

Kane grunted as the egg imploded as the sea had its way. He didn't know many real ace ways to die. This didn't look like one of them.

"Stay close, Baptiste," he commanded on their restricted sideband.

"No worries, Kane," she answered.

"Baptiste, break left now-now-now," he barked. He did likewise, banking the machine as if it were an aircraft. She obeyed, turning even more sharply, although molasses slow compared to what he was used to.

She did a creditable job, too, actually turning inside and behind him. That had been his intent. He could see in a full globe around the craft without even turning his head, which was a good thing since he, like the other pilots, lay flat on his belly on a couch that filled itself with some sort of gel to conform snugly to his proportions. He could see an egg craft behind him and to his right, maneuvering to get in behind him, 155 yards away according to the numbers on the screen. That was why he had changed course and ordered Brigid to follow. It would complicate the targeting solution of the bastard trying to get on their tail.

All around he could see a twisting dogfight. As he surveyed the battle, he banked and turned to reverse into the egg craft trying to line up on his six. Baptiste, he was pleased to see, followed his lead with only a little lag. She'd always been a quick learner.

Even after hours on the simulator, tucked away inside the *Sneaky Bastard* en route to Lemuriaville, Kane could not get entirely used to flying the DeepFighter. As its designers apparently intended, it handled much like an aircraft. With the added benefit that it couldn't fall out of the sky, but maintained neutral buoyancy and dived and climbed under power using "seafoil" vanes except in certain emergency situations. Of course, the very medium it "flew" through was constantly trying to crush it and its occupant as quickly and comprehensively as a catastrophic rendezvous with the planet's surface would an airplane.

But by his reflexes the thing flew like a lead pig. Only good thing was, as the simulators had indicated, the DeepFighters flew far faster and maneuvered more rapidly than their ovoid opponents.

Another muted boom and protracted distant-thunder rumble: a second sub had bit the big one. He grinned. He'd have loved to nail one of those big bastards himself, but he wasn't down here for R&R. It'd be the next best thing, though, once he got his undersea dogfight missiles and antimatter machine gun lined up on the Lemurian now desperately locked in a vertical turning duel, trying to outspiral the more agile craft....

"Kane." It was the voice of Lakesh, back in Cerberus, who was taking advantage of a communications satellite that would relay the transmission via *Sneaky Bastard.* "Kane, come in, please. It's urgent."

"It always is, Lakesh," he said. "Snap it up. I'm busy here. Having a dogfight and everything."

"Kane, you must attack Lemuriaville itself. You must destroy the dome at once!"

And as his brain strove to assimilate the fact he had just been ordered to commit genocide, Brigid Baptiste's voice rang in his skull: "Kane! Above us! They're attacking us!"

Chapter 29

"So the big bastard himself is down there?" Grant asked.

"That's what our bug friends say," Domi replied.

The displays inside their helmet visors showed a false color rendition of the seafloor. Ahead a black chasm slashed across a plain of what appeared to be faintly greenish gray silt.

Not six miles away, although far past the ability even of their manifold scanners and onboard artificial intelligence to resolve an image, the Lemuriaville dome rose from the ocean bottom. Grant's sensors showed him a swirl of lights that represented the dogfight raging off in the distance. It was just stray energies resolved into discreet blobs, not real identifiable images. He hoped Kane and Brigid were doing well.

The *Sneaky Bastard* had dropped the four DeepFighters of Grant's element, Sea Snake, six miles before letting go Kane's twelve ships. As planned, the Lemuriaville craft that had apparently been guarding, or at least scouting for, the monstrous underwater creature had turned tail and fled quickly to protect their home from attack.

"Straight shot from here, looks like," came the voice of Zander, currently doing business as Sea Snake Three, lead pilot of Grant's second DeepFighter pair.

"Yeah," Grant said. "All we have to do is chill a half-billion-year-old squid in a hardhat."

"Strike," Domi said.

"COMMANDER?"

The man looked up calmly at the opened door. His holding cell was as white as polished bone and bare but for a sink, a toilet, both in stainless steel, and the comfortless steel-frame cot on which he sat. Its air bore the faint smell of mildew, and the residue of a thousand sets of lungs, which the ville's electrostatic scrubbers were never able to purge altogether. And in the cell something else: the harsh stink of strong disinfectant, and beneath it, the odor of despair.

"Yes, Senior Warden Cotswold?" The words rang like spent cartridge casings on tile.

The jailer was middle-aged, medium height, slumped and soft, had gray-and-white side whiskers and an eye that looked off in some random direction. The physical disability, as minor as it was, had relegated his thirty-odd-year service career to menial tasks in support of the internal and external patrol elements. The less than heroic assignments had well suited his less than decisive nature.

He worked his pink-and-gray lips doubtfully in and out, showing that indecision now. "Commander, there is trouble. Trouble in the city. I know I shouldn't be doing this. But I feel you are needed."

"How are you able to open my cell like this?"

"The others have gone. There is rioting in the Habitat. Worse, the dome itself is under attack from without."

Zeno stood. He stretched, bent his head first to one side and then the other. "I must have a uniform," he said. "Weapons."

"I shall get them, Commander."

Zeno nodded briskly. "We go."

"SET SQUID," Kane directed. "Execute."

Tiny vents all over the DeepFighter instantly ejected a cloud of black inklike fluid, englobing the craft in a flash. Kane was about to order Brigid to follow suit— he'd opened their private frequency even as he gave his own AI the oral command—when he saw blackness puff out to surround Black Snake Two.

The visor's central image, of two descending egg craft almost lined up for the faster-than-light kill shot on him and Baptiste, never flickered. The terawave radar saw right through the synthetic "ink." Nothing else did for a good ways above and below the brief visual spectrum, conventional radar included.

The object wasn't so much to hide them from the enemy's prying eyes—even their cruder sonar would penetrate the murk—as to foil his laser beams.

One of the eggs turned into a boil of bubbles even as Kane looked up. "What the fuck?" he asked aloud.

"Yee-haa!" The second attacking egg broke right, to be intersected by dazzling antimatter pulses from at least two sources. It actually broke in two rather than imploding. Momentum carried the pieces a few more yards before the dense water sucked it out. Then they simply began to drift toward the bottom.

Kane didn't know most of the pilots well enough to recognize their voices when distorted by transmission, not to mention caterwauling like a scalding cat. The visor display obligingly identified the speaker as Green Snake One, Shannon Leary, a short, mustached pretty-boy outlander recruited from what had been Spearfish-ville. Kane now saw the four green blips of his reserve element dropping from above: seeing their leader in trouble, Green Snake One had taken it upon himself to commit his team to the fight.

It was poor discipline, but Kane didn't have it in him to bust the kid's hump for that. And anyway, any fighter jock, fixed-wing, rotary wing or, Kane guessed, under-water, who didn't have the initiative and balls to toss *procedure* when it came time…wasn't really a fighter jock.

"Thanks, Green Snake One," he called back. "Now try to stay high and eyes open." Even if a fight did de-velop relatively slowly down here, the same consider-ations applied as with air combat. You didn't want to run low on altitude, speed or ideas.

He turned his DeepFighter's nose out of the furball and accelerated away. Separating was one way you bought time to access your options in air combat—and kept them open. He checked to make sure Baptiste followed. There she was, keeping her "wing tip" twenty yards from his with the near-obsessive precision she brought to all aspects of her life.

In a moment he saw that the available Lemurian defenders seemed to be paying attention to the newcomers with the height advantage and not to him and his wingie, since he had deliberately steered them away from the dome. Which he still couldn't yet see with the naked eye, scarcely surprising under these conditions. He turned his attention back to the long-range communications with Lakesh.

"Sorry, Cerberus. Had a little bit of staying alive to do. Now, I thought I heard you order me to commit murder on a pretty mass scale."

"Do you think I would direct such a thing casually?" Lakesh demanded, his voice brassy with outrage.

"Yes. If it suited some hidden agenda of yours. Spare me the fake emoting and cut to the bone—what's the deal?"

"I thought in your prior existence you had been trained to follow orders instantly and without question."

"Yeah, well, that was then. And anyway if I'd stuck to following orders like a good little Mag I wouldn't be here, would I? Talk to me, Lakesh."

"There is no time—"

"No, there's not. So cut the bullshit."

A pause. The crackle of static seemed to have gotten worse than even a moment before.

"Very well. As you may be aware, a coronal mass ejection from the sun is headed directly toward Earth. It is of scale and energy unprecedented since measurements began being kept, although of course records are somewhat spotty from the years between the nukecaust and the Program of Unification."

"What does that mean for suffering mankind?"

"Under most circumstances, little. Our satellites are well hardened against the accompanying radiation, or they would never have survived this long. Earth's atmosphere will absorb most of the harmful quanta—those unprotected on the surface may experience perhaps a five percent increase in the risk of cancer over the next thirty years."

Kane grunted. Most people who were susceptible to disease, including cancer, had been weeded out of the gene pool by the plagues following the nukecaust and ensuing skydark. "Then why—?"

"Energy, Kane. Unprecedented energy input. Leviathan has apparently foreseen such an irruption from the Sun's surface for some time, through means I cannot even speculate upon. So upon Leviathan's instruction Baron Lemuria is preparing within the next very few minutes to kill—sacrifice—the entire human population of Lemuriaville except for himself, his Trust and a few key guards and technicians. And direct their prana to Leviathan."

"But why?" Brigid exclaimed. "If Leviathan can use the energy from the coronal mass ejection…"

"Precisely for that reason—he intends to use the life-force of a thousand people as a sort of lens, to channel and focus the enormous energy input of the CME."

"To do," Kane asked, "what?"

"Our deep-sea friends cannot be absolutely sure. Or insofar as they can make clear to me. They hypothesize that Leviathan intends to deprive the overlords of their human servitors—and possibly destroy or severely injure the overlords themselves."

"How exactly?"

"Essentially disruption of every cell of every organism on Earth's surface. Possibly beneath the sea, as well—quite possibly including, or so I speculate, the vent-forms. Old Tower informs me Leviathan's actions could produce a global extinction event."

"You mean like the nukecaust and skydark?"

"Ah, no, friend Kane. Far greater. On the scale of the Permian-Triassic extinction 250 millions years ago."

Brigid gasped. "The Great Dying?"

"So scientists called it." Kane could just see the balding head nod. "You will no doubt recall that seventy percent of land-based life, and ninety percent of marine life, are believed to have been wiped out in that catastrophe."

Of course Kane recalled no such damn thing. He whistled. "Impressive, Lakesh," he said. "Why? What's it get him?"

"The overlords, it would appear, or so he seems to believe. The self-enhancing pulse—one might call it a feedback system—of psychic disruption may well serve to destroy them."

"But doesn't Leviathan want to rule everything?" Kane asked. "What good is it to rule over a lifeless mudball?"

"Even the extinction of ninety percent of life isn't the extinction of all life," Lakesh said crisply. "As we have seen in a succession of great extinctions, most recently skydark, life does rebound. It may takes years, centuries even. But the surviving life expands to fill every available niche once more, adapting as necessary. And Leviathan is nothing if not patient."

"Okay, so Leviathan's going to go scorched earth on, well, Earth," Kane said. "What do you want me to do about it?"

"You must disrupt Baron Lemuria's timing, Kane. The only way to do that is to extinguish all life within the dome first."

"You have got to be shitting me," Kane burst out.

"I only wish I were," Lakesh said. His voice actually sounded sad, or at least wistful.

"Why not Grant? He should be readying to make his attack run right this moment." *Or our pals here are dying for nothing.* The defending blips were far fewer in number than moments before, although others now emerged irregularly from the dome to join them. But two more Snake flight images had vanished.

And the worst, it seemed, was yet to come.

"The coronal masse ejection will strike Earth's outer

atmosphere in approximately 323 seconds. Earliest projected time for Grant to land a shot upon Leviathan is 411 seconds."

"And that half minute isn't enough margin for error?"

"The effect, Old Tower assures me, will propagate at the speed of light."

"Damn," Kane said.

"With respect, friend Kane, why do you hesitate? You have not heretofore been a man to shrink from taking life."

"Damn it, Dr. Lakesh," he heard Brigid snap. "That isn't fair!"

"I'm ready as any man to kill whoever needs killing," Kane said. "But as for wiping out a ville full of innocent people…I still wear the coat and armor sometimes. Even the Sin Eater. But the Magistrate's badge—I took that off a long time ago."

"Little as I like to fall back upon the doctrines of utilitarianism," Lakesh said, "I am forced to consider this equation—one thousand noncombatant lives, or the lives of all humans, and possibly all life-forms above the viral level, in the blink of an eye."

Kane took a deep breath. "Baptiste," he said over their private frequency.

"You may not want my advice, Kane. I am not as sentimental as is common for females of the human species. I am trained to evaluate things dispassionately— even matters such as this."

"Don't need your input," he said almost tenderly. "I carry the freight on this one.

"I just wanted to hear your voice."

Anam-chara. He didn't say aloud.

"Snake Flight," he said on the general frequency, "Snake Lead. All Snakes switch to the heading and velocity I am transmitting…now. Green Snake, stay high and out front. Yellow Snake, out ahead of me. Keep the bastards off me and Black Snake."

The acknowledgments crackled back. He had not sent a course directly for the dome, which he could not yet see. That would bring out last-ditch ferocity in the defenders, might lead to suicide-ram attacks. Instead it would take them within five hundred yards of the undersea city.

At the last possible instant, Black Snake would dive on the dome itself. He had already confirmed that only he and Baptiste still had their big ship-killing missiles, which were all that had a chance of cracking the giant armaglass bubble. Once its structural integrity was weakened, the relentless pressure of the sea would do the rest. But it would take a lot to crack that egg….

The unimaginable undersea monster had been invading their dreams for weeks—trying to recruit them to his last crusade against his inhuman rivals. But Kane suspected the nightmares Leviathan sent would be nothing to what would rack his sleep the rest of his days if they pulled this off.

If.

Chapter 30

"My Lord," Director of Internal Operations Malatan said, "the preparations are complete. The inner sanctum is sealed. At your command, the nerve agent will be released into the dome at large."

Baron Lemuria nodded gravely. It took supreme effort to keep his features impassive.

Inside he was almost as passion racked as an apekin. All our work! he thought. The power we have built up over decades, hiding away down here in the depths of the sea—all gone in a breath.

Yet their new ally had promised a reward greater than they could imagine—and certain destruction, did they not obey. Immortality or oblivion: the choice was obvious. Only one rational course lay open.

He remembered an apekin expression his chief enforcer, Bennett, was fond of quoting: "You can't make an omelet without breaking eggs."

He sat in a special circular chamber deep beneath the foundations of the dome, dug out of the rock of the seabed itself. Five seats were arranged around his central throne, right beneath the apex of the chamber. Lines of some yellow metal, possibly gold, connected the five outer seats in the form of a five-rayed star.

"But my Lord," Director MacArthur asked plaintively as the other five members of the Lemuriaville Trust took their seats in response to the baron's gestures, "there are only five seats."

"You speak truth, MacArthur." The baron caught Bennett's eye and nodded.

Twisting in his seat, the marshal drew his side arm and pointed it at the standing Trust member.

MacArthur paled. "You can't—"

The maser disrupter's buzz sounded harsh in the thirty-foot-wide chamber. A steam jet of blood and other body fluids boiled in a millisecond by the coherent microwave beam burst out the front of his tunic and knocked him onto his back. He lay in a graceless sprawl with the outflung fingers of one hand just touching the smooth curve of the interior dome, toward the top of which he stared with bulging, sightless eyes.

The lines in the floor glowed with golden radiance.

Baron Lemuria's alabaster fingers tightened on the arms of the throne as ecstasy surged through him. He closed his eyes and put his head back.

It's true! he thought. The apekin's life-force flows into me!

He opened his eyes. The others stared at him, eyes wide and faces flushed. Their manner suggested not so much shock or fear as—what did they call it?—embarrassment.

As if they all had been caught indulging in some secret, nasty pleasure.

"A token of what awaits us, gentleman," he said. "Let the countdown commence!"

"I'M SORRY, WARDEN COTSWOLD," Commander Zeno said to the figure slumped on the floor by his booted toes. He had intended merely to stun the jailer with a blow to a certain meridian at the back of the neck that should render him unconscious for a period of ten to fifteen minutes. Unfortunately for all his iron self-control the commander's system was highly adrenalized. He feared he had struck too hard and broken the man's neck.

Not, he suspected, that it would matter greatly.

Checking the side arm in the holster the now still warden had returned to him, Zeno donned his blue-green lacquered helmet and turned to the airlock-style door that gave out upon the Habitat. It was sealed against the possibility of a breach in the dome caused by the attackers, whose identities Zeno could not even hazard a guess at. He doubted, should the enemy succeed in cracking the mighty bubble, whether such precautions would do more than delay the inevitable by a smattering of heartbeats.

A code punched quickly into the keypad beside the door by a gauntleted fingertip overrode the electronic seal. With a hiss of air pressure equalizing the valvelike door opened.

Outside, bedlam awaited.

"HOLY SHIT," a voice said in Grant's ears.

It might have been his own.

From the black depths of the trench, a denser blackness was rising. Tendrils swung with seeming laziness before a rounded mass. An eye glared red from the middle of it.

His four DeepFighters hugged the bottom. The terrain was tortured here, sinuous knifeback ridges and sudden narrow crevasses. Sea Snake was making use of the relief, bobbing and weaving around the high points. They surrendered the height advantage by doing so. Grant reckoned the protection from detection conferred a lot more advantage than being in open water well above their target.

Seeing the monstrous nautilus for the first time, with his own eyes, he felt relief they'd played it this way.

At least the eye, oddly human despite glowing with its own bloody light, not to mention being as wide as a five-story building was tall, wasn't looking at them. It seemed to be turned upward.

"I wonder if it can see all the way to the surface," came the voice of Bobbee Klammer, Sea Snake Four. Grant's and Domi's two companions were both biologists from Manitius who had long been fascinated by Earth's oceans, even though until migrating to Cerberus they had been unable to study it except by way of the Moonbase's databases. They weren't the hottest Deep-Fighter pilots; those had gone with Kane. That was fine with Grant. His element wasn't supposed to be doing a lot of fancy dogfighting on this sortie.

Lakesh believed knowledge of marine biology might come in handy on the Leviathan-hit flight. Grant couldn't see it. But then he wasn't a whitecoat.

Right now, he almost wished he was.

THE OVERHEAD FLUORESCENT lights deep in the Bilge flickered irregularly, but the rioters didn't seem to notice.

Weapon in hand, Zeno strode among the vast hulked shapes of machines and pipes. He saw no other wardens. They had either been pulled out or pulled down.

He might have tried slipping from shadow to shadow: shadows were about the one thing never in short supply in the Lemuriaville Bilge—shadows and misery. Neither had ever been more plentiful than they were now.

Zeno passed within fifteen feet of a party of mostly naked Bilgers engaged in the mass rape of a victim of indeterminate age and sex. The victim neither struggled nor screamed, and appeared quite likely dead. It was crossing the line even for the Bilge, about the fate of whose inhabitants the masters of the ville cared but little. But Zeno paid no heed.

He no longer served the masters he had all his life. He knew, without knowing how he knew, that all trusts had been betrayed. It was time for him to do something he had rarely done in all his years: look out for himself.

Skulking had never been his way. The rioters seemed to ignore him, their eyes sliding past his upright striding form as if it were optically slippery. Easier prey abounded here, after all: and the Bilgers had never been backward about preying on one another. For many it had been their only means of surviving at all.

But though he would not let them see him run any more than cringe, he strode rapidly. For time was short, his mission vital.

BEFORE AND BELOW Kane the dome gleamed dully in simulated light. He was surprised by how large it looked.

"Black Snake, Snake Lead," he radioed. "Only shoot at the defenders. No one fires at the dome. Repeat, no one fires at the dome."

"Throwing a feint at 'em, are we?" came back Black Snake Four.

"Affirmative."

"You insist on bearing this burden alone, Kane?" Brigid asked.

He didn't answer.

No big subs showed on his display. When he keyed a search for their distinctive characteristics—mass, profile, energy emissions—his AI reported none within range. He was surprised they had no more than three. Perhaps some were elsewhere on missions that had taken them too far to return for this fight. Or maybe the baron hadn't felt a need for that many of the larger craft, costly in resources to build, crew and maintain. It wasn't as if they'd faced a lot of enemies down here on their own turf.

Not until now.

The egg craft seemed taken by complete surprise when Kane's three surviving ships broke away to dive on Lemuriaville itself. Yellow Snake Two and Green Snake One and Four, the only survivors of his Snake elements, engaged a dozen egg craft in a desperate, twisting brawl, trying more to distract them from lining up for kill shots on the three craft diving toward their homes. Toward their families and loved ones if they had them. Although if this near-baron was like the genuine article Kane had worked for in Cobaltville, he discouraged forming of close bonds beyond the ranks of his Magistrate equivalents—and wasn't too eager to foster camaraderie even among them if it might compromise their loyalty to the baron.

Enough thinking. The dome now lay a thousand yards away. It was time to lock on and launch.

Except he found he couldn't.

"Damn," he said.

"What is it, Kane?" Brigid asked. He cursed himself briefly for his carelessness at leaving his mike hot.

"My system won't lock up the dome," he said. "My sensors see it, but the AI doesn't recognize it as a target."

"Could that be deliberate? The builders may have wanted to prevent any accidental launches against it by these secret undersea fighters," Brigid said.

"Or not so accidental," Kane said. "Yeah. Damn, I'm going to have to take the shot ballistic."

"Unguided? But that means—"

"Yeah. The missile's basically a big streamlined rock. I'll have to close within two hundred yards to make sure of a square hit. I want you to peel away when I get within five hundred, Baptiste."

She said nothing.

"Baptiste," he said in a throaty growl. "I told you—"

"Snake Lead, Black Snake Four. Three bandits have broken away and are lining up behind us. They're—"

A burst of noise. Then static. Then silence.

The purple arrowhead symbol of Black Snake Four went out.

"I'm on them, Kane," Brigid said. Her craft nosed up and banked to its right into a climbing turn.

He opened his mouth to order her back into formation with him. Then he realized they were within a handful of seconds of the point at which he had directed her to leave him regardless.

But now she was headed into deadly danger either way. There was nothing he could do about it.

He felt a cold hand of powerlessness close around his gullet and guts.

Chapter 31

Initially the Lemurians ignored Brigid, likely because they were too focused on the threat to their dome, she thought.

She was thankful not for her own sake, but ironically for Kane's. Because by concentrating totally on trying to crush his fragile eggshell craft and take away the life that, at times like this, she knew was as dear to her as her own, they made it possible for her to prevent them.

Even to her the undersea craft seemed slow. Yet it was much more agile than the hostile eggs. Her DeepFighter's nose came around as three went by, intent on coming into range to kill Kane with their lasers.

Her targeting pipper crossed the lead craft. It turned from yellow to white and began to pulsate. Her finger tensed on the trigger.

Brilliant pulses streaked toward the ovoid: electrically propelled antimatter packets. Hits flashed dazzling violet-white. The craft imploded.

The enemy craft nearest shied away from it and from Brigid. The third continued in Kane's wake. She sent a spray of three dogfight rockets after the ovoid that had sheered off, in hopes of keeping it off her tail. Then she turned after the pursuing craft.

With a certain fatalism she watched as the minitorpedoes missed the egg. It started to turn back to intercept Kane—or her.

If the pilot wants me, he's got me, she knew. Yet if she could somehow keep them from coming within range of Kane's DeepFighter before he launched his one ship-killer missile, nothing else would matter. She turned her display to center on the foe closest to Kane.

KANE HEARD THE THUD and crumple of an undersea craft dying. His gray eyes flicked aside for the single second needed to register that Baptiste's purple pip still shone in his display. While one of the three egg craft engaging her had vanished, two more had broken loose from the scrum above and were closing with her fast.

One of the nearer ones slipped past her and came on after Kane, lining up for a shot.

But the dome filled his field of vision now. The terawave radar rangefinder clicked off the distance: 210, 205…

It hit 200 and began flashing red. He pressed the red button with his right thumb.

In the belly of his craft an elongated longitudinal segment rotated. The ship slowed slightly but perceptibly as the missile thus exposed, streamlined as it was, exerted drag.

A blast of compressed gas started it on its way out

of the launch tube, which as soon as it registered the missile was clear, rotated back inside the DeepFighter, leaving the hull as unbroken and apparently seamless as before. Kane saw a spark in his display as the rocket's motor lit.

He followed it down. He was the one shot now. If he missed—or if the rocket didn't crack the dome—he would kamikaze his ship right in after it.

It might even be easier that way.

LIKE A GIGANTIC SHADOW made solid, the monster stretched black tentacles toward the surface. Though the seabed here lay three hundred meters fathoms, well below the crush depth of a conventional prenukecaust submarine, it looked to Grant as if the tips of the longest might actually breach into the sunlight.

With Domi hanging doggedly on his wing he had climbed back up to one hundred fathoms above the average seafloor level for his firing pass.

"Damn," he said on the TBS to Domi's fighter. "I expected to be above the son of a bitch."

"He's huge." The albino outlander sounded awed.

Below and in front of them their two companions had launched their long-range ship-killing missiles. They vanished into the looming blackness without so much as a flicker visible to Grant's instruments. Now Sea Snake Three and Four were blasting off all the smaller dogfight missiles loaded in their wings and firing their antimatter projectors. They were still out of range for the antimatter weapons, whose projectiles flared into momentary brilliance and vanished after two hundred yards.

None of it made the slightest impression. "We're just gnats to that thing," Domi said in a hushed voice.

"That's why we got the implosion bomb," Grant said. "Now if he just stays nice and oblivious to us till we get in range…"

BLUE-GREEN BLAZED PAST Kane on the right. Fortunately the visor video would transmit no harmful levels of radiation, and filtered out the potentially blinding cyan laser glare that shone in through the small side viewport. He heard a crack like a giant ax striking wood. The DeepFighter rocked and gurgled as steam bubbles boiled from the beam's wake. The egg jockey had gotten rattled and squeezed off before he had Kane dead to rights. Or he had been aiming to burn the ship-killer.

He missed.

The rocket didn't.

White flared in Kane's vision. There was no afterimage; the display emitted no light bright enough to dazzle. For a moment nothing happened.

"All right, you bastards," he said aloud. "Here I come." The hairs at the back of his neck rose. He could feel the gunner of the pursuing craft sighting him in tight. This shot wouldn't miss.

A roughly circular patch of the dome sagged. The cracks that had initially been too small to see deepened and thickened into a tracery of dark lines crazing the crystal perfection.

And then the weakened spot gave.

Kane pulled up hard as he could. Ferocious turbulence rocked the DeepFighter. So enormous was the pressure differential that in the first few seconds no air escaped. The water crowded in regardless, in a stream as hard as solid steel.

Then a great turmoil of bubbles erupted from the hole. Climbing now, Kane saw a crazy kaleidoscope of darting cyan beams as the bubbles broke up the laser beam the pursuing craft had fired at him. He caught a glimpse of the egg, jostling wildly amid the commotion. Then, struck by debris or simply stressed beyond its terrific strength, it folded like a cheap plastic toy beneath a boot heel.

Switching his point of view, Kane sought Baptiste. But the dome had turned into a bubble volcano. Lights flashed within it as the water rushed in at the velocity of a high-powered rifle bullet. Not even his fighter's miracle sensor array could penetrate the fantastic turbulence.

A rushing roar enfolded him as he arrowed toward the surface. Perhaps it was a ville dying.

Or maybe it was just his own blood in his ears.

"THE MOMENT HAS COME," Baron Lemuria proclaimed. He stood and flung his arms out to his sides, feeling for the first time in his life as if he were physically as strong as a bull human. He felt the presence of Leviathan, and for the first time felt no accompanying fear. The power the ancient being had promised him surged through his veins like liquid electricity. "Release the gas in thirty seconds! The sacrifice begins."

A Klaxon blared. The dim yellow lights around the base of the chamber wall and the single light directly above the baron's head began to flicker.

The baron turned in place, hands open as if in supplication. "What is it? What's this? *What is happening?*"

Director Malatan had a computer pad in his hand to initiate the release of the nerve agent into the dome above. Now he stared at it in horror.

"The dome itself is attacked," he said in a tone of disbelief verging upon awe. The pad fell from suddenly numb fingers and he raised his head to the ceiling of the deeply buried chamber.

"There is a breach—"

"A breach?" the baron said. "Impossible!"

The top of the hemispherical chamber split open. A sheet of water struck down. The baron's body was torn in two.

The world fell in upon the Lemuriaville Trust.

The sacrifice was complete.

It was also premature.

A LONE HUNTER-KILLER EGG accelerated away from the stricken dome. Beside him in the cockpit, Commander Zeno heard faint whimpering.

He half turned to tousle Robert's sweat-matted

bronze hair. "Don't cry," he said softly. "We're free. For the first time in our lives, we are free."

OUT AT THE EDGE of the atmosphere an invisible jet struck. The efflorescence of agitated atoms was not visible to the naked eye here on the day side. The Aurora would be spectacular at night all the way down to the equator. If anyone survived to see it.

Inside Cerberus the arrival of the coronal mass ejection was greeted by spikes on banks of readouts in the operations center. It was all Lakesh, standing and staring at the giant map display as if he could somehow see what was happening beneath the ocean eight hundred miles away, could do to keep his face impassive.

Then he cringed as blackness exploded in his mind.

GRANT SCREAMED as the wave of fury washed through his mind like black lava.

For a moment he lost control of his senses. When he came back to himself, he felt flash relief that the craft had not strayed from its course too badly.

Mostly he felt relief he was still alive. He had been convinced for a moment that the psychic disruption Leviathan planned to bring about had come to pass. That he was dead, along with everybody else.

"What," he said, "was *that?*"

"Big fucker mad," Domi said. "Big time."

"Outstanding," Grant said. He felt an urge to pump

a triumphant fist in the cramped cockpit. "Kane must've busted the dome."

"Look out," Domi called.

The monster thrashed the seafloor with its tentacles, raising clouds of silt like the smoke from burning cities. And now, in its rage at being thwarted, it turned its attention to the nearest scapegoats: those tiny craft that had been stinging at it with their puny futile weapons.

A shadow tentacle slammed down to crush Sea Snake Three into the side of a stone tower. Sea Snake Four had sheered off and was streaking away. Its pilot broke hard to her starboard, successfully eluding the downward stroke of a tentacle as big around as a redwood.

Her escape was momentary. A blue sheet discharge crackled from the tentacle. It enveloped the fleeing Deep-Fighter. The little craft buckled as its structural integrity failed under the whiplash of colossal energy release.

Grant laid his targeting reticule on the center of the monster's bulk. His visor display scrolled down to the optimal launch point. He saw the flare and, on the side display, Snake Four's red pip go out. "Fuck!" he exclaimed. "I didn't know he could do that!"

"It's like a monster from an old Japanese vid," Domi said.

"Well," Grant said, "he's screwed now."

He pickled off the implosion bomb. "Break right!" he ordered Domi.

For a wonder she obeyed. Grant cranked his Deep-Fighter hard the other way.

A tentacle cut at a transverse angle between them. It flashed off another lightning sheet. But the two small craft were already too far away to take its full effect. Despite the Faraday cage formed by the DeepFighter fuselage the hair stood up on the back of Grant's neck.

The two combat craft lined out directly away from the monster's bulk. Grant felt fresh relief that Domi, like him, had sense to "fly" level instead of climbing for the seeming safety of the surface. That would bleed off speed. Grant had no clear notion of what an implosion bomb that size would do, much less to something like Leviathan. Right now their best chance of escaping whatever its effects were lay in maximum separation.

He kicked the rear-cam feed into central display. A vast tentacle unreeled after him like the pyroclastic flow from an exploding volcano.

The world twisted.

It was as if reality itself became momentarily plastic. Warped to unimaginable forces. The giant triangular shadow that was Leviathan distorted. Then it began to flow inward toward the center of its own titanic mass.

For one final moment the tentacle continued to reach for Grant's fleeing ship. Then it attenuated like molten glass being drawn out into a pipette. And then it was sucked backward into the contracting shadow behind.

A psychic blast smashed into Grant's mind, a hundred times stronger than the rage that had followed Leviathan's sensing of the destruction of his plan. Grant blacked out again.

He came back to himself just in time to fight the shock wave caused by water rushing into the replace the enormous volume occupied moments before by Leviathan. "Domi!" he shouted into the roar.

KIRI RECOVERED from the psychic shock before anyone else aboard *Great Sky Reef*. She leaped to her feet.

"Children of the Great Wave!" she shouted, throwing wide her arms and projecting her voice to reach the whole of her flotilla, which had now moved almost above the point at which the mainlanders said the enemy city lay. Bits of wreckage, torn metal and plastic and limp bodies, residue of the subsea battle, bobbed on the waves around and among the small ships. "Children of the Wave, stand up! Arise and face our destiny!

"Our great enemy is destroyed. The great path of light on water lies open before us. We shall make ourselves masters of the wide Pacific, and none shall be able to resist us now!"

The others rose to their feet and cheered until it seemed their lungs would burst.

The giant air bubble given off by the catastrophic rupture of the Lemuriaville dome rose up directly beneath them.

It hurled the ships in all directions, shedding men and women like water drops from shaking dogs. Where the two hundred-yard-wide bubble burst it left a crater in the water. And when the water rushed in again to fill that emptiness, after the fashion of water, Kiri and all the people of her fleet were sucked down, and down, and down, to a blackness no light ever penetrated.

As the vacuum in her lungs grew too great, and broke down her control so that she drew them full of fatal water in one convulsive heave, she thought she saw the face of Reva, bruised and bloated, floating before hers.

Epilogue

Tupolu, war leader of the Wave Children, met them at the water's edge in the greenish twilight.

"I am sorry," he said. "You are not welcome here."

"But we've come to see if there's any way we can help," Brigid called from the Zodiac boat Grant had steered up inshore until the bottom scraped sand and the retreating surf foamed around it, vaguely phosphorescent. Behind them *Sneaky Bastard* rode at anchor, a loaf of shadow in the gathering gloom.

Behind Tupolu stood the Wave Children. Those who survived. Most were either very young or very old. They held torches in an almost eerie silence as they stood gazing at the four mainlanders with expressions unreadable in the orange light of sunset.

The island warrior's big bare chest rose and fell in a sigh. Like the rest he wore a simple grass skirt. "We cannot survive very much more of your help," he said. "Our fleet mistress, who should have been war leader, has been taken by the sea to join her son. I, the war leader who should have been fleet master, am now faced with the task of navigating our way into a future that looks racked with fearful storms."

He came forward a few paces, until the water sloshed around his ankles. "I know that you mean well. You did not intend the disasters you caused to be visited upon us. But still you brought them.

"If you would be kind to us—please go. Leave us to mourn our many dead in peace. And do not return."

"DATA DELIVERY CONFIRMED," Sally Wright said, turning from the operations center console. She ventured a shy smile. "It looks as if the vent-forms have kept their end of the bargain."

"Damn well better," Grant said. "After what we went through."

"Please double check, Sally dear," Lakesh said. He seemed nervous. "Is there any possibility the transmission could have been…tampered with?"

She shook her close-cropped head. "I don't believe so, Doctor. The colony creatures provided us with a protocol to ensure data integrity. Our computers have already verified the accuracy of the transmission."

"So all we have to do is build the sumbitch, and we can go to the stars?" Domi asked. "Cool."

Lakesh's eyebrows squeezed together. "Domi, my sweet, it might not prove so simple. We must thoroughly test the system before attempting to make use of it."

"While I agree we need to exercise proper caution to make sure we have followed instructions properly,"

Brigid said crisply, "I think we can rely on the reliability of its functioning. It sufficed to bring the vent-forms to our world. And they seem to have been using it for many years."

"Yeah," Kane said. "If we trust them. And speaking of trust—"

"Yeah," Grant said. "I'm waiting for the shoe to drop, too."

"Shoe?" said Brigid. "I'm afraid I don't understand."

"Bates," Kane supplied. "We're just waiting to see how he's screwed us."

"What is strange," Lakesh said, "is what the dog did in the nighttime."

Grant shot a scowl to Kane, who shrugged. "What are you talking about, Lakesh?" the wolflike man asked.

"It's a reference to a Sherlock Holmes story," Brigid said. "*Silver Blaze.* Holmes mentions, 'the curious incident of the dog in the nighttime.'"

"What the dog did in the night that was so strange," Lakesh said with an air of grand satisfaction, "was nothing at all. It did not bark, you see, when it might have been expected to."

"What's strange," Grant said, "is the two of you."

"You mean we can't even trust Bates," Kane said, "to be untrustworthy?"

"It would appear," Lakesh said, "that he got what he desired from our deep-sea vent-dwelling friends, and was satisfied with it."

"That'd be a first," Kane said.

"I don't know I'm too thrilled about the prospect of Bates having star travel," Grant said.

"What's shaken?" Domi asked, biting into an apple she'd snagged from the commissary on the way to the command center. "Mebbe he'll go away for good. Leave us alone."

"I wish I could be so sanguine as you, my child," Lakesh said.

"Much as I hate to," Kane said, "I agree with you, Lakesh. Once a megalomaniac, always a megalomaniac. He's not going to be satisfied until he owns Earth. Even if he has to conquer the rest of the universe first to do it."

"Or until he gets chilled," said Domi, ever practical.

"Now that," Kane said with a sinister grin, "is what I call positive thinking."

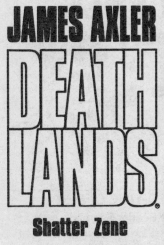